DAMAGE
CONTROL

JEFFREY GALLI

This book is a work of fiction. Names, characters, places, and incidents are products of the author's imagination and are used fictitiously. Any resemblance to actual events, locales, or persons, living or dead, is entirely coincidental.

For my late Uncle Bob, aeronautical engineer extraordinaire, whose crowning achievement was the development of the B-2 Spirit, otherwise known as the Stealth Bomber.

Three may keep a secret, if two of them are dead.
Benjamin Franklin

1

Los Angeles. A city of angels? Doubtful even once upon a time, and certainly not during the sweltering summer of 1965.

Jack Murphy slid onto a stool at the polished mahogany bar, trimmed in gleaming brass. His sport coat was torn at the breast pocket and streaked with dirt. A paisley tie hung loose and askew at his collar. He fished a cigarette from his half-depleted pack, tapped the end a couple times on the back of his hand—more out of habit than to settle the tobacco—then fumbled for the Zippo in his pants pocket. Once lit, he drew the unfiltered smoke deep into his lungs, held on for a moment, and then expelled it slowly through his nostrils. It had been another one of those days.

He gave a quick survey of the place. Mondays were generally slow, but tonight seemed to be an exception. And judging by the noise level, everybody was having a good time.

Without being asked, the bartender filled a glass with dark ale from the tap and placed it in front of him.

"You look like you could use this, Jack."

"Thanks, deShazo. Guess I should've picked today to go fishing."

"Better have a doctor take a peek at that eye. It's gnarly."

Murphy shrugged. "I've had worse."

Liam Clancy, the regular bartender, a cantankerous Dubliner, was undergoing hospital treatment for liver cirrhosis. Rumor held he wouldn't be back, the perils of a lifetime of hard drinking.

His replacement—at least for the summer—couldn't have been more different: young and tall and bouncy. Men would gladly confess their sins to her and then beg an indulgence for the impure thoughts they'd be having later on in her regard.

Laura deShazo was her full name. When first introduced, Murphy asked if she might be of Czechoslovakian ancestry. French, she'd explained. When her great grandparents and their brood of children had debarked in New York at the turn of the century, an enterprising Ellis Island immigration officer had simply written down what he'd heard: de Chazeaux became deShazo. As for being called by her last name, she said there were probably millions of Lauras in the world but only a handful of deShazos. She preferred the uniqueness.

Tonight, she was decked out in a green bare-midriff outfit with her brunette ponytail held in place by a shamrock barrette. No one would've guessed that this stunning hard body, bronze beach bunny was also top of her class at USC, majoring in chemical engineering. Only in California.

An authentic Irish pub, O'Neill's had only been in business since the late 1940s, upstaged by Casey's—downtown on Grand—which had opened its doors in 1916. Yet its reputation had elevated it to a southern California landmark, nonetheless. In fact, no self-respecting descendent of Erin's Isle, living within a hundred miles, would ever admit to not having bent an elbow there on one occasion or another.

Its location on Gower Street, south of Paramount and Columbia studios, also insured that the *Who's Who* of Hollywood stars and movie moguls were routinely counted among its clientele. As proof, the paneled walls were littered with framed publicity photos autographed to the proprietor, known by all as "Mickey."

Then four months ago, in the early morning hours of March

eighteenth, after closing up from St. Patrick's Day celebrations at the pub, Michael "Mickey" O'Neill was shot to death. The following day, the LA *Times* headline read: NOTED BUSINESSMAN GUNNED DOWN. The story had gone on to say that as nothing appeared missing, authorities had ruled out robbery or burglary as possible motives.

It was only after reading the account in the paper, and the history given of the famous watering hole, that Murphy had made a pilgrimage to O'Neill's, though he didn't have far to travel. He lived only a few blocks away, and figured he must've passed the place dozens of times since moving to LA the previous November. But while it may've been morbid curiosity that had first brought Murphy to O'Neill's, it wasn't pints of Guinness that kept him coming back; rather, it was Mickey's daughter who had left her position in haute couture to take over the management reins.

Murphy felt a hand on his shoulder at the same time that a woman slipped onto the stool next to his.

"I'm sorry. I didn't see you come in," she said.

Although Tara—shortened from the Irish spelling of Taragh—O'Neill had come to the United States with her father when she was sixteen, she still—now at thirty-five—spoke with an endearing brogue. A slave to fashion, she wore a pastel yellow mid-thigh jumper over a sheer white long-sleeved blouse. With emerald eyes and strawberry-blond hair done in a bouffant—à la Jackie Kennedy—she was dynamite. Any other time, Murphy would've longed to light her fuse. With some regularity, they'd been sharing each other's bed for three months now. But he'd have to forego tonight in his battered state.

She leaned over to kiss him on the cheek, then registered his eye and disheveled appearance.

"My God! What happened to you?" She turned his face to hers and gently touched the reddish-blue welt that adorned his left cheekbone.

"The husband of a client took exception to the photographs I took of him with a buxom stripper. Must've done a quick calculation of what his peccadilloes were going to cost him."

"And so he took it out on you."

"He and two of his country club buddies, each wielding a putter. They jumped me in the parking lot behind my office about an hour ago."

She noticed his raw knuckles.

"So what do *they* look like? Anything like you?"

"No comparison. When I last saw them, they were being loaded into the ambulance I called for from the corner phone booth. The husband is going to be taking his meals through a straw for a while. The others will be on crutches until Thanksgiving. Then I phoned my client and told her what had occurred. She said it wasn't half of what the 'rat' deserved. Said she was going to triple my fee; it was her husband's bank account, after all. So you see, a dark cloud turned out to have a silver lining."

"What about the police?" She had a look of concern on her face.

"What about them?"

"Won't they come looking for you? I mean the hospital staff will demand to know how they got that way."

Murphy shook his head. "The husband is a bigwig at AT&T. He's not going to want his already dirty laundry dragged further through the mud. It could cost him his job, and he'll need that for the child support and alimony. He'll concoct a plausible story about him and his friends being mugged by a street gang, and that'll be the end of it."

She took his hands in hers. "I hope so—for both our sakes. I'd hate to have to go see you in jail. Do you suppose they have conjugal visits?" She laughed.

"Is that a proposal?"

"I doubt I'm going to get one out of *you*. So, yes. Neither of us is getting any younger."

"Well, that's certainly true for me. I can't even remember when I was your age," he joked, though there was only an eleven-year difference.

"C'mon, darling," she whispered, her lips to his ear. "Make

an honest woman of me."

"And we'll live happily ever after, is that it?"

"I know you love me."

"Sure, you're every man's fantasy, but…"

"But what?"

"Maybe you won't understand, but being an investigator—first in the Army and now private—is all I know how to do. You'd want kids. And hell, so would I, even though I'd be a doddering old codger before they graduated from high school."

"That's not true; you wouldn't be *doddering*." She chuckled.

"Be serious, Tara. They'll be days like today. Only maybe I won't come out on top. It wouldn't be fair to you *or* them."

"Jack, my father ran a bar for a living, and look what happened to him. There are no guarantees in life; I know that. But I want us to be together, no matter what."

Murphy's eyes locked on hers, but he said nothing.

Tara finally said, "Do you really expect to go on like it is now? A roll in the hay when our schedules allow."

"It's been good, hasn't it?"

"The *best*, but I want permanence. I want commitment."

"I *am* committed. There's no one else but you. How could there be? You totally exhaust me."

"Now who's trying to be funny? You know what I mean. Think it over, Jack. But don't wait too long to come to your senses. I'm the best thing that ever happened to you. Don't lose out." She paused, then, "Now let me get those blood stains out of your shirt."

2

It didn't take much urging for Murphy to leave much earlier than customary. He felt as lousy as he looked and readily accepted Tara's stern instructions to go straight home and get a decent night's sleep. He didn't even kiss her before heading out.

It was shortly after eight o'clock when Murphy turned into the driveway of his circa 1926 two-bedroom, one-bath California Spanish cottage on a quiet street off Melrose. Six months ago, when he'd run across the real estate listing, it was described as a "rustic fixer-upper." After seeing it in person, he wondered where "rustic" left off and "ramshackle" began. But the price for the abandoned property was too good to pass up. At only $15,000 and back taxes, his loan sailed through without a hitch. It was the first time he'd ever set down roots. His previous twenty-three-year career as a military policeman mandated that he be mobile, always ready for a new assignment at a moment's notice.

Now, thanks to the labor of a few hungry students from LA City College, the flawed stucco had been patched and painted with a fresh coast of whitewash. A dozen missing roof tiles had been replaced, as had the dead shrubs front and back. The palm trees had needed pruning but were otherwise healthy, and the lawn had come back through the efforts of a Japanese gardener who came weekly to apply his magic. Maybe the house, with its arched doors and windows, wasn't quite ready to grace the pages of *Sunset* magazine, but its curb appeal had come a long way.

Murphy recognized the tricycle blocking his way as belonging to the toddler next door and got out to move it aside. He then parked in the detached garage at the end of the driveway. Making his way to the back door, he heard the telephone ringing. He was unlisted, so except for the occasional wrong number, the only calls he received were from whom he'd expressly given his number; and those weren't many. Once inside the kitchen, he switched on the light and reached for the wall phone.

"Hello."

"Mr. Murphy?" A male voice he didn't recognize.

"Speaking."

"You don't know me. My name is Clayton Hayward. I spoke to your secretary around noon and told her it was quite important that I reach you."

"Did she give you this number?" He'd have to clarify the rules with Andrea if she had.

"No, she said she'd give you mine when you came in. I waited all afternoon, but when I didn't hear from you, I began calling your home number that I'd obtained from my daughter: Alynn."

"Alie?"

"Oh, yes, I forgot she prefers that now."

Former Chief Warrant Officer Alie Hayward had been another Army cop with the Criminal Investigation Division. They'd worked together on his last big case before he'd retired. And though their paths had crossed only briefly, she'd been the woman of his dreams until Tara had displaced her. Even now, just thinking of her—with her cute Doris Day features—caused him to smile.

"How is she?"

11

"She's fine and I suppose doing well in the Bureau. That was her childhood dream come true."

Murphy knew she'd left the Army, just before his own departure, to attend the FBI Academy. The last time they'd spoken was on the phone soon after she'd graduated and received her first duty assignment.

"So what can I do for you, Mr. Hayward?"

"It's Clayton—or better yet, Clay. No reason to be formal. After talking with Alynn, I feel as if we're already friends."

"All right, Clay. How can I be of service?"

"Well, it's a complicated story, I'm afraid. I think it would be better if we spoke in person. Would tomorrow morning be convenient?"

"I'm sure that can be arranged. Do you have my office address?"

"I'd rather you come to my home."

"Okay. Where do you live?"

"Bel Air. I expect you know where that is."

"I've certainly driven past the sign often enough."

"Never taken the bus tour of movie stars' homes?"

"Maybe I'd have gotten around to it, but I've been kind of busy since coming to LA and setting up shop."

"Understandable. Well, the easiest way to my place is to take…"

"I think I've got it," Murphy said after he'd scribbled the directions on a pad by the phone.

"Then I'll say goodnight and look forward to meeting you tomorrow morning. Say ten o'clock."

The connection was broken before Murphy could confirm the time. He sensed Clayton Hayward was used to getting things his own way.

3

The next morning, Murphy sat on the edge of his bed, wondering if anyone had gotten the license number of the truck that had hit him. Every muscle ached. In his mind, he labored under the delusion that he was still twenty-something. Clearly, he was not. He shook a cigarette from the pack on the nightstand, fired it up, took a deep drag, and blew a couple smoke rings toward the darkly stained beamed ceiling. He then found his slippers by the side of the bed and forced himself to stand. Even his hair hurt.

He shuffled out of the room in his underwear and down the hall to the bathroom where he made an obligatory pit stop before popping a mouthful of aspirin to quell a splitting headache. A trip to the kitchen was next, where he filled a teakettle with water and turned a gas burner on the stove to low. Then back to the bathroom for a shower.

Afterward, he wiped the condensation from the mirror and took a good look at his eye. "Gnarly" was how deShazo had described it. Even with the ice pack he'd used last night, it was still puffy, and the bruise had now spread down his cheek. But like he'd told her, he'd had worse, as was evidenced by the scars on his five-ten frame, the last the result of being shot a year ago. The slug had entered just below his collarbone, represented now only by a mere pucker in the skin. The scar from the exit wound out his back, however, was a ragged affair.

When at last he emerged, a towel draped around his waist, his face tingling from Old Spice after-shave, and a dab of Brylcreem worked through his salt and pepper hair, he felt a hundred percent better.

The kettle on the stove was whistling as he opened a jar of instant coffee, spooned a fair amount into a ceramic mug, and added the scalding water. No cream or sugar. Just straight up—the military way.

He took the coffee back with him to the bedroom where he donned his only suit—a gray pinstripe. Tara thought he looked like a mobster when he wore it. He would've looked even more so if he'd worn his fedora. It seemed that men's hats had been passé in southern California since the late fifties. He couldn't say he missed not having to wear one; they were always being misplaced. Besides, they were hardly utilitarian in a temperate climate. Then there was the bulge of his shoulder holster, cradling a Model 1911 Colt .45 pistol. The same make and model he'd carried throughout his Army investigator years. There were doubtless more sophisticated weapons since its introduction before the First World War, but none with more stopping power. Being hit with a .45 caliber slug was like stepping in front of a train. Down and out. But his training had taught him that a pistol's primary function was to kill at close range; and unless that was your intent, it was better to keep it holstered. Less messy that way.

Murphy retrieved the newspaper from the flowerbed out front. The delivery boy's aim from his bicycle seldom got it to the porch but on occasion had put it on the roof. It was going to be another hot one today, he thought. And smoggy. He could tell by simply looking across the street. The houses were already in soft focus. Coming back inside, he phoned his office, indicating he had an appointment at ten and would be in afterward.

Tara would want to know of his improved condition, but

that news would have to wait. Running a bar that didn't close until two a.m. had its drawbacks. She was seldom out of bed before noon.

He had plenty of time before his meeting with Clayton Hayward, and traffic would be light at mid-morning. He settled in at the kitchen dinette and turned to the sports section of the paper. As was his habit, he found the baseball box scores. The Brooklyn Dodgers had been the team of his youth, but even as an adult, he'd felt betrayed when the "Bums" abandoned their fans for Los Angeles after the 1957 season. He'd vowed then never to root for them again.

But then the "when in Rome" scenario came into play, and he'd repented of his wrath. Now it looked like Walt Alston's transplanted "Boys of Summer" had a good chance of clinching the National League pennant if Drysdale and Koufax could keep their arch rivals, the San Francisco Giants, off their backs. And if they came out on top, the World Series match-up would likely be with the Minnesota Twins, no slouch of a team with "Mudcat" Grant and Jim Katt throwing their best stuff. If the stars aligned, he was certain he could score some tickets. Being a private eye, his circle of acquaintances grew wider each day, and every once in a while someone wound up owing him a favor.

4

Bel Air's west gate was found at the intersection of Sunset Boulevard and Bellagio Road, adjacent to UCLA. Murphy waited at a red light while an open-air tour bus traveling in the opposite direction made a left turn in front of him, its passengers—mostly Oriental, as far as he could discern—ever alert for a glimpse of any movie star who called Bel Air home.

He then made a right turn and followed at a comfortable distance, not knowing if the bus would be making any sudden stops. When finally it pulled to the side of the road, presumably allowing the tour guide to expound on a particular residence, Murphy proceeded cautiously to the left, noting that a few tourists had snapped his picture.

Who did they think he was in his dark glasses? Tara had once told him he resembled Alan Ladd in *Shane*. But that silver screen idol was dead, so when the tourists got back to wherever they came from and developed that film, they'd identify him as no one in particular.

Besides, what celebrity would be driving a ten-year-old four-door Chrysler Desoto, even if it did look brand new with its wide white-wall tires and moon hubcaps. He'd bought it at an estate sale. It really had belonged to a Pasadena octogenarian who'd only driven it to church, to her canasta club, and to Safeway for her groceries. The speedometer had shown less than 3000 miles, and judging by the residue on the dipstick, she'd never added oil or had it changed. He'd offered $300, and the late woman's nephew jumped at the deal. Murphy had subsequently taken it to a mechanic who'd swapped out the sparkplugs and fluids and pronounced the car to be a genuine "creampuff."

Consulting the directions he'd written down last night, he made his way haltingly through what might've been a maze. Except for gaps to accommodate gated driveways, most estates were secreted behind stone walls and tall hedges. Clearly, the rich and famous valued their privacy to the extreme.

Murphy stopped in front of the given address on Stone Canyon Road. A twelve-foot high solid metal gate blocked his advance. A camera peered down from atop a gate post. Leaving the car to idle, he walked to the call box and pushed the button.

"May I help you?" A male voice with an accent that Murphy took to be Mexican.

He faced the camera. "I'm Jack Murphy."

"Yes, Mr. Hayward is expecting you. Please proceed."

While walking back to his car, a large dog, straining at its long leash, passed by in the street. There were no sidewalks. At the other end of the tether was an attractive woman, casually dressed, her hair hidden beneath a brown polka dot scarf.

"Looks like you're the one being taken for a walk," Murphy called.

The woman turned and smiled broadly. "Good morning. Yes, it would appear so." Then she was gone, the dog continuing to drag her along.

When he turned back, the gate had swung inward revealing a brick driveway that traversed manicured lawns surrounding stands of full-grown pine trees and red sandstone boulders that could've been transported from any John Wayne western shot in southern Utah. The drive looped by a ranch-style house with a shake shingle roof. Saddled horses hitched to a rail in front wouldn't have looked out of place.

As Murphy got out of the car, a dark-complexioned man with boyish features appeared on the porch that ran the length of the façade. His jeans and Hawaiian shirt had a freshly ironed look.

He waited until Murphy had scaled the wide steps. "If you'll follow me, sir."

5

Removing his sunglasses, Murphy was led through a spacious knotty pine, leather-appointed living room. Wooden wheels that looked as if they might've come from ancient covered wagons had been fitted with lights resembling candles and hung from a vaulted ceiling. He didn't recognize all the paintings, but those he did belonged to Frederick Remington and Charles Russell. Western-themed bronze castings adorned the rustic mantle above the stone fireplace, and colorful native woven rugs were scattered across plank flooring. If Hayward's intention had been to create homage to the Old West, he'd succeeded. And if simply being a resident of Bel Air hadn't been enough to tell Murphy that Hayward had money—and lots of it—this western museum drove that notion home.

Double glass doors opened onto a large red brick patio, protected from the sun by an ivy-covered pergola. Beyond was a sparkling swimming pool.

"Mr. Murphy," the escort announced to a man reading a newspaper. He sat at a linen-draped table with silverware set for two.

Murphy approached and offered his hand which the man shook, saying, "You'll excuse me for not getting up." He then laughed.

It was only then that Murphy saw Hayward's wheelchair. Now he understood why Hayward hadn't wanted to come to the office. Despite that, however, dressed in white trousers and a navy polo shirt that fit snuggly over his broad shoulders, he had a robust air. The image was further accentuated by a well-tanned face. In fact, still with a full head of auburn hair, it was difficult to assess how old he was. Given Alie Hayward's age, Murphy pegged her father to be in his mid-sixties.

"Please have a seat." Hayward gestured across the table. "And feel free to take off your coat. You'll be more comfortable. The heat is already bordering on unpleasant."

Murphy hung it on the back of the chair and sat down. He noticed during the process that Hayward's attention had focused on his shoulder holster and pistol. That was a common reaction for the uninitiated who'd only seen them in movies or on television.

Hayward then asked, "Will you join me for breakfast?"

"I'm not much of a morning diner, but a cup of coffee would go down nicely."

Hayward looked over at the young man. "The usual for me, Alberto; and coffee for our guest."

"Right away." He retreated into the house.

"That's a nasty-looking eye you've got there," Hayward said. "I'll bet there's a story behind it."

"Hazards of the trade, sir."

"Please, the name's Clay, remember?"

"All right. And turnabout is fair play. I'm just Jack to my friends."

"Well, Jack, that injury appears to be of recent vintage."

Murphy nodded. "Yesterday afternoon. It's why I didn't get word of your phone call to my office."

"I trust whoever did that to you is in even worse condition. Alynn said you were sort of a tough guy."

"Really? Those were her words? A 'tough guy'?"

"No, I'm sorry. That was a paraphrase. I believe she said you weren't someone to trifle with."

"Well, I've never run from a fight; that's true enough. Better to meet the opposition head on, so there's no misunderstanding later about what can be expected. The three guys responsible for this," he gestured to his eye, "got the message."

A brief lull, then Murphy changed the subject: "You have a magnificent home."

"Some think I've overdone it; that I'm a frontier fanatic. And they may be right. I think I was born seventy-five years too late. I would've been entirely satisfied living in the rough and tumble West: in the saddle from dawn till dusk. Then again, maybe I've been influenced by too many western films. It may only be the West of my imagination.

"In any event, I wish I could say everything you see came as a result of my own hard work. But, alas, I inherited my good fortune to live a celebratory lifestyle. And I dare say I'm not the only 'trust-funder' who lives in Bel Air. On the other hand, there are many who got here on their own talents. Those would be the Hollywood show business types, of which there are quite a few."

"It's funny you should bring that up," Murphy said.

"Oh?"

"Because I'm almost positive I saw Maureen O'Hara out front before driving in."

"It's certainly possible. She and her husband live on the next street over. She didn't by any chance have that mangy, ill-tempered beast with her, did she?"

"As a matter of fact..."

"Then that was Maureen, all right. And that hairy brute with her is Tommy, an Irish wolfhound. I've seen smaller ponies. It drags the poor woman everywhere. I offered once to pay to put the son-of-a-bitch in obedience school, for its own good, as well as hers, but Maureen declined—rather rudely I thought. I'm afraid her feisty screen persona may not be an act."

Alberto eventually appeared with a tray containing a silver carafe, a plate of scrambled eggs and bacon, and two buttered pieces of toast. He placed the food in front of Hayward and then poured two cups of coffee.

Hayward said to Murphy, "You sure I can't get you something more?"

"No, really, I'm good just the way it is."

"I guess that'll be all then, Alberto."

When he'd gone, Hayward said, "I don't know how I'd manage without him. The son of a friend whose family escaped from Cuba right after Castro came to power. He's been my lifeline since the accident."

Murphy said, "I hope the wheelchair is only temporary."

Hayward forced a laugh. "You can hope all you like—God knows I did at the beginning—but my doctors say nothing more can be done. I'm stuck in this confounded contraption until someone dumps me into my grave."

Murphy nodded and then said, "If you don't mind me asking, what kind of accident was it? Automobile?"

"No, nothing so mundane. It happened at White Sands, New Mexico. Northrop was testing a prototype aircraft. As project director, I was there to view the flight. A careless crane operator struck the scaffold I was standing on. It collapsed, pinning me underneath."

"Damn!"

"You can say that again. But it was being rousted about by emergency personnel and a bumpy ride in an ambulance that sealed my fate. At first I was angry. Or maybe it was self-pity. I'd been in aeronautics for most of my adult life. Designing things that flew was my passion. I would've liked to have stayed on, if only in a diminished capacity. Management saw it differently. That was five years ago."

"I'm sorry," was all Murphy could think to say.

"But burdening you with my 'sour grapes' isn't why I asked you here this morning."

"Why did you ask me?"

Hayward took a deep breath. "It's about my son, Charlie. He's disappeared, and I want you to find him."

6

"Missing persons is more the domain of the police," Murphy replied. "They would have greater resources than I."

Hayward nodded. "I went to them first. They made some inquiries, but I don't think their hearts were in it."

"Why would you say that?"

"They saw a pattern. You see, Charlie's gone missing before."

"Oh? When was that, and what were the circumstances?"

Hayward thought for a moment, then, "I'd say about a year ago and then again six months before that. He had a problem with drugs, or maybe it was just alcohol. Talking with him, I was never sure. I begged him to get into treatment the last time, but he said everything was under control. And it looked to me that he might be right. When he'd visit, some of the 'old' Charlie was evident."

"When was the last time you spoke with him?"

"The evening of July second. I specifically remember that date because I'd had an appointment with my doctor late in the day, and Alberto and I had gone to dinner afterward. We hadn't been home long before Charlie called. I'd say it was around seven o'clock. He'd often check up on me."

"Could you tell where he was calling from?"

"No, I... Wait. He turned down the television so he could hear better. He must've been at his apartment. After a few days when he didn't call again, my thought was that he'd perhaps gone out of town on assignment for the *Times*."

"*Times?*" Murphy questioned, then, "Right. Charles Hayward. How could I not have made the connection? I've seen his byline often enough."

"Of course, I made an inquiry with the paper's city editor; he's a friend of mine. He was polite, but it was obvious that he thought Charlie's absence was a result of having fallen back into his old ways. But to be fair, in his shoes, I'd have probably seen it that way, too."

"I know this sounds trite, but does your son have any enemies?"

"If he does, he never said anything to me. It's not hard to imagine though, given the stories he's written. When Charlie smells corruption, he doesn't rest until he's found the source."

"Previously, when the police were involved, where did they find your son?"

"That's just it; they never did. When Charlie got sober or whatever, he showed up as if nothing had happened. That's why the police were reluctant to get on board this time. Said they had better things to do than traipse all over town looking for a spoiled rich kid with an addiction."

"But you feel this time is different?"

"Call it a father's intuition."

"I assume you called Alie about him. What did she think?"

"I'm embarrassed to admit this, but she can barely give me the time of day. It's been that was since she was a teenager. A divorce is at the heart of her resentment. Then to make matters worse, my ex-wife contracted a terminal illness. Somehow in Alynn's mind, I was responsible for that, too. Anyway, yesterday morning, when I turned to her for help, she was as disinterested as LA's finest. She gave me your office and home numbers, vouched for your abilities, and hung up."

"I wouldn't have thought that of her. What kind of

relationship does she have with her brother?"

"Only minimally better than with me. You see, after my ex-wife's passing, Charlie elected to stay here rather than live with Alynn. I think she felt betrayed; that I'd influenced his decision. But regardless, Jack, will you humor an anxious father and take the job?"

"All right. Count me in."

Hayward then leaned to his left and reached down, coming up with an attaché case that Murphy hadn't noticed. He pushed aside his breakfast plate and placed it on the table. Then snapping open the lid, he withdrew a photograph.

"This is Charlie's graduation picture. Class of '62. University of Southern California."

"Does he still wear the beard and mustache?"

"Only the mustache. Says it makes him look older and more credible as a journalist."

Hayward returned to the case and extracted a sheet of paper and a metal ring with a single key attached.

"I wrote down the address of his apartment, and this is a spare key he gave me. I've also listed the names of as many of his friends as I could remember him mentioning." Murphy looked at the short list. "All right, I'll see if I can track them down."

"I've included my phone number. Keep me informed of your progress. Day or night. I'm seldom not here."

"Certainly. Do you have anything else that might help?"

Hayward thought for a moment. "He drives a '53 Corvette, if that's in any way important. White with red interior, the only color scheme it came in. His favorite car since he was a kid. I bought it for him as a graduation present. It turns heads."

"I can imagine," Murphy mused with a smile.

"Oh, and one last thing." Hayward again went to the case. This time for a thick stack of currency, secured with a rubber band. He slid it across the table.

Murphy was taken aback as he thumbed through the bills.

"Five thousand dollars, Jack. And I'll pay whatever it takes to find my son. I've already lost Alynn; I couldn't bear losing

Charlie."

Murphy swiveled in his seat, reached into his coat, and came away with a spiraled pad of paper and a pen.

"Let me write you a receipt."

"That's not necessary, Jack."

"No, it's best that I treat you like any other client." He then tore the signed and dated page from the pad and handed it to Hayward. "So unless there's something more I should know, I'd better start earning this money."

Walking back through the house, with Hayward rolling at his side, Murphy said, "I noticed there are signs of an old fire on the hillside beyond your yard."

"Yes, a large one at that. It was four years ago this coming November. The surrounding area was tinder dry when it started. Residents with shake roofs scrambled to hose them down. I was already relegated to this damn wheelchair, so Alberto did all the work to save this place. Some, however, weren't so lucky. Burt Lancaster lost his home, I know. And I think Zsa Zsa Gabor. Three thousand of us were eventually evacuated. The media referred to it as 'a tragedy trimmed in mink.' Assholes. They'd have sung a different tune, if *they'd* risked losing everything."

When they at last exited the house to the front porch, Hayward exclaimed, "I can see that you know your cars, too, Jack. A Desoto Coronado Fireflite would be perfect for someone in your line of work. Not at all ostentatious, so it doesn't draw any attention. Plus, it's got a V-8 under the hood. It'll outpace any of the competition. Of course, I don't need to tell you; that's why you undoubtedly have it. The Chrysler engineers really knew what they were doing when they designed that mechanical marvel. I'm actually surprised it wasn't a bigger seller in its day. You've kept it in pristine condition. I respect a man who takes care of the tools of his trade. It tells me a lot about him. I'm feeling even better now than I did a few minutes ago when you took the job."

"And I'll do my best, Clay." Murphy shook his hand.

"I know you will."

26

But then Murphy held on and said, "You were certain—even from last night's phone call—that I'd sign on, weren't you?"

"I never figured it any other way, Jack."

7

The office of Murphy & Doyle, Private Investigations was located on the third floor of a Great Depression-era granite building at the corner of Broadway and Temple, literally across the street from the Los Angeles County Criminal Court Building and within walking distance of a half-dozen other private and public agencies that routinely contracted for investigative services.

Murphy had met Matthew Doyle during the war. Both were recovering from battlefield wounds at an Army infirmary in Tripoli. As military policemen assigned to different units, they'd kept in touch by letter as the Allied offensive pushed into Europe.

After V-E Day, Murphy remained with the Criminal Investigation Division, while Doyle returned to Los Angeles, the city of his formative years, and joined the LAPD. He retired from Robbery-Homicide about the same time Murphy decided to pull the plug on his own career. It had been Doyle's idea to team up for a private run at what they knew best. And so far, the fledgling detective agency had done remarkably well, due primarily to Doyle's reputation and connections in the city. The reason Doyle received second billing was simple to explain: He'd lost the coin toss.

Most of their work came from defense attorneys who hired them to find exculpatory evidence for their clients. Though coming from different orientations, both men recognized that the judicial system was stacked against defendants. Judges, by and large, were former prosecutors who laughed at the notion of the accused being innocent until proven guilty.

The balance of their cases came from insurance companies that wanted outside investigations of alleged fraudulent claims where internal collusion was suspected. There were far more of these incidents than might be expected. And, of course, there were pre-divorce cases, where aggrieved spouses wanted the "goods" on their partners.

These latter cases, which usually involved sneaking around with a camera to catch couples *in flagrante delicto,* was unsavory business and gave private investigators a bad rap as "low-life gumshoes." And window peeking was not without its hazards, as Murphy could readily attest since yesterday.

Andrea was at her typewriter, transcribing a dictated report from her shorthand pad, when Murphy entered the office. Blond and petite and vivacious, with great legs, she was still the quintessential cheerleader who, over her parents' protests, had dated the team quarterback—and notorious bad boy—during their senior year in high school. They'd eloped that summer. Two kids—boys—came in rapid succession. The husband, Johnny Duncan, worked as a grease monkey for a transmission shop. Murphy had met him only once and judged him to be far from the campus hero that Andrea had fallen for. She maintained their marriage was still a bed of roses, but who did she think she was fooling? The occasional bruise emerging from a layer of heavy makeup told Murphy a different story. Sure, life wasn't fair, or he'd still have been married to his former wife, whose "forsaking all others" vow had lasted only until she met a fast-talking musician while he was chasing Rommel across the Libyan Desert. Nevertheless, Andrea deserved better than what she was getting from the schmuck she lived with.

Looking up, she removed the cigarette that had been dangling from her lips, and rested it on an ashtray.

"Holy smoke! Tara said you looked a mess last night. I see now what she meant."

"Thanks for the second opinion," he joked. "You'd have been the first to see me, but you'd already gone for the day. I was intending on finishing up some paperwork when Florence Baldwin's husband figured he was going to teach me a lesson— maybe even a permanent one. He figured wrong."

"You can't let him get away with this. You've got to press charges."

"I don't think so. What his wife has in store for him will be his punishment for years to come. Plus, I got my pound of flesh, even if one of his buddies did manage to tag me once."

"It's your face, but if it were me, I'd want him booked and behind bars if only over night while his lawyer arranged bail. Why should he get off scot-free for an assault? What if it had gone the other way? Who knows what kind of guy Matt would hire as your replacement? Maybe I wouldn't like him as much as I do you. In fact, if it hadn't been for Tara, I might've made a play for you, myself." She winked.

Murphy didn't doubt that for a second, knowing her marital situation. He'd have been her ticket out—despite being old enough to be her father.

When he didn't respond, she said, "Well, a girl can dream, can't she? And speaking of girls, Tara has already phoned twice this morning, looking for you. She seemed put out that you hadn't checked in with her."

He looked at his watch; it was ten minutes to noon.

"Normally, she wouldn't even be awake until about now. What did you tell her?"

"That you had an early appointment out of the office, and that I was sure you'd call her as soon as you were free. That was the first time she called. The second time was just a few minutes ago. I was forced to agree with her that you were an unfeeling brute who deserved to be cut off from any intimate activity until you had performed adequate penance."

30

"I know what that middle part means, but what would 'penance' entail, do you suppose?"

"Do I look like a social worker?"

"But you're a woman; you undoubtedly speak her language. Help me out here; I'm on the ropes."

"You really are hopeless. You are the love of her life, and I think the feeling is mutual. A diamond ring would smooth over any rough patch between you two."

"Oh, brother! She told you to say that, didn't she?"

"She didn't need to. Apparently you're the only one who doesn't have a clue. What kind of a detective are you, anyway?"

Murphy reached into his coat pocket, extracted the stack of money, and tossed it on her desk.

"This kind," he said without affect.

She whistled and started to thumb through the bills.

"Compliments of Clayton Hayward, our new client," Murphy said. "I kept five hundred for expenses."

"What kind of person pays with a wad of cash?"

"A rich one."

"And what does he want you to do for this moolah?" She still held the bundle. "Rub someone out?"

"Nothing that dangerous. His son has dropped out of sight. He wants me to find him."

"We've never handled a missing persons case before, but if they pay this good, maybe you and Matt should specialize."

"Where is Matt, by the way? I saw his car in the lot."

"In court, remember? The Vargas girl murder."

"Oh, that's right. Freddy Harmon is no more guilty of murder than you are, Andrea. Matt and I pawed through the alleged evidence. It's too pat; to the point of being manufactured. And what's worse, the DA has to know it. Yet he's going forward anyway. He's got to prove to his constituents that he's tough on crime, even if it means sending an innocent Negro kid to the gas chamber."

"That's a sad commentary, Jack."

"It's been a particularly difficult case for Matt. He prided himself on being an honest cop. Now he has reason to believe some of his former colleagues in Homicide have been playing fast and loose with the rules. And more than likely going back a ways when he was still on the force.

"You know, Andrea, this make me wonder why I spent my best years in the military, keeping the world 'safe for democracy,' when I see blatant attempts to subvert those principles. Let's just hope that Harmon's public defender can derail a guilty verdict with what Matt has come up with."

Andrea nodded, then grabbed her purse from the bottom drawer of her steel gray metal desk and tossed in the money.

"I'd better deposit this. Can you hold down the fort? I won't be long."

"Sure. I've got it covered, and while you're gone I'll call Tara and beg forgiveness of my sins."

"You do that. And I'm not kidding about a ring, Jack. You can't say you're strapped for cash." She waved her purse at him. "Not with all this on the books."

8

Murphy drifted back to his own office, a sterile affair with only a calendar on the wall as decoration. A venetian blind-covered window looked out over the alley that ran the length of one side of the building, and a radiator kept the room warm when the outside temperature dipped to the mid-forties a few mornings a year. Doyle's office didn't look much different, and the furniture—what there was of it—had come from secondhand stores. When they were just starting out, it seemed imprudent to deplete their capital on office accommodations.

Now that theirs had shown itself to be a rising star among a score of fly-by-night LA detective agencies, better digs were in the planning stages. Despite the fact that cases were resolved by good field work—not sitting in plush offices—prospective clients generally associated affluent trappings with success. Soon they'd have them.

Murphy sat at his scarred wooden desk and reached for the phone. First, he tried Tara's apartment. No answer. He then dialed the only other number he had for her.

After five rings, he was just about to hang up, then, "O'Neill's"

"deShazo, it's Jack."

"Hey, so how are you feeling today?"

"Much better, thanks. But you wouldn't guess that by looking at me. I think I'm going to make up a story that I got the chance to spar a few rounds with Sonny Liston and came up short, like he did a couple months ago against Muhammad Ali."

She laughed.

Then Murphy got down to the matter at hand.

"Listen, is Tara there?"

"It's still a little early for her. In fact, I just got here, myself. Have you tried her at home?"

"Yes, but she wasn't there, either."

"I can take a message if you'd like."

"My secretary says that Tara has been trying to contact me, but I was away from the office. I'm here now but don't know for how much longer. When she comes in, tell her I called and that I'm in great shape for the shape I'm in." He chuckled.

"Will we see you later on?"

"I'm counting on it, but I picked up another case this morning and don't know where it's going to take me."

"Okay, I'll let her know. Now you take care." She then broke the connection.

The next call was one Murphy knew he'd have to make even before leaving Hayward's patio. He consulted his Rolodex, flipping through the entries until he found the one for the FBI's Atlanta Field Office. He hoped Alie would be at her desk, or at least in the building. He committed the number to memory and dialed. A woman's voice, dripping with southern charm, answered.

"Federal Bureau of Investigation. How may I direct your call?"

"Special Agent Hayward, please." Equally charming.

"One moment, sir. And have a wonderful day." Click.

Two rings, then, "Hayward."

"Is it now? This is a voice from your not-too-distant past." Murphy's tone was mock-serious.

"Jack. I figured you'd be calling sooner or later."

"Consider this 'sooner.' I just returned from a visit with

your father."

"Well, that was fast. I only gave him your number yesterday."

"I think he would've actually preferred to meet yesterday, but I was dealing with another matter and missed his call. Anyway, we had a nice chat."

"And now you're wondering why I pawned this off onto you, is that it?"

"I wouldn't have put it quite like that, but I suppose so. I can maybe understand your feelings for your father. I mean, the divorce and all that, but—"

"Oh, so he dragged that into the conversation, did he? I'll bet he didn't take any responsibility for my mother moving out. About how he couldn't keep his dick in his pants. About how his little 'conquests' would blatantly call the house at all fucking hours."

Murphy was silent for a moment and then replied, "Yes, that's unfortunate, but what does it have to do with your brother?"

Now it was Alie's turn to be quiet.

Finally, she said, "At the beginning, *nothing*. Mom packed her bags, and with Charlie and me in tow, moved into an apartment in Beverly Hills. She sued for divorce and received enough alimony and child support that we never went without. In time, her health began to fail, slowly at first, but with a vengeance near the end. Cervical cancer. I was in my junior year at UCLA when she died. I hadn't seen my father for years until he came to the funeral, all contrite. Not once had the son of a bitch ever made an attempt to see her in those agonizing last days, though he sure as hell knew about her desperate condition.

"It was then that he made his play for Charlie. He was now off the hook for alimony, and if he could convince Charlie to go back home and stay with him, the child support would go away, as well. It was money in the bank."

"Or maybe he was doing you a favor. Did you ever consider that?"

"You mean doing double duty as sister and guardian? Yeah, I thought about it. For about two seconds. In any event, back to court we went, and the judge sided with him. Besides, Charlie was only too happy to reclaim a life of privilege. He had few real friends, only freeloaders who encouraged his addictive behaviors.

"Brushes with the law were inevitable, but high-priced lawyers always found ways to wipe the slate clean. When it looked like Charlie wasn't going to graduate from high school, Father donated new lights for the football stadium and, as if by magic, a GPA worthy of a valedictorian miraculously appeared on his transcripts.

"Then it was off to USC, where his drug usage continued, as did my father's enabling. And when he graduated—no doubt somewhere near the bottom of his class this time—it was Father's connections that got the LA *Times* to hire him."

"Well, your father isn't writing Charlie's stories for him. I've read some of them. Your brother has real talent."

"I wouldn't know. Now as to his disappearing act, is this one his third or fourth? I've lost count."

"His third, if you father has it right."

"And Charlie always showed up eventually, didn't he? The cops looking for him spun their wheels for nothing. But has he gotten help for his addiction? No. He denies even having a problem."

"Your father feels he may've turned the corner; that his disappearance is due to something else."

"Wishful thinking. More likely someone will find him OD'd."

"That's pretty harsh, Alie. He's your brother, not some nameless junkie."

"He might as well be. He made his own bed with my father's help. They can both go to hell."

"Well, my job is to find him—if I can—and I was hoping you might be able to give me something more than what your father provided."

"Which was?"

"A key to your brother's apartment and a very short list of his current friends."

"Read me their names."

Murphy pulled the sheet of paper from his coat hung over the back of his chair and recited off the list.

"No, I don't recognize any of them, but then Charlie's life is a blank to me. So how much are you being paid for this 'quest,' if you don't mind me asking?"

"Five thousand dollars."

"You came cheap. You could've negotiated twice that."

"I'd already committed *before* any talk of money. Knowing he was your brother sealed the deal for me. You saved my life last year. I figured I owed you."

A long silence.

"You're a good man, Jack. I knew that from the first day we met. I'm now sorry I've been such a shit about this. I'm a big girl who ought to get over it. Maybe I'm the one who needs therapy."

The conversation went on for a few minutes more, until Andrea came in from the hallway, announcing, "I'm back, Jack. Did you miss me?"

9

Murphy delayed leaving until after he'd brought the Baldwin Case up to date, culminating in his encounter with Frank Baldwin the day before. Should anything happen to his wife as a result of Murphy's investigation into infidelity, this report would no doubt sway a judge as to Frank's propensity for violence.

Standing at Andrea's desk, he crushed out his cigarette in her ashtray and put on his coat.

"I haven't been able to make contact with Tara, so if she calls again, tell her I'm feeling much better."

"Have you thought about that diamond ring?"

"Did anyone ever point out that you have a one-track mind?" He chuckled.

"Women are hardwired that way, and the sooner you understand it, the better."

"I'm beginning to see that. Anyway, if she does call, tell her I'm planning to see her later tonight."

"Okay."

"In the meantime, I've got to jump on this Hayward case. If there's a trail to follow, I don't want it getting any colder."

The address given for Charlie Hayward's apartment turned

out to be opposite Farmer's Market at Third and Fairfax. Murphy had been there a couple times with Tara. Her father had always bought his corned beef and cabbage there for the pub, and she saw no reason to find another vendor.

The Market had begun in the 1930s simply as a vacant lot where local growers brought their produce. Eggs, meat, poultry, cheese, and butter followed. Now it was a Los Angeles landmark, complete with boutiques and eateries, visited yearly by hundreds of thousands of tourists—or locals who just wanted to chat over warm croissants and cups of café au lait.

Murphy parked in the lot and walked across the street to the seven-story building that had the appearance of having had a recent facelift. Double glass and brass doors opened onto a lobby with a polished marble floor. Behind a matching marble counter sat a gawky kid in an LAPD-blue uniform with a security guard patch on each sleeve and no name tag.

"Can I help you?"

He took leave of his stool, but not before stashing a *Playboy* magazine in a drawer beneath the counter. Murphy knew it was a *Playboy*, because Doyle had the same edition in his desk at the office. He said he the articles stimulating.

"I'm here to see Charles Hayward." Getting the ball rolling.

"I can tell you right now he isn't in."

Murphy held up the key that Clayton Hayward had given him.

"I think I'll check for myself, just the same."

"Okay, but you'll need to sign." He gestured to a logbook on the counter. An adjacent pen was affixed by a length of chain.

After Murphy filled in the requisite information, the kid pointed and said, "Elevator is down that hallway. Apartment 704, if you don't already know."

Murphy rode to the top floor and stepped out onto a carpet that felt like walking on a cloud. Four doors, two on each side, flanked the wide corridor. 704 was at the far end on the right.

As he inserted the key into the lock, he wondered what he'd find behind the door. Alie had painted her brother as a hopeless drug addict. If his disappearance was the result of having died from an overdose, then maybe his corpse was inside, waiting to be discovered.

Murphy took a handkerchief from his pants pocket and held it over his nose as a precaution. A moment later, he knew the truth: If Hayward had overdosed, he hadn't done it here.

He closed the door behind him and began a slow, methodical walkabout, as if the apartment were a crime scene. Right off, he didn't care for the choice of furniture. Every piece, even the television console was Danish Modern. Or maybe the style was just Scandinavian. It had been all the rage in Europe while he was there. He preferred couches and chairs that gave the impression you might actually want to sit on them, like the overstuffed variety in his own house. But he had to admit the carpet was amazing and made the kind in the corridor feel like burlap by comparison. He wasn't sure he'd have gone for white, but its contrast with teak and red leather was stunning.

On the coffee table were copies of three subscription magazines. He picked up the closest and thumbed through the opulent pages. Maybe it was true that money didn't buy happiness, but it sure as hell covered the cost of whatever else was on the list. He tossed the magazine back onto the table and turned his attention elsewhere.

It appeared that Hayward was fond of French Impressionism. Fine prints by Monet, Degas, and Renoir were exquisitely matted and framed. Murphy felt proud of himself. He wouldn't have known a Claude Monet from a Norman Rockwell if his last Army duty station hadn't been near Paris.

The design motif continued into the bedroom, with an equally uncomfortable-looking bed. But what Murphy noticed most was the mirrored ceiling. He didn't have to guess what that was about. Hayward senior had said that his son's Corvette turned heads. Maybe it did more than that. Maybe it was a "babe magnet," as Matt Doyle referred to sports cars. A half-depleted box of condoms and jar of Vaseline in the nightstand seemed to lend credence to that notion.

The only other item in the drawer was a loaded .38 caliber Colt Detective Special. Murphy tipped out the cylinder and looked down the revolver's snub-nose barrel. He could tell it hadn't ever been fired, and it still had that factory-fresh smell. He jotted down the serial number and put it back.

Then he went through the dresser drawers. A stack of starched dress shirts were still in cellophane, the way they'd come from the cleaner, and socks and underwear were arranged by color. The closet held an impressive array of suits, sport coats and trousers, and casual attire. Hugging the back wall was a floor rack of shoes for all occasions. He was about to slide the closet door shut when he spied a briefcase tucked away in back. He lifted it out. A colorful decal of Mickey Mouse adorned a corner of the lid. Beneath the handle was a three-digit combination lock. The two brass clasps were bent, presumably from having been pried open. A look inside found it empty.

The bathroom smelled squeaky-clean, no doubt helped by the lavender air freshener atop the toilet tank lid. By this time, Murphy suspected what he'd find in the medicine cabinet: nothing of consequence, but everything stowed in its assigned location. He wasn't disappointed.

What was now obvious was that Charlie Hayward lived a very organized life that seemed incongruent with that of an addict; hence, the possibility that he could be holed up somewhere in a drug-induced fog was beyond remote.

Murphy strolled back to the living room. On a built-in bookcase was a collection of literary classics—a few hardbound but most in paperback. They looked well-used. He slid one out and rifled through the pages. Scribbled notes in the margins led him to conclude that they'd been made as a result of classes that Hayward had taken in college.

A snapshot in a gold metal frame then caught his eye. It had been taken at the beach and showed a thin bikini-clad girl flanked by two equally skinny bare-chested boys—a much younger Charlie Hayward being one of them. Their outstretched arms were draped over each other's shoulders and they were laughing, high school kids having a good time. On closer examination, the person who'd taken the photo appeared to be partially reflected in the mirrored aviator glasses of the other boy. Crossing the room, he drew the drapes to let in more light and squinted to make out the image: a girl holding at her waist what looked to be a twin lens reflex camera. Murphy couldn't discern any facial features, but she wore a one-piece swim suit. He wondered if she's been part of the fun or merely a passerby who'd been commandeered to take the picture. Regardless, the outing had been important enough for Hayward to keep a memento of it—the only item of a personal nature that Murphy had found in the apartment.

He returned the photo to the bookcase and exited the room by the French door to the patio. Only then did it dawn on him that Hayward's was a penthouse apartment with spectacular views from outside. He concluded that the other three apartments on this floor were similar. The one next door was separated by a six-foot concrete wall. The rent had to be beyond what even a reporter of his stature could afford, not to mention the expensive décor. What's more, the clothes in the closet all had the kind of designer labels that put them out of the reach of most mortals. Was Clayton Hayward subsidizing his son's lifestyle? Most likely, unless Charlie was selling drugs— not using them.

Returning from the patio, he pulled the drapes closed. He hadn't yet given the kitchen a looksee. It was separated from the dining area—actually part of the living room—by a breakfast counter and stools. As he'd come to expect by now, everything was spotless; one could have eaten off the tile floor. The cabinets were well-stocked with food and also housed a selection of china and crystal glasses and stemware. Only the best. This was further evidenced by a sizable cooler, built into one of the base cabinets, fully stocked with fine wine and champagne.

"What? Nary a bottle of something rot gut?" Murphy said aloud. "C'mon, Charlie, live a little. Don't you have any average friends?"

Curious, he pulled open the refrigerator door to find an assortment of domestic and foreign beer labels, as well as soft drinks. Maybe Hayward was a proper host, after all. He also found a half-empty carton of milk. As was his habit in his own kitchen, he squeezed open the coated cardboard spout and sniffed. The stench watered his eyes. He wondered how long the souring process would've taken and decided it depended on how fresh the milk was to start with. In any event, Hayward hadn't been around to dispose of it.

He thought briefly of pouring the smelly liquid down the drain and flushing away the odor but then figured if Hayward's absence eventually turned into a police matter, the apartment should be left the way he'd found it.

Murphy took a final tour of the apartment, hoping he'd missed something the first time around. He came up empty.

10

Murphy by-passed the lobby and rode the elevator to the underground parking level. He wasn't a connoisseur of automobiles, despite what had been said about his Desoto, but he recognized the '53 Corvette, just as described, tucked in the corner of the lighted garage. Wherever Hayward had gone, he hadn't driven there. The car was unlocked. Smart. It was foolish to secure them. All a crook had to do was slit the cloth top and open it from inside. And even if there wasn't anything of value to steal, the owner was still out the cost of repair or, worse yet, a new top.

The registration card in the glove box identified the car as belonging to Charles V. Hayward. A flashlight, an open pack of Beemans Chewing Gum, and a dog-eared book of maps for LA County rounded out the contents. He didn't have a key for the trunk, but that didn't pose much of a problem. Murphy was pretty good with lock picks—a skill he'd honed in the Army—and he always carried a set for just such an occasion. He needn't have wasted his time. Nothing but a spare tire and jack, and a folded plaid car robe in a plastic carrying case. Murphy had one, too, for those spontaneous trips to the beach with Tara to watch the sun set.

He wanted to talk with the security guard but first made a stop at the bank of mailboxes farther down the hallway from the elevator. He found the one labeled 704 and, again using his picks, had a look inside. Nothing but two throwaway ads addressed only to "current occupant."

"You called it, all right." Murphy walked toward the kid. "So when was the last time you saw him?"

"You a cop?"

"Private. Name's Jack Murphy."

He flashed his badge and ID. He'd found by experience that people were conditioned to acquiesce to a show of authority. The police had government credentials, more often than not uniforms, and flashing lights and sirens on their vehicles. A private investigator's status was substantially different, the most notable being the absence of any power of arrest or even detention. Nor was there any easy access to official law enforcement channels of information. For these, there was a reliance on the cultivation of friendship with those in the "system" who did have access. That's why most PIs came from the ranks of local, state, and federal police organizations.

Murphy and Matt Doyle's badges resembled the silver and gold shields of the LAPD, absent the image of the city hall in relief, and were clearly stamped "Private Investigator" in blue letters. Seldom did anyone want to examine the pictured license that accompanied the badge in the black leather bi-fold.

"I never met a private eye before." The kid's eyes lit up. "Must be exciting; like in the movies."

"No, I'm afraid nothing in real life is like the movies. So let me ask you again: How long has it been since you've seen Charles Hayward?"

"The Fourth of July." There was no hesitation.

"You seem pretty sure about that. How come?"

"For two reasons: He had a bash at his place. You know, to watch the fireworks. From the rooftop you could see several displays. Anyway, the downstairs tenant complained about the noise, and I had to go up and ask him to keep it down. He was

45

pleasant about it and apologized."

"What was the second reason?"

"My mother died on the following day. I took a few days off for her funeral in Kansas City. I haven't seen Mr. Hayward since I got back."

"Three weeks, give or take, huh? So is someone picking up his mail, because the box is empty?"

"He has his mail delivered elsewhere—maybe at his work. Several of the tenants do the same thing, for whatever reasons."

"You mentioned a shindig on the Fourth. Does Hayward have many of those?"

"No, mainly just sleepovers."

Murphy chuckled. "A ladies' man, huh?"

The kid stifled a laugh. "I take it you don't know him very well."

"What do you mean?"

"Because if you did, you'd know he was queer. But then, whatever floats your boat, I always say."

Murphy was taken aback. He wondered if this revelation was germane in any way. But one thing was certain: Alie didn't know about it, or she'd have thrown it into her rant. And there was a good chance the father was in the dark, as well. In any event, the mirrored ceiling suddenly took on new meaning.

Recovering, Murphy said, "These 'sleepovers' as you call them, did they always involve the same person, or does Hayward mix it up?"

"I haven't been on shift every time, you understand, but from what I saw, I'd say he had a couple of favorites."

"Are their names in there?" He gestured to the logbook.

"No."

"Why not? I had to sign."

"Because you weren't with a tenant. The ledger is only for unaccompanied visitors."

"Look, I'm fairly new to LA, and up until a minute ago, I had no interest in the homosexual community. So let me ask you this: Where do these folks hang out? There must be places that cater to them. Any idea where Hayward might go?"

"I once overheard him mention the Garden of Eden."

"Well, that's easy enough to remember. I'll look up the address in the phonebook."

"I can save you the time. It's on Venice Boulevard, almost to Pacific Avenue. Right hand side of the street. There are naked statues of Adam and Eve in front. You can't miss them. I pass the place when I go to Venice Beach."

"I'll check it out; maybe someone there has seen him."

"Is Mr. Hayward in any kind of trouble?"

"Hard to say. His family hasn't heard from him in a while, and I've been asked to make inquiries. Like I'm doing now."

"I certainly hope there isn't a problem, because whatever else he might be, he's a hell of a nice guy."

Thinking back on the gun he'd found in Hayward's bedroom, Murphy asked, "What about crime in the neighborhood?"

"Well, I wouldn't call it 'crime-free.' All the tenants are well-heeled. Several have connections to the movie studios: screenwriters, assistant directors, technicians; you know, worker bees, but plenty of money. They prefer to have a guard at the front door."

"Has there ever been an instance where someone got past security and broke into an apartment?"

"I've only been here a year, you understand, but I don't think so. Besides, my job is to make sure nothing like that happens." He came around the counter and stood opposite Murphy.

"I don't want to burst your bubble, son, but you're paid to give tenants an *illusion* of being safe."

"What do you mean?"

"Well, take me for example. What if I were really a burglar intent on ransacking apartments for whatever easy loot I could find? All you did was have me sign in. What if I'm not who I say I am?"

"But you had a key to Mr. Hayward's apartment," the kid countered.

"Could've been to anything; you had no way of knowing.

47

You even pointed me to the elevator. So you see, you think you're doing a good job of keeping the wolf away from the door, but it's only an illusion for the tenants *and* you."

"Okay, I get your point. But I'd do all right in a real pinch." His hand went to the butt of his revolver. "I know how to use this, if I have to."

"Really?" Murphy was skeptical. "Well, I'm betting that if a guy came in here who knew what he was doing, you'd be dead on the floor before you could even get that weapon out of its holster."

"I don't think so."

Murphy shrugged. "Who knows? Maybe I haven't given you enough credit. Anyway, it's been good talking to you; you've been helpful."

Murphy turned to leave, then swiveled back on his heel. Before the kid could respond, Murphy had him off balance against the counter, the kid's own sidearm tucked under his chin.

"See what I mean? You want to march into battle, and you're about as combat ready as a Boy Scout. You need to challenge more and be a little less trusting."

Murphy lowered the weapon and held it out butt first for him to take.

"Damn! That was fast." His eyes were still wild with terror as he holstered the revolver.

"Practice, practice, practice. It doesn't apply just to playing the piano at Carnegie Hall. If you want to stay alive in my business, you've got to be better than anyone you come up against."

"Then what about that bruise on you face? You forget to duck?" He chuckled nervously.

Murphy cradled his cheek with his hand. "Only a scratch. You ought to see the other three guys. I doubt any of them has left the hospital yet."

11

Murphy left one of his cards and told the kid to keep his eyes and ears open for anything that might help with Hayward's disappearance. He said there'd be a C-Note in it for him if he struck gold. The kid nearly tripped over his own feet getting the door open.

It was mid-afternoon and Murphy had only been running on coffee and aspirin since getting out of bed. He headed for one of the interior open-air delicatessens at the Market. Liverwurst on rye, an icy bottle of Michelob to wash it down with, and a cigarette was about as good as it got on a hot, smoggy day. There were plenty of empty tables under canvas canopies that shielded patrons from the elements and contributed to the cozy ambiance. He found one near a newly misted produce display that filled the air with the scent of fresh citrus.

While in Paris with the Army, he'd loved to sit at sidewalk cafés and watch passers-by. He claimed it honed his skills of observation. Thus, out of force of habit, he surveyed the few people that occupied tables in the vicinity. The closest were obviously Oriental—Korean to be more exact. He recognized a word of conversation every so often from being stationed in Soule during the Korean War—or "police action," as it was frequently referred to, despite the fact that 36,000 American soldiers died there. Mother, father, and three kids out for lunch. Immigrants, because the only Korean spoken was between the parents. The kids spoke perfect English.

Much too easy, Murphy thought.

The couple that had taken seats three tables away was more challenging. Having only coffee, they spoke German from what Murphy could hear, but the man had an accent that might've been Armenian. There was a large enclave of Armenians in Los Angeles that had immigrated immediately after World War II, before the Iron Curtain had descended. But their clothes seemed too heavy for the southern California climate, and their shoes were definitely old world—thick-soled, clunky. Next to Las Vegas and San Francisco, LA was a western mecca for manufacturing shows. He concluded the couple could well be part of an overseas trade delegation off on an afternoon excursion.

Murphy finished his sandwich with the last swig of beer and then checked his watch. No reason to make the trip back into town when his next destination was out toward Venice Beach. Still, he wanted to call his office for any messages and to speak with Doyle, if possible. He found a payphone on the outskirts of the Market.

"Murphy and Doyle, Private Investigations."

"Andrea, it's Jack."

"Are you okay? I was worried."

"Of course I'm okay. Why wouldn't I be?"

"I happened to be looking out the window when you drove away. Just as you left the lot, a car parked on the street pulled out into traffic behind you and nearly caused a wreck. I thought maybe Frank Baldwin hadn't learned his lesson, after all, and was following you."

"Baldwin won't be working the pedals of a car for some time. You worry too much."

"Listen, there are only two women in your life, as far as I know: Tara and yours truly. It's our job to worry about you, but I'm the one getting paid for it."

"Well, as long as you brought up her name, has she called?"

"No. I thought maybe you eventually got hold of her."

"Too busy, up till now. But is Matt in?"

"Not currently, but I expect him back. You want me to give him a message?"

"Yeah. I want him to try to run down the registration on a handgun purchased by Charles Hayward."

Murphy took the notebook from his coat pocket and read off the serial number. He knew that state legislation was underway to require gun dealers to report handgun purchases, but as of today the reporting process was only voluntary.

"Are you going to be back in today?" Andrea asked.

"No. I've got another stop to make." He looked again at his watch.

"You know, with you and Matt gone so much, I get lonely."

"How about buying a goldfish? You can put the bowl right on your desk."

"That's what I like about you, Jack: You're all heart."

Murphy's next dime was spent on calling O'Neill's and not without some trepidation. It was Tara who answered.

"It's about time, don't you think?" she started in after finding out who it was.

"Didn't deShazo tell you I called?"

"Yes, but I thought you'd have called me first thing this morning. You left here last night looking like crap. When I didn't hear from you, I called you at home but got no answer."

"Really? What time was that?"

"A little after nine."

"I'd already left on a case by then."

"So Andrea said. You can call her, but you can't call me?"

"Honest, I thought about calling but figured you'd still be in bed. You usually are, right?"

"Not today. I had an appointment to get my hair and nails done."

"How was I supposed to know that? But, hey, I'm sorry."

There was a long silence, then, "Apology accepted. So will I see you tonight? I thought that maybe we could...you

51

know…if you're up to it?"

"That's the best proposition I've had all day. And yes, I can hold up my end. But—"

"But what?"

"I need to check out a club on Venice Boulevard. It's part of that case I'm working."

"What club is that?"

"I'm sure you've never heard of it."

"Try me."

"The Garden of Eden."

"You've got to be joking. That's a notorious haunt for—"

"Yes, so I've been told. But duty calls. And the sooner the better. I'm thinking it must have an afternoon happy-hour. I don't expect to be long."

"Yeah…well…if you don't turn up at the pub, I'll assume you got a better offer." She laughed.

12

Rush hour traffic was light by Los Angeles standards, although visitors from North Dakota or Wyoming would've found it maddening. Movement from Point A to Point B was one of the downsides of living in LA. A state highway engineer had once confided to Murphy that by the time new traffic arteries could be designed and built, they were obsolete. The reason, he'd explained, was that the infrastructure simply couldn't keep up with in migration. Southern California was a magnet for those looking for prospects of a "better life." The climate was undeniably superb, even when smoggy days were factored in. Well-paying jobs were plentiful. Housing prices and rents were low. Excluding a few neighborhoods, it was relatively safe. It was a wonder that anyone chose to live elsewhere.

Roads that terminated at ocean fronts were always backed up, regardless of the time of day, and Venice Boulevard was no exception. It seemed to Murphy that he'd hit every red light. The Garden of Eden was right where the kid at Hayward's apartment building had said it was: almost to the beach on the right side of the street. In fact, Murphy now recognized he'd seen it before on the day he'd gone fishing on the Venice Pier. Apparently, patrons arrived early, because it was only four o'clock and there were no vacant stalls in the parking lot. Instead, he found a spot on the street around the corner.

He transferred the photo of Hayward and the list of his friends into his shirt pocket, then ditched his tie and shrugged out of his suit coat and shoulder holster, leaving them in the trunk. From what he'd seen, the dress standard for the club was casual attire. No reason to draw any undue attention to himself. He kept his dark glasses on.

As he walked past the stone statues of Adam and Eve in the buff, he marveled at the detail. Anatomically correct in every way. Michelangelo could've taken lessons from the artist who'd sculpted them. Murphy followed the two women who'd just entered when he was challenged by the doorkeeper.

"Hold on there, buddy. This is a private club for members only."

His black head was shaved, and he wore a single earring. Under his silver-studded leather jacket, his muscled body must've resembled a professional wrestler's. Obviously the first line of defense against the inquisitive. Murphy had seen two Harley-Davidson motorcycles parked in the lot and wondered if one of them belonged to this guy.

"Yes, I'm quite aware of that," Murphy lied. "I'm new to LA, and this place came highly recommended. I noticed there are more cars out front than at Disneyland." He reached for his wallet. "So how about I buy an E-ticket for twenty bucks, and if I like the ride, I'll buy a season pass." He held out the bill.

The guy hesitated a moment, than snatched it from Murphy's hand.

"You're kind of a wise-ass, you know that?"

"I've been called worse."

"I'll bet you have. E-ticket, huh?" He laughed. "Pretty funny. Okay, go on in. You play your cards right, you might even score."

My sentiments exactly, Murphy thought.

Once inside, he removed his sunglasses to acclimate his eyes to the ambient light, filtering through a thick layer of cigarette smoke. He felt like he needed a flashlight to find his way around. Drawn from the pages of Genesis, murals adorned the walls and ceilings, though the figures of winged naked angels were less explicit than the statues outside. Nonetheless, the biblical renditions would've been at home in the Sistine Chapel.

Mingling couples and singles of either sex seemed to be having a good time. Some had drinks in their hands, while others swayed on the parquet dance floor to a song chosen by what appeared to be the resident disc jockey. Murphy's attention was then caught by two individuals in black leather jackets kissing as then leaned against the wall. Because of their close-cropped hair, he'd at first identified them as men. He now saw he was wrong. Did they belong to the other motorcycle? Dykes on a bike? In any event, only Murphy seemed to pay the slightest bit of attention to them.

With most of his adult life having been spent in the Army, Murphy was a man of the world and not prudish by any standard. He knew such establishments existed—no matter the city—but he'd never been remotely curious enough to venture inside one. Until now, when circumstances demanded it. He couldn't get close to the bar to order a drink but caught the bartender's eye and pointed to a vacant booth on the opposite wall. The man nodded he understood.

Murphy had just ensconced himself on the green Naugahyde fabric when a sharp-featured man with curly blond hair sauntered over. More pretty than handsome. The top three buttons of his shirt were undone, exposing a hairless chest and a thick, dazzling gold chain.

He cleared his throat. "Buy a girl a drink?"

This was all new for Murphy. No man had ever come on to him before, but he'd used similar lines hundreds of times on female barflies. He wondered if they'd sounded as lame to them as it did now.

"That all depends on whether you're good for answering a few questions."

The man nodded and then slid in next to Murphy.

"My name's Craig. What's yours?"

"Jack."

"Pleased to meet you, Jack." He offered his hand. "I don't believe I've seen you around before."

At that moment, a waitress appeared at the table and stood ready to take their order. Her working uniform consisted of a long-sleeve white shirt with a black bowtie and gold cufflinks. A red satin cummerbund and black slacks and Oxfords finished off the ensemble. Her dark hair was slicked back in a pompadour reminiscent of Rudolph Valentino, *the* silent movie heartthrob. Masculine appearance or not, she had a perfect nose, and even through the smoke, her twinkling eyes were the brightest shade of blue that Murphy had ever seen.

Murphy said, "I'll have a Jack Daniels and soda. Plenty of ice. Give my friend here whatever he wants."

"A strawberry margarita. Extra salt." After she left Craig said, "So I was saying that you must be new to our little home away from home."

"You're right. And I'm only here now on business—not pleasure."

Craig furrowed his brow, apprehension showing.

Murphy slid the photo of Hayward toward him.

"Have you ever seen him before?"

Craig glanced at it briefly but didn't move to pick it up. He looked over at Murphy.

"A cop. I might've guessed. That's the way my life's been going lately. You got balls coming in here and asking us for anything." He started to extract himself from the booth.

Murphy grabbed him by the arm.

"Hold on! Don't jump to conclusions. I'm no cop. I'm a private investigator."

"Birds of a feather." He tried to pry Murphy's hand loose, but Murphy tightened his grip and yanked him back.

The foursome in the next booth craned their necks to get a better look. Murphy gave them a withering scowl, and they went back to minding their business.

As if on cue, their drinks arrived, the waitress taking them from her tray and setting each on a paper doily. Murphy gave her a ten-dollar bill.

"Keep the change."

She smiled and then winked, as if to give him an "atta boy" for scoring a date.

Craig then said, "Okay, you bought me a drink, so I owe you for that." He sipped at the pink liquid over the salt-rimmed, shallow glass.

Murphy said, "I'm curious. What's your beef with the police, anyway?"

"This." He pulled open his shirt at the neck, revealing a scar near his shoulder blade. "Shattered collar bone. Just for being at the wrong place at the wrong time."

"Are you saying you were attacked by the police? Without provocation?"

"You must be a stranger in town . Cops don't need a reason to rough us up. It's sport for them. And it's always open season on 'faggots.' There's safety in numbers, but let them catch you alone..."

"The guy at the front door looks like he could hold his own." Murphy took a swig of his whisky.

"Tiny? I guess he'd be an exception, all right. He's a body builder. Won a couple of local competitions. They'd think twice about pushing *him* around." Craig laughed.

"And he goes by 'Tiny'?"

"His real name is Alfonse, but to his friends, he's just Tiny. So what is it you want?" His tone was again defensive.

"For you to take a closer look at this picture." Murphy repositioned it. "Do you recognize him?"

This time he picked it up—reluctantly.

"He's lost the beard," he said at last, "but he still wears that ridiculous pencil-thin mustache. Says it makes him look sophisticated like David Niven or Clarke Gable. If you want my opinion, it's what porn stars grow."

"So I take it you know him, then."

"Of course. Charlie Hayward. The LA *Times* reporter. Usually comes in maybe three times a week, but come to think of it, I haven't seen him lately."

57

"Can you remember the last time?"

Craig sat back. "I'm not answering any more questions, until I know what this is about. Why is a private investigator interested in Charlie?"

"He's dropped out of sight, as you said. I've been hired by his father to find him."

"Well, in that case, the simplest thing would be to look for his car. Charlie almost never lets that Vette out of his sight. When he's here, he pays Tiny extra to keep an eye on it."

Murphy nodded but already knew that wasn't true. He shook out a cigarette from his pack and offered it to Craig.

"No thanks. I don't smoke. I have to draw the line somewhere." He laughed.

Murphy lit up. "So let me go back to my previous question: Do you remember when you last saw him?"

Craig thought for a moment. "The Fourth. He'd invited a few of us over to his place for a barbeque and to watch the fireworks. The party broke up about midnight. I'm pretty sure I haven't seen him since."

"At that time, did he give any indication that he was planning a trip or would otherwise be gone for any length of time?"

"Not that I'm aware."

Murphy changed direction. "Did you spend a lot of time with Charlie? I mean—"

"You mean were we ever a 'couple'? God knows I would've liked that, but no. It came down to not being Charlie's type."

"And what type is that?"

"Charlie prefers more manly companions. And let's face it; I'm a bit swishy. So when I saw you come in—"

"Yes…well," Murphy was flustered, "we can put that to rest. So what can you tell me about Charlie?"

"You mean apart from being one of *us*?"

"Yes."

"Well, he's got more money than Carter has liver pills, but he's not stuck up about it. Knows how to spread it around. If someone's short on rent, for example, Charlie rides to the rescue. Doesn't even seem concerned about being paid back. He has lots of friends here."

Murphy removed the folded sheet of paper from his shirt pocket and held it out for Craig to take.

"According to his father, these are some of Charlie's friends. Could they be club members?"

Craig perused the list of three names and nodded. "All of them. In fact, I saw them here earlier."

"Maybe you could introduce me later."

"Sure, why not?"

"Thanks. I'm kind of grasping at straws for any leads. What about narcotics? I've been led to believe he may have a problem."

"I've heard rumors to that effect but assumed that if they were true, it was in the past and that he'd cleaned up his act. I never saw any evidence to the contrary. And I ought to know, because I once dabbled a little, myself."

"Might there be someone who'd like to do him harm? You know—a jealousy thing. He jilts one guy for another."

"That scenario plays out from time to time, sure. LA's hardly the City of Brotherly Love. But I never heard anything like that with regard to Charlie."

They finished their drinks and then Craig vouched for Murphy as he was introduced to the three guys on the list, men who'd actually been intimate with Hayward. Murphy went through the same line of questioning, with the same disappointing results. He gave each of them a business card and requested that they call if they thought of anything more.

Craig eventually walked Murphy to the front door and shook his hand.

"You're an okay guy," he said. "Sorry I was so rude at the beginning."

"Nonsense. You've been a great help, and I appreciate it."

Outside, the doorman asked, "Did you enjoy the ride?"

Murphy patted him on the shoulder. "Alfonse, it was everything I hoped it would be—and then some."

Walking back to his car, Murphy thought about something he'd seen while being introduced around by Craig. He'd read that everyone has a double somewhere in the world—a person who could be an identical twin, but isn't. Well, as strange as it seemed, he'd seen Rock Hudson's double. The light hadn't been good from across the room, and it was only for a fleeting moment, but still... He wondered what Rock's reaction would be. He'd probably laugh himself silly at the notion.

13

Make up sex is great! Murphy thought as Tara slid off, both of them sweaty and spent.

"That was the best ever," she panted.

"'Customer satisfaction' is my motto." He chuckled, a bit winded himself. "Glad to have been of service, Miss."

The fireworks had begun the night before. He'd gone to O'Neill's from the Garden of Eden in plenty of time for dinner. The *entrée du jour* was shepherd's pie, artfully prepared by Paddy Malone, chief cook and bottle washer and a good friend of Tara's late father. They'd subsequently left the pub around ten, deShazo tasked with closing up, and headed for Murphy's place.

"Reckless abandon" was the term that had come to Murphy's mind as they'd torn at each other's clothing, letting the items fall to the floor as they'd haltingly made their way to the bedroom. He'd feared Tara might be writing checks that his aging body couldn't cash, but in the end, he'd come through like a champ. Exhausted, they'd drifted off to sleep. Then twenty minutes ago, just before first light, Tara's engine had fired up again. A slow purr at first, but eventually revving to a high pitch.

After regaining her breath, she pulled up the satin sheet to cover them.

"Jack, I need to talk to you about something." She stared at the ceiling, her fingers laced behind her neck.

"What is it? Another sermon on marriage, because—"

"No, not this time. It's a secret that I've never shared with anyone."

Murphy rolled onto his side to face her and propped himself on his elbow.

"Okay. You've got my attention."

She took a deep breath. "For my part, it began during the first winter after the war. I remember the day was bone-chilling and windy, as only Belfast can get that time of year. I had arranged to go to a friend's house after school. It was already dark when my father came to pick me up. I expected him to come to the door, but he just honked from the street. When I got into the car, I could tell something was wrong. That's when he told me my mother had been killed in an explosion that had destroyed our house. I must have been in shock, because I only remember having an empty feeling. I didn't cry."

"What further explanation did he give?"

"That's just it. He said I was better off not knowing. I pressed him, but he would only say that he had made his own bed and now both of us had to lie in it. He then told me never to ask him more. By the tone of his voice, I knew he was serious. He'd never spoken to me that way before.

"We followed another car to a farmhouse far out into the countryside, where we stayed for the better part of a month. Other people came and went every day, but I was never allowed outside. For my own safety, they said. We were given new identification documents. Our name had been Maguire. Michael and Taragh Maguire. But now it was O'Neill. Even our birth certificates reflected the change. Then one night we were loaded into the back of a covered truck and driven to the coast. From there a cargo ship took us to Canada. Then by train to Los Angeles, where we were met by one of the men I'd seen at the farmhouse. He made it plain to us that any ties we

62

had to family or friends in Ireland were to be severed. No one could know our whereabouts. So I did what I was told and put my prior life behind me. I had just turned sixteen.

"As you might imagine, I secretly struggled to make some sense of it all. We'd fled like criminals. Why? But it wasn't until I was in college that my quest for the truth began in earnest. First, I thought I might be able to find an account of my mother's death. I went from library to library on the chance that they subscribed to a Belfast newspaper with archived copies going back that far. There were none.

"But from what else I had read, I learned that immediately after the war, special units of the British Army were tasked with hunting down and eliminating German collaborators, especially in the North, where they took pleasure in the use of explosives to do their duty."

"Are you suggesting…?"

"Yes. I believe my father was a Nazi spy. I think the intent was to kill him and anyone else in our house, but my mother was the only casualty."

"You'd have been in your early teens during the war. Yet you had no idea what he was up to?"

"None whatsoever. Of course, being a liquor salesman, it seemed like he was gone more than he was home. Whatever he did for Germany, he could have done while he was away."

"Do you think your mother knew?"

"I'd like to believe she didn't, but it doesn't matter. They murdered her just the same. And as for my father's financial situation after the war, I know there was never any excess cash lying around. So how was it that he had sufficient resources to procure a pub in Los Angeles? I think the answer is obvious. The Nazis not only arranged to get him out of the country with a new identity but also provided him with funds to start a new life. And once I'd come to grips with his past, not a day went by that I didn't feel complicit.

"Then you walked through the front door and stole my heart. I knew from the onset that I'd eventually have to shine a light on the skeletons in the closet but was afraid of losing you when I did."

Murphy embraced her.

"What's past is past, Tara. A lot of regrettable things were done during the war—on all sides. Your father would've been reminded of that every time he thought of your mother. And I'll bet he never remarried because it would've betrayed her memory. I'm just sorry you've carried this burden all these years."

"Oh, Jack," she cooed. "I love you so much."

Then she pushed him onto his back, and her engine started to rev again.

14

They showered together. Afterward, wrapped in a towel, Tara used a blow dryer on her hair while Murphy retrieved their clothing—complete with Colt .45 and shoulder holster—that littered the living room floor, evidence of a night of passion.

He had just deposited the items on the bed and was on his way back to the bathroom when Tara stepped out, wearing nothing but a smile.

"How about we make a day of it?" she said. "Get out of the heat and drive down to del Mar."

Corona del Mar was a beach about fifty miles south of LA. The half-mile narrow stretch of sand was framed by cliffs to the east and rocks that jutted into the ocean on the north and south, giving the area an air of seclusion. It was a favorite destination for sunbathers and surfers who wanted to avoid the crowds of tourists that inhabited the more commercial beaches.

"It's going to be another scorcher; that's for sure," Murphy said. "But I really need to stick close to this case I just picked up."

She ignored his response. "We could swing by my place and pick up my swimming suit. Remember that little cove we found last time on the other side of the tide pools?"

They'd stayed to watch the sun set and had been cut off from returning to the main beach by high tide. Making the most of their situation, for hours they'd skinny-dipped and made love in the moonlight.

"There's nothing wrong with my memory." He grinned.

"Well...? Let's say we do an encore performance." She approached and threw her arms around his neck. "Practice makes perfect." She ground her naked body against him and kissed him hard on the mouth, her tongue searching.

At last, Murphy pulled away and held her at arm's length.

"You really know how to close a deal, but I still have to decline the offer. How about a rain check?"

"You're taking a pass on all this?" She slowly ran her hands down her body. "You're not just another private eye, Jack. You must be Superman."

They laughed.

"What's so important about this case, anyway" she finally said, "that it can't wait a day?"

"A guy has gone missing; I've been hired to locate him."

"Who?"

"I can't tell you his name. It would be a breach of professional ethics."

"Does Andrea know who it is?"

"Yes, but she—"

Tara cut him off. "Is this the way it's going to be after we're married? You out and about, maybe risking your life for God knows what, while I mind my own business?"

"I—"

"Oh, I forgot. You haven't yet made up your mind if you want to marry me or not. Don't let me pressure you, but I'd have thought that after last night and this morning..." She left the thought unfinished, but Murphy caught the drift.

"Well, you see, that's just the problem," he replied. "I was this close," he used his thumb and forefinger, "to checking into a hospital for exhaustion. I don't know how much more of a good thing I can take."

"A rough and tumble guy like you? I find that hard to

believe, but maybe you're right. Maybe I should be looking for someone much younger, someone who can hold up his end," she winked, "if you know what I mean, big boy?"

Before he could think of something witty to say, she walked past him toward the bedroom and patted his butt, as she did.

They'd taken separate cars when they'd left the pub the night before, so after breakfast—Tara had wanted to fix him bacon and eggs, but he'd begged off in favor of toast and coffee instead—he went directly to the office.

Andrea hardly looked up from her typing when he came in and crossed the room to his partner's office. Matthew Doyle, about the same age as Murphy, looked years older—due to balding gray hair—and tipped the scale at a shade under three hundred pounds, the last thirty piled on since his retirement date in October. He hadn't always been a heart attack candidate, but when his wife of twenty years had dumped him and taken his high school-age kids with her to Florida, he'd fallen into a dark pit of despair. In fact, he'd confided to Murphy that he'd given a lot of thought to just "eating his gun" after the divorce was final and being done with it once and for all.

But since joining forces with his old Army buddy, he seemed to be on the way to recovery. He still drank more than he should, but that fault had its roots in going home to an empty apartment every day. Murphy dragged him to O'Neill's at least once a week in hopes that he'd meet someone, but as yet he'd had no success. And his weight wasn't helping his self-esteem.

Doyle sat with his feet on his desk, reading the newspaper. A cup of coffee and a half-eaten donut were at his elbow.

"Has the world blown itself up yet?" Murphy asked from the doorway.

Doyle came to an upright position and folded the paper.

"I don't know about the world," he said, "but everywhere you look, there's a fuse burning in LA. Those race riots last year back east were only previews of what we can expect."

"You've worked here your whole career. You got anything specific in mind?"

Doyle shook his head. "No, that's just it. No telling for

sure where it's going to explode, but if I were a betting man, I'd say East LA or South Central. Chief Parker believes the Negroes and Mexicans have to be taught who the boss is. Which translates into aggressive patrolling in those areas. Too aggressive, if my sources have it right."

Murphy pulled up a chair.

Doyle said, "Andrea told me about your encounter with Frank Baldwin. I see now that she wasn't exaggerating. As far as I'm concerned, that son of a bitch ought to be in jail, along with his pals. But if you want to go soft on them..." He left the thought unfinished.

"Locking them up wouldn't do my eye any good. And besides, I gave a lot more than I got. A slick lawyer might even suggest I went overboard to resolve the situation. So I'll just leave it like it is. But you mentioned your sources. Did you have any luck finding where Charles Hayward purchased the revolver I found in his bedroom?"

"You must be living a charmed life, my friend. Most sporting goods stores haven't seen fit to voluntarily report their sales, but Hayward bought his at one that did." He picked up a 3x5 card from his desk and read what he'd scribbled. "Colt .38 Detective Special. Purchased the afternoon of June seventh of this year at Mel's Sporting Goods. That's located on Crenshaw Boulevard at Imperial. I looked it up."

"That's in Inglewood, isn't it?"

"Yep."

"Yet Hayward lives in West LA and works downtown. He must pass a dozen sporting goods stores on his way every day. Why would he go all the way out to Inglewood to buy a gun?"

"Doesn't make much sense to me, either. So tell me what else you've got?"

They always staffed each other's cases. Two brains and four eyes often paid dividends that going solo lacked.

When Murphy was through, Doyle said, "Homosexual, huh? You think it figures in somehow?"

"Too early to tell."

"You going to bring it up with the father?" Doyle took a bit of his donut.

"I told him I'd keep him up to date on my progress, but I think I'll hold off on *that* bombshell. Unless I find it has meaning to the case."

"So what's your next move?"

"Well, you've probably had more experience with missing persons cases than I have. I had AWOLs to find in the Army, but in most instances I don't think the two are comparable. I don't expect to find Hayward holed up in some cheap hotel room because he doesn't like the rules and regulations of working for the *Times*." He laughed. "But that's where I'm headed now. Shake the tree. See if anything falls to the ground." He got to his feet. "Getting Hayward's phone records and any credit card transactions would certainly come in handy."

"No doubt. But even the police couldn't get a warrant for that information without reasonable suspicion that Hayward's disappearance is tied to a crime. Private eyes are just shit out of luck."

"Yet another downside of working outside the 'system.' And in that regard, I could use some help on another matter."

"And what's that?"

"The Mickey O'Neill murder last March. What are the chances you could score a copy of the investigative file from one of your ex-buddies?"

"Slim to none after my testimony on the Freddy Harmon case yesterday. I'm now officially a leper in some circles."

"For telling the truth?"

"For exposing cockroaches to sunlight. It just so happens that the cockroaches in question were once my friends. It's 'The Code' thing. And I violated it. Simple as that. Didn't CID have its own version?"

"We watched out for one another, sure, but I can't think of an instance where anyone deliberately falsified evidence with the expectation of everyone else turning a blind eye. Maybe that's why we were transferred around so often—to avoid forming those kinds of ties."

"Well, in my case, those attachments began when we were rookies. We've got history."

"And they'd be part of gassing an innocent kid? Shit, they missed their calling by twenty-five years. They should've been rounding up Jews for the Nazis. Well, fuck 'em then. I'll go at the O'Neill murder a different way."

"You won't have to, because I already have a file copy. It's in a cardboard box in my bedroom closet."

"I don't understand. Why would you have the file? You didn't work the case, did you?"

"No, a couple of detectives who now consider me persona non grata were assigned the case. Not the sharpest knives in the drawer, so when they officially declared it unsolvable, I made a copy. It's not uncommon for homicide cops to take a few cold cases with them into retirement. Just for something to do. And sometimes, they get lucky; they see something that others missed. In any event, I'll bring it in and we can go over it together. I assume your interest has something to do with Tara."

"You don't know the half of it."

15

As in most metropolitan cities, downtown parking is a bitch. Los Angeles was no exception. Consequently, Murphy decided to hoof it. It was already uncomfortably warm and the prospect of triple digits later in the day loomed large. He regretted now that he hadn't succumbed to Tara's invitation to a day at the beach. Even panhandlers, who were normally in evidence, had abandoned their respective street corners for shadier locations.

Murphy had become accustomed to seeing large numbers of homeless people during his tours of duty in Europe. Directly or indirectly, millions had been left adrift in the wake of Hitler's Third Reich's march across the continent. The bulk of LA's homeless were likewise tied to the war, but in a much different way. They were the walking dead, soldiers who'd never recovered from their experiences, permanently scarred by what they'd seen and done. The worst tended to be Marines who'd served in the South Pacific. But regardless of the theater of operations, returning GIs had subsequently turned to alcohol and drugs to mask the pain of their nightmares. In fact, they were hardly strangers to narcotics. Addiction had begun in the foxhole. Benzedrine tablets had been passed out like candy by company commanders to keep the men alert for enemy activity.

Being strung out had become second nature to them in combat. But now, without a purpose, suicide was not uncommon for them.

Murphy was always good for spare change. *There but for the grace of God*, he figured. He'd even been told that if it hadn't been for Jimmy Cagney's concern, Audie Murphy, the bravest and most decorated soldier of them all, would've likely drowned in a bottle of whisky. Now, with Cagney's help, he was a famous movie star, but rumor held he slept with a pistol under his pillow to keep away his war-induced demons.

The *Los Angeles Times* Building, on the corner of First and Spring streets, was a massive structure of limestone and granite that had been awarded a gold medal at the 1937 Paris Exposition for its modern architecture. Its double glass front doors opened onto a marble-tiled floor depicting a huge compass. At the center was a revolving world globe about five feet in diameter. Originally, the walls had been adorned by great murals depicting various aspects of newspaper production. They were now covered by decorative aluminum paneling. There was, however, a larger than life portrait of Otis Chandler, the current owner of the newspaper, which looked down from its perch.

On his walk over, Murphy had rehearsed his approach. He had no official standing; thus, no one was obliged to talk to him. That was another of the downsides of being a "private" detective. In the Army, CID agents were considered to be one rank higher than anyone they spoke to. Cooperation was, therefore, understood to be a direct order.

Although a uniformed security officer surveyed the lobby, the Keeper of the Gate appeared to be a gray-haired woman in the upper reaches of sixty. As Murphy approached, she looked up from filling in the squares of a crossword puzzle with a stubby pencil and adjusted her tortoiseshell horn-rimmed glasses.

"May I help you?" Her eyes went immediately to his battered face, and she winced involuntarily.

"Yes, my name is Jack Murphy." Now for the lie. "I have

an appointment to see Charles Hayward this morning."

"I'm sorry, but Mr. Hayward is no longer employed by the *Times*."

"But I spoke to him earlier in the month."

"Yes, well he left us about two weeks ago."

"Some other paper made him a better offer, huh?" Murphy chucked. "I'd have figured he was one of your best reporters. I'm surprised you'd let him go that easily."

"Sometimes a change is best for all concerned."

It was plain she knew more than she was letting on.

Murphy said, "Nevertheless, I have certain information that the newspaper will want to follow up on. At least that's what Mr. Hayward thought. Perhaps I could speak with his replacement."

"I'm afraid his position has yet to be filled, but maybe Mr. Klinefelter is available. He's City Editor. Mr. Hayward reported to him."

Murphy was suddenly thrust back into time.

"That wouldn't happen to be Morris Klinefelter, would it? The famous war correspondent?"

She smiled for the first time.

"None other. The *Times* attracts only the best. Though I doubt the name would mean anything to our younger employees. They have no concept of history. It's a shame, really."

"I won't bore you with the story, but he and I once came into contact during the Normandy Campaign. It was a on a day neither of us will forget."

"Why don't I just ring his secretary for you?"

A few moments later, the receptionist was on the phone.

"Hazel. Gladys. I have a gentleman here who had an appointment for this morning with Charlie...A Mr. Jack Murphy...No, I don't know what it was about, but I thought if Morris wasn't too busy, he could meet with him."

Murphy said above a whisper, "It'll only take a couple minutes of his time."

She nodded. "He says it won't take long. And what's more, he knew Morris during the war...Fine. I'll send him right up." She cradled the phone receiver, then reached into a desk drawer and withdrew a clip-on visitor's pass.

Handing it to Murphy, she said, "Take the elevator," she pointed behind her, "to the third floor. It'll open onto the City Newsroom. You'll be met by an escort."

Murphy clipped the tag to his lapel, then said, "Thank you for going out of your way to help me."

"Entirely my pleasure, Mr. Murphy."

On the third floor, the elevator doors slid open to reveal a sprawling room filled with the sound of typewriters, phone conversations, and hectically scurrying men and women. Sunlight from banks of windows near the ceiling barely penetrated the layer of tobacco smoke that hung over the proceedings like an indoor cloud.

The promised escort wasn't what Murphy expected. Standing beside the elevator was a teenage boy with red hair, freckles, and glasses fitted with thick lenses that created a bug-eye effect. A white shirt, striped tie, dark trousers, and wingtip shoes gave him the appearance of a junior executive.

"Mr. Murphy?"

"Yes, that's right."

"My name is Kevin." He reached out his hand which Murphy shook.

"Pleased to meet you, Kevin. The paper must be hiring younger and younger reporters."

Kevin laughed. "No, I'm just a high school summer intern. I get to see how a newspaper is run, and I've learned a lot. After college, I'm going to be a journalist."

Murphy grinned. "And I bet you'll be a good one."

"Mr. Klinefelter is waiting, so if you'll just follow me, I'll take you to him."

No one even glanced their way as he and Kevin threaded the labyrinth of desks strewn across a linoleum-tiled floor. At last, they entered a small anteroom outside Klinefelter's office. A tall, slender woman—presumably, Hazel, his secretary—stood at a file cabinet, her back turned.

Kevin announced, "Ma'am, Mr. Murphy is here to see Mr. Klinefelter."

She turned and gave Murphy a once-over. Like a general inspecting his troops. Murphy couldn't tell if he'd passed muster, or if the black eye made him suspect.

"Thank you, Kevin." All business. She then walked to her desk and picked up a pile of manila envelopes. "Take these down to the mailroom," handing them to the boy. "And tell Steve that they're to go out Special Delivery."

"Yes, ma'am, right away." Then at the doorway, he turned and said, "Nice to have met you, Mr. Murphy."

Murphy nodded, and Kevin disappeared into the newsroom.

"Nice kid," Murphy said.

"And very industrious. We've had some interns who were more trouble than they were worth." A pause. "Mr. Klinefelter just stepped out on a matter, but he shouldn't be long. You may wait in his office." She ushered him to the door.

Once inside, a framed poster-size black and white photograph caught his attention, and he walked across the room to study the image more closely.

Moments later, a voice from behind said, "Omaha Beach. June 6, 1944."

Murphy turned to see a stocky, dapper-looking man in shirt sleeves and suspenders. He leaned slightly on a burled wood cane. More than twenty-one years had passed, but Murphy would've recognized him anywhere.

"Yes, I know. I was about a hundred yards farther up the beach with my MP Company. Did you take this picture?"

Klinefelter joined him.

"As it turned out, it was the last photograph I took during the war. Moments later, a German mortar round blew off my right leg, just below the knee. I probably would've bled out if it hadn't been for an enterprising medic. I owe him my life but never got his name."

"I'd say that was more the rule than the exception. Angels of mercy with tourniquets and morphine."

Klinefelter laughed. "I never heard it explained that way before. But you're right." He paused, then, "So my secretary tells me that we were acquainted during the war. Jog my memory, Mr. Murphy."

"'Acquainted' might be too strong a word. I knew who you were from the picture over your byline in the *Star and Stripes*. You or Ernie Pyle had a story in every edition. Or maybe it just seemed that way. In any event, you and I were lying side by side on that hospital ship that took us back to England. I'd taken some shrapnel, myself. You were more drugged up than I, in and out of consciousness for the trip, but I felt I was in pretty good company. I'd never been that close to anyone famous before—or since, for that matter."

"Fame is fleeting. And for the record, compared to Ernie, I was a hack. But I appreciate the compliment." He pointed to a dark brown leather sofa, cracked with age. "Please have a seat."

Murphy did so, and Klinefelter settled comfortably into an adjacent matching chair.

"I think the expression was 'smoke 'em if you got 'em,'" Klinefelter said.

"Thanks. I've been trying to cut back, and I've already reached my limit. But what the hell." He pulled a half-pack from his shirt pocket and lit one.

Klinefelter came up with a cigar.

"Cuban. There's an embargo on, but what good are friends in high places if they can't skirt the rules for a worthy cause." When he'd finished laughing, he said, "I understand you had an appointment with Charles Hayward." He shook his head. "Too bad he didn't have the courtesy to call and tell you he no longer worked here. I hope you didn't travel far."

"No, I walked over from my office. And I would've loved to have found him in, but from what I'd already been told, I knew he wouldn't be. My real purpose in coming was to talk to anyone who might have an idea of his whereabouts. I apologize for the subterfuge. I've been hired to find him, if I can."

Klinefelter leaned forward and tapped the end of his cigar

on a table ashtray. When he leaned back, he said, "You're working for Clayton Hayward, then?"

"Yes. Private investigator."

"Is that shiner of yours work related?"

"Unfortunately, but the other guys only *wish* they looked this good."

Klinefelter laughed. "Were you a cop before?"

"Army CID. When everyone else went home after the war, I stayed on—until my retirement last November."

"You think there's more to Charlie's absence than meets the eye? Is that it?" He sounded skeptical.

"I only took the case yesterday, so I haven't yet formed an opinion. But I've already spoken to some of his friends, and they seem baffled that they haven't seen him."

"I suppose you know that the police were already here, asking questions."

"I assumed as much. Clayton Hayward said he'd contacted them about Charlie's disappearance. Did they speak with you?"

"No, I was out of the office when they showed up. A couple of plainclothes detectives. That was last Thursday, I believe. They apparently had a look around his office, went through his desk, talked to some of the staff. If they discovered anything of value, they didn't say." He paused, then said, "I know Clayton. Quite well, as a matter of fact. At one time or another, we've sat on the boards of some charity organizations. He has a bundle of inherited money. Charities always prefer board members who can singlehandedly take up the slack in case of shortfalls. I was the exception on that score, but I could deliver media attention. Anyway, it was Clayton who pestered me to hire Charlie right out of college. His grades were abysmal, but I agreed to try him out. I moved him around to see what he could do: a flower show; a debutante ball; a couple obituaries; even a roller derby game.

"He may not have impressed his professors, but I sure as hell took notice. It was like having Hemingway on staff. The kid was that good. He could write rings around anyone else. But investigative reporting was his forte. I started him out in earnest on the political beat. He took to it like a fish to water. If the official version of events didn't add up, he wouldn't rest until he'd discovered the truth.

"This isn't to say he didn't have his shortcomings. First it was booze; however, I can think of a few Pulitzer Prize winners who drank with both hands. He started to drag himself in at all hours, usually missing the sacred daily briefing. Then he'd be gone for a day or two without any explanation. I even sat him down right where you're sitting and asked what was going on."

"What did he say?"

"I can't remember his exact words, but the gist of them was that I worried too much, and that he'd never missed a deadline. So what was my problem?" He took a puff on the cigar. "I'm not a psychologist, but my feeling was that he was suffering from depression and was self-medicating via alcohol and then narcotics."

"When I talked to Charlie's sister, she pegged his problems on drugs, too."

"He has a sister? I didn't know that. I thought Charlie was an only child. Clayton never let on."

"There's some bad blood between Alie—that's the daughter—and her father. She was Army CID, as well. She's now an FBI agent and the one who actually recommended me for the job. She couldn't care less about her brother's well-being. If he dies of a drug overdose, good riddance."

"What's that old saw about blood being thicker than water?"

"I was equally surprised to hear how down she was on him, but oh, well… Clayton Hayward told me that Charlie had gone AWOL twice before now. What can you tell me about that?"

"Not much more than what you've said. Both times he was gone for about a week. And both times the cops arrived as the result of Clayton notifying them. Though on the second go-around, they struck me as less enthusiastic. Then on both occasions Charlie simply showed back up to work bright and early, as if nothing had happened. I let the first time slide. After the second, I told him he was fired. He must've gotten on the phone to Clayton, because within minutes he called and begged me to give Charlie another chance; that he'd even pay Charlie's salary until he'd proved himself to me. I declined the offer of money but relented on firing him. I felt sorrier for Clayton than I did Charlie. That was about a year ago, and I have to say that Charlie was as good as gold right up until about three weeks ago. That's when we last heard from him. The proverbial straw that broke this camel's back. We're running a newspaper here, not a rehab clinic."

Murphy nodded that he understood. "You said he was good at investigative reporting, and I'd have to agree. I've read his stuff since coming to LA. Surely, he could've ticked off some people."

"You can say that again. Some are under indictment, and some are even doing time."

"Might any of that have resulted in people wanting to do him harm?"

"Anything is possible in LA—you'll find that out the longer you live here—but Charlie never mentioned feeling at risk for what he wrote."

"Was he currently working on anything explosive, so to speak?"

"Maybe. For weeks he'd been very hush-hush on a story he was pursuing. He was supposed to read me in on it after the long Fourth of July weekend. Said he wanted the story to be rock solid before presenting it for review. But he never came back to work."

"You said 'review'?"

"The *Times*, or any major newspaper for that matter, wants to avoid legal challenges to its stories. I'll give you an example: After the Kennedy assassination, one of our cub reporters claimed to have sources within the FBI and CIA who had confided to him that the federal investigation was being compromised from on high; that extensive evidence of multiple shooters was being quashed. And not only that. These sources also alleged the act of assassination, itself, had been conceived and overseen by individuals whose names you would surely recognize. It's a story that would've toppled our government.

But we didn't print it, because Otis Chandler had cold feet. In hindsight, now that the Warren Commission Report is final— Magic 'fucking' Bullet, my ass—I wish we *had* run the story."

"Can't you still?"

"Only theoretically. The reporter in question was killed in a house fire, the result of a freak natural gas explosion. And all his notes apparently burned up with him."

"I'd say that sounds like—"

Klinefelter held up his hand. "Don't go there. I had a knot in my stomach for weeks afterward. You see, I'm not a big fan of coincidences."

"Neither am I—especially *now*."

"You think there's a parallel with Charlie going missing? That he got into water too deep for his own good?"

"My gut says so, for whatever that's worth."

Hayward's purchase of a gun now took on proper perspective: He hadn't thought his previous stories had put him at risk, but this one had made him cautious, or even afraid.

Klinefelter shook his head. "And I rushed to judgment and fired him. I should've been smart enough to smell smoke."

"Is there anyone who Charlie might've confided in about the story he was working on?"

"It's hard to say. He was always pretty tight with his copy girl. I've seen her around this morning. How about I pair up you two?"

"Sounds good. With Charlie gone this long, the only game for me to play is catch up."

16

The copy girl wasn't at her desk. Kevin, the summer intern, was summoned to find her. Shortly thereafter, the paper's owner requested Klinefelter's presence at an impromptu meeting. This left Murphy in the care and keeping of Hazel, who'd necessarily been read into the situation. He didn't have long to wait before a woman appeared at the doorway. Murphy judged her to be in her mid to late twenties—and possibly single, given the absence of a ring on her left hand. A blonde, she was strikingly attractive, even without makeup or lipstick. Undoubtedly an example of a "natural beauty" that he'd heard about since coming to LA. Her gentle tan was complemented by a yellow floral-print sundress that accentuated her curves—all of them in the right places. And what's more, she looked vaguely familiar.

"I understand Mr. Klinefelter wants to see me," she announced, quickly glancing at Murphy, then back to Hazel.

"Actually, it's Mr. Murphy here who wishes to speak with you. It's about Charlie."

Murphy approached. "Jack Murphy." He smiled widely.

She shook his hand. "Shannon Rigby."

Hazel said, "The briefing room is vacant. Why don't you

take Mr. Murphy there for a chat."

They traversed the beehive of activity, and Shannon ushered Murphy into a glassed-in room, the center of which contained a scarred wooden conference table surrounded by a dozen leather high-backed swivel chairs. Closing the door behind her, she motioned Murphy to a chair at the head of the table and then sat down, as well.

"Hazel said you want to talk with me about Charlie. He's all right, isn't he?" There was genuine concern in her tone.

"That's what I'm trying to find out. I'm a private investigator working for his father. So far I've found no one who's seen or talked to him in a while. Klinefelter thought if anyone at the paper might've had contact, it would be you."

"I would've thought that, too. We go back to our high school days. He even got me this job."

"I know he's pulled disappearing acts before, and the consensus appears to be that his absences were drug related."

"Sadly, I have to concur, but he's since put his self-destructive behavior behind him. Of that, I'm absolutely certain."

"As a result of coming to grips with being homosexual?" No reason to sugarcoat it.

"You know about that?"

"I didn't until I spoke to some of his friends of a similar persuasion. Do you suppose his father is aware?"

"Oh, he knows, all right. And it's driven a wedge between them. Mr. Hayward simply can't accept Charlie for who he is."

"Is that right...? I was led to believe they were extremely close."

"Hardly. They seldom speak. Needlessly tragic. And all Charlie wants is to be true to himself."

"So when was it that you last had contact with Charlie?"

"The last time I *saw* him was here at work on July second. Then the following Monday morning he called me at home to ask if he could come over. He wanted me to type up an outline of a story he'd been working on. He said he was sorry for the short notice, but he needed to make a presentation to the

Review Committee on Tuesday. I told him I didn't have anything planned, so sure. He said he'd show up around one and that he'd bring a pizza. He never arrived. And I've had no word from him since."

"I may be jumping to conclusions, but it's beginning to look like whatever Charlie was working on plays a role in his disappearance. Klinefelter says he wasn't privy to the substance of that story. Did Charlie give you any indication?"

"No, and that's strange. Normally, we worked closely together on the research of his stories. But this time he'd shut me out. Said it was going to be the story of his career and that he needed to keep it under wraps until it was ready to be published. So when he called that Monday, I was excited to eventually see what he had."

"Did you know he purchased a revolver last month?"

"No. That surprises me. Charlie hates guns. Doesn't think the Second Amendment argument has any validity for this day and age."

"There's no mistake. The police department has the paperwork on file. That tells me he was willing to put aside ideology to maybe protect his own life."

"Are you suggesting Charlie might be…dead?" She started to tear up.

"Circumstantially, that possibility has to be ruled in, given the fact that no one has heard from him, but there's no hard evidence to that effect. I'm still hopeful, and you should be, too."

Murphy didn't like lying to her, but who knew, maybe there'd be a happy ending that, as of this moment, he hadn't envisioned.

He pushed on. "Klinefelter said he'd terminated Charlie's employment. I'm assuming he had some personal items that must've been cleared out."

"Yes, after the police were here last week, I boxed up everything that was his. It isn't much."

"Could I take a look? Maybe there was something the police missed."

"Sure. It's all in a cardboard box under my desk. I'll get it; it'll just take me a minute."

When she returned, she placed the carton in front of Murphy. He removed the lid, tipped the box on its edge, and began extracting the items: a framed Bachelor's Degree in Journalism from the University of Southern California; a ceramic ashtray from his alma mater, embossed with the image of a Trojan warrior. He set them aside. Next were two small wooden display cases, each containing a fountain pen.

Shannon explained. "Those are gifts from Charlie's father. One's a Visconti; the other is a Mont Blanc. Both expensive."

"Neither looks to have been used."

"Charlie doesn't like fountain pens. Says no matter how much they cost, they still leak. He originally had more than these two, but he gives them away as retirement gifts. They're certainly worth more than the gold-plated watch that the *Times* provides."

He then hefted out a Philips compact cassette tape recorder.

Shannon said, "It can be plugged in or run on batteries. Charlie likes to take it along for interviews. That way he doesn't have to rely on his memory, and he's a lousy note taker."

Murphy opened the cassette compartment to find one in place. He pushed the Play button and the spindles began to turn, but the only sound was a soft hiss. He rewound it a bit. Nothing. Then Fast Forward. Still nothing. He flipped the cassette over and tried again to no avail.

"I know he has other cassettes," Shannon said, "but I didn't find them when I cleaned out his desk."

The final item extracted from the box was a cheap daily appointment book. Murphy flipped through the pages. All appeared blank.

He said, "Apparently, he kept his schedule elsewhere."

"The *Times* issues one like that every year to all its employees. But Charlie has a leather-bound notebook where he enters his meetings and other appointments. He keeps it in his briefcase."

Murphy thumbed through it again and this time came up with a notation on June 7. No more than hen scratching as far as he could decipher. He handed it to Shannon.

"What do you make of this?" he asked.

"That's my shorthand." She laughed. "And a good thing, too. Even I can't read my own handwriting. I flunked penmanship in elementary school. Anyway, it says 'confirming meeting at Lighthouse. 1:00 p.m. Bob Reed.'" A pause. "Oh, I remember now. Charlie was away from his desk when the call came in. I needed something to write on. I found this appointment book in the top drawer and wrote down the message. When Charlie got back, I relayed the information. He said Reed was an old family friend who worked at Northrop Aircraft."

"Did he go to that meeting?"

"I assume so."

"I may want to follow up on that appointment. Do you mind if I keep this book?"

"No. Be my guest."

Murphy took a moment to jot down in his own handwriting what he couldn't decipher in shorthand. When he was finished he returned the other items to the carton and replaced the lid.

"Is there anything else that you can think of that might help me? No matter how insignificant it might seem."

She shook her head. "I wish there were."

Murphy started to get up, then sat back down.

"When I first saw you, I thought I recognized you from somewhere. And I've been racking my brain about it. Now I know. In Charlie's apartment, there's a picture of him at the beach with another boy and girl. You're wearing a lot more clothes now, but you're that girl, aren't you?"

Shannon laughed. "Guilty as charged, but I can assure you I've since graduated to one-piece swimming suits. Charlie and I were an item back then. Everyone—including me—figured we'd eventually get married. But Charlie would never commit. Of course, now I know why."

"It's none of my business, but you haven't been carrying a

torch for him all these years, have you? I mean—"

"I know what you mean: a pretty girl, sitting around brooding over lost love."

"Something like that."

"No.   As a matter of fact, I've been married twice. Currently divorced.   I may've set the bar too high.   I've got Charlie to blame for *that*."   She wiped her tears with both hands. "Promise me you'll find him, Mr. Murphy."

"I'll do my best."   Murphy got to his feet and extended his hand.

While riding the elevator down to the lobby, he reflected on Shannon Rigby: polite—she hadn't once looked at him as if expecting an explanation of his black eye; loyal, as well as compassionate—she cared deeply about Charlie Hayward; and glamorous, but not full of herself—a trait she shared with Tara.

17

When Murphy returned to his office, he was surprised to find Doyle seated at Andrea's desk.

"Why, Andrea, how you've changed since I've been away. And not for the better, I might add."

"Very funny."

"Where is she, out to lunch?"

"That and she's shopping for a present for one of her kids. It's his birthday next week. Maybe we should chip in a couple bucks apiece."

"Good idea." Murphy took a ten from his wallet and tossed it on the desk.

"I'll match it and get a card."

Murphy shrugged out of his suit coat and draped it over his shoulder.

"It's brutal out there," he sighed. "When I was growing up back east, we called it the 'dog days of summer.' When does fall kick in around this part of the country?"

"Fall? What's that? I thought you would've figured it out by now. We've only got three seasons in southern California: pre-summer, summer, and post-summer. I gave my oldest boy a surfboard for Christmas one year. That afternoon, he went right down to Manhattan Beach and tried it out. If I remember, the temperature was 85 degrees. There aren't many places in the country that can boast of that. As a matter of fact, I've never understood why LA news channels even bother to employ weathermen. I mean, what's the point? The forecasts are always monotonous shades of ideal."

"Well, I have to admit it's better than what we experienced in North Africa, huh?"

"You mean where the fire hydrants—if they'd had any—would've been fighting over dogs?"

Murphy laughed.

Doyle then said, "Oh, by the way, I haven't just been sitting here twiddling my thumbs. I called a buddy of mine over at Rampart. I was his training partner when he was a rookie, fresh out of the Academy. He still likes me, despite the fact that others are calling me a turncoat for my testimony at the Harmon trial. Bad news travels fast. In any event, he's a sergeant now who works Missing Persons. I thought he could fill me in on the ground that had been covered the last two times Hayward bugged out."

"What did he say?"

"Only that Hayward showed up on his own accord before they even got geared up."

"That's what his father intimated. He said they weren't particularly excited this time about getting a report that he was gone again."

"Well, that's just it, you see."

"What?"

"No one filed another report. My guy didn't know anything about Hayward going missing."

"Maybe the father filed the report elsewhere—at another division."

"Negative. Even if he had, it would've been forwarded immediately to Rampart. That's where the Missing Persons Unit is housed for the entire city."

"Your buddy is obviously mistaken, because two detectives showed up at the *Times* last week. They talked to the staff and went through Hayward's office."

"Are you sure?"

"I got it straight from his boss and confirmed by his copy girl."

"That's weird. Oh, well… It wouldn't be the first time the left hand didn't know what the right was doing. So what did you find out at the newspaper?"

Murphy filled Doyle in, then retreated to his office and withdrew a phonebook from his desk drawer. He found the requisite listing and dialed.

A pleasant voice answered, "Northrop Corporation."

"Would you connect me with Robert Reed, please?"

"Do you know his department, sir?"

"No, I'm sorry, but I don't?"

"That's quite all right. One minute, while I consult our directory."

The phone went dead, as she apparently put him on hold. Only a few seconds passed before she was on the line again.

"For future reference, Mr. Reed is assigned to Special Projects. His extension is 205."

"Thank you very much." Murphy jotted down the number in case he needed it later.

"I'll connect you now, sir. Have a pleasant day."

One ring.

"This is Bob."

"Mr. Reed, my name is Jack Murphy. I'm a private investigator looking into the disappearance of Charles Hayward and—"

"Charlie's missing? I saw him not that long ago."

"Yes. I understand he had a meeting with you on June seventh."

"That sound about right. I'd have to check my schedule to be sure."

"Did you have any further contact with him after that date?"

"No, just that one time. Look, I've known the Hayward Family for years. Clay is a good friend and former colleague."

"Yes, he mentioned in passing that he'd worked for

Northrop when he'd had his accident. I'd forgotten that until just now."

"A tragic turn of events for a gifted engineer, and a great loss for the aeronautical community."

"Listen, would it be possible for us to talk in person? I'd like to pick your brain about Charlie."

"Certainly, if you think it'll help. Just tell me when."

"Today, if possible. I'm already behind the eight ball on this case."

"There isn't any way I could get you cleared into the plant on such notice. National security, and all that. I'll meet you at the Lighthouse Drive-in on the corner of Hawthorne Boulevard and Rosecrans Avenue. You can't miss it. It's not called the Lighthouse for nothing."

"I'll find it."

"Now, I've got a fire or two to put out here before I can leave, so let's say we meet in 90 minutes. That okay?"

"Perfect."

"How will I recognize you?"

"That's easy. Look for the guy who appears to have gone a couple rounds with Floyd Patterson and lived to regret it."

18

Reed was right: You couldn't miss the Lighthouse. It could be seen from blocks away, its white plaster façade, capped in red, jutting from atop a vintage circular-style diner. Turning into the lot and parking near the sidewalk, Murphy saw that carhop service was offered under a canopy that had the appearance of having been built as an add-on. A good call by the owner, judging by the amount of eating and socializing in and around the cars.

There were far more people outside than in as Murphy pulled open the front door and stood in the shallow foyer. He removed his dark glasses, stashed them in the breast pocket of his suit coat, and surveyed the dining room made up of booths along the exterior walls and stools affixed to the floor around a curved counter, occupied by two old men, hunched over their plates. Another man, seated at one of the booths where he could see the front door, caught Murphy's eye, motioned him over, and got to his feet.

He offered his hand. "Bob Reed."

"Jack Murphy."

"Pleasure to meet you, Jack." He pointed to the opposite bench.

Handsome, six-four, lean, with a full head of dark hair—
though receding—Murphy pegged Reed's age at about forty. A
plastic pocket protector adorned his white short-sleeve shirt,
and his striped tie was worn loose at his neck.

Reed said, "I recognized you immediately from the
description you gave. You weren't kidding, were you? I think
I'm obligated to inquire what the other guy looks like, if you
don't mind telling me."

"You're not the first to ask. There were three. And the last
time I saw them, they were being loaded into an ambulance.
They didn't look that chipper."

"A long time ago, I dated a girl whose father was a private
detective. He always had stories of derring-do that impressed
me. But I don't remember him ever being bruised up."

"Then he was extremely lucky. Normally, in this line of
work, it's only a matter of 'when,' not 'if' the shit hits the fan.
I was an Army investigator a lot of years, and it's all I know
how to do, so I picked up this gig with a buddy from the war.
He's a retired LA cop." Murphy reached for one of the menus
that stood upright in a metal condiment caddy.

"You going to have anything to east?" he asked.

"No, just this cup of coffee for me."

"But you've eaten here before?"

"Twice a week, or so. It's a regular lunch hangout for
Northrop engineers. You can't imagine how many aircraft
designs got their debut on a paper napkin from this place."

"Really?" Murphy was still engrossed in the menu. "I
always figured that kind of stuff was reserved for drafting tables
and slide rules."

"Nope. Remember the flying wing? Could have been
designed right here or at another diner. It was flown a time or
two over the city in the 50s. A lot of *avant garde* technology
went into it. Didn't catch on, though. Currently, it's in one of
our hangers, gathering dust. But one day, someone is going to
find value in that design."

"Uh huh." Murphy was still focused on the menu.

Reed said, "I'm not a gourmet by any measure, but the

corned beef on rye with shoe string potatoes is well worth the seventy-five cents."

It was then that the waitress showed up, a motherly type in a light green and white uniform. She carried a half full coffee pot.

"Sorry for the wait." She topped off Reed's cup. "Seems like there's always a bit of kitchen drama going on." Then looking at Murphy. "And what can I get for you, hun?"

"The corned beef on rye and coffee." He replaced the menu.

She grabbed a clean mug off the table of the adjoining booth and filled it with steaming brew.

"Do you take cream?"

Murphy shook his head. "Just black and strong."

"Like my men," she said, more to herself than to them. Then she was gone.

They both laughed.

At last, Murphy said, "That was more information than we needed. But it's nice to know where she stands on interracial relationships."

Reed crushed out the butt of his cigarette in the ashtray and lit another. Then he offered the pack to Murphy, who hesitated briefly before taking one.

"I really shouldn't. Been trying to cut back." Murphy then fired it up using his Zippo. "But old habits die hard, as they say."

"Tell me about it. I'd never smoked until I joined the Army right out of high school. I was assigned to a rifle company that went straight to Europe after basic. My training didn't prepare me for squat. It's one thing to shoot at paper targets; it's another to draw a bead on an actual person—even if he *is* the enemy."

"And to have that target shooting back at you."

"Exactly. When buddies at your left, right, and rear are shot to pieces, it makes you wonder when your own number will be up. I was scared to death every day. And if it hadn't been for these coffin nails," he held up his cigarette, "to take the edge off my nerves, I wouldn't have made it. But enough reminiscing. What is it you'd like to know about Charlie Hayward?"

"On the phone, you indicated that you'd known the Hayward Family for some time. Maybe you could start by elaborating on that."

Reed tapped his cigarette on the edge of the ashtray, took another deep drag, then expelled the smoke through his nostrils.

"When the war was over, I came back home and used the G.I. Bill to get into college. I wanted to be an aeronautical engineer, and USC had an excellent program. I'd just started my sophomore year when I was summoned to the department chairman's office, where I was introduced to Clayton Hayward—a representative from Northrop. It seems that one of my professors was also a talent spotter. He felt the University was holding me back; that I'd be better off learning while doing. Northrop had been sent samples of my work, and Clay was there to offer me a job at more money than I ever thought possible."

"Which you accepted."

"And never regretted my decision for an instant. That was 1947. Clay was assigned as my mentor but became a close friend. As such, I was often invited to his home in Bel Air and got to know his wife and kids. There's not much more to say, other than Clay and I worked together on numerous occasions at the plant, right up until his accident."

"I only met Clayton Hayward a couple days ago, but he struck me as a smart guy."

"'Brilliant' is more like it. It was a real loss when Northrop decided to let him go."

"So why did they? He might be confined to a wheelchair, but other than that, wouldn't he be all that he'd ever been?"

"His colleagues—me included—thought that, as well, but we didn't get to vote. Of course, Clay filed suit, alleging wrongful termination. Northrop eventually settled his claim for an undisclosed amount, but allowing him back wasn't part of the deal." Reed sighed. "I suppose it came down to Clay being his own worst enemy. While it's true that he was an extraordinary design engineer, he often found himself at odds with Management. You see, for security reasons, much of what goes on at Northrop is compartmentalized. By that I mean there isn't a need to know what everyone else is working on. Clay felt that his tenure with the company should've exempted him from that 'paranoid nonsense,' as he called it. After all, his fingerprints were on virtually every aircraft design that Northrop had produced over the past thirty years. If *he* couldn't be relied on to keep a secret, he maintained, then who could?" Reed shrugged his shoulders. "But what's done is done."

As if on cue, the waitress arrived with Murphy's order. She topped off their coffee mugs and scurried away.

Murphy eyed the mountain of corned beef between thick slices of toasted rye bread, cut on the diagonal.

"How do you get your mouth around this beast?"

"I've always had to resort to knife and fork."

Murphy lathered the top layer of beef with a liberal amount of mustard and sliced off the first bite.

"Even if I wasn't starving," he said after a moment, "this would still be the best corned beef I've ever had. And that's saying something, considering I'm in a relationship with a woman who owns an Irish pub, with that very item on the menu."

"You're dating a woman who owns a bar?" Reed seemed impressed. "You must be living right to deserve something like *that*."

Murphy laughed. "A woman who has every intention of turning me into a bartender, after she gets me to say 'I do.'"

"It might be safer, you know?" Reed gestured toward Murphy's eye.

"You'd think that, wouldn't you? But her father, the previous proprietor, was murdered a few months ago right out behind the place. Moral of the story: Shit happens—no matter what."

"Point taken."

Murphy took a sip of coffee. "So let's get down to the real reason I called you: your meeting with Charlie. How did that

95

come about?"

"Well, his phone call came from out of the blue. And it *was* on the morning of June seventy, just like you said. I verified that before I came here. We hadn't spoken in years. In fact, he wondered if I even remembered him. I told him it would be hard not to, since his name was in the *Times* quite regularly. He said he was in the preliminary stages of a story and wanted to 'pick my brain' before he went any further. He asked if it would be possible to meet that afternoon. I told him I'd have to see about rearranging a few things before I could commit, and that I'd have to get back to him. Truth be known, I was as curious as he was anxious. Within the hour I called his office. He wasn't available right then but called me back a few minutes later to confirm. I met with him right here for lunch."

"What did he have to say?"

"First it was just a lot of small talk. Catching up, really. As I said, it had been years since I'd seen him. Then he turned solemn. He asked my opinion of a former Northrop employee. A man by the name Gordon Kane. He'd been part of the security unit for many years but had quit some time back to take the job of director of security for the Flamingo Hotel in Las Vegas. I specifically remember that, because he joked at his going away party that he'd be rubbing shoulders with both show business people and crime bosses. In any event, I told him that Kane had had a reputation for taking his work seriously."

"What was Charlie's connection to Kane? Did he say?"

"Not directly, but he mentioned winning a hundred dollars at roulette when he'd gone to Vegas recently. I assumed that he'd met Kane there in some capacity. Then Charlie inquired generally about projects that Northrop had worked on over the years, some going back to before I even hired on."

"Anything specific?"

"No, just timelines, mainly. Innocuous stuff that he could probably have found at the library."

Murphy thought for a moment. "Why go to you when he could've spoken to his father? Surely Clayton Hayward knew

96

Kane and had been working at Northrop much longer."

"I asked him that, myself. He said they weren't on the best of terms. He didn't elaborate, and I didn't pursue it. It was none of my business."

"Did Charlie seem ill at ease talking with you?"

"His tone was a little conspiratorial at times, but I figured that was standard behavior for investigative reporters." He chuckled.

Murphy ground out his cigarette in the ashtray and hastily finished off the last two bites of his sandwich, then extracted a handful of change from his pocket and dumped it on the table. "That should cover everything." He reached across and shook Reed's hand. "You've given me a piece of the puzzle I didn't have before, Bob. Next stop: Gordon Kane."

"Are you going to call him and explain the situation? He was a decent guy when he worked for Northrop. He'd surely fill you in on his meeting with Charlie, like I have."

"Doubtful. I have a feeling their conversation wasn't the kind you have over the phone. That's why Charlie made the trip to Vegas."

"So now you're headed there, as well?"

Murphy nodded and checked his watch.

"In that case," Reed said, "let me give you some scientifically proven advice: If blackjack is your game, double down on eleven. Odds are you'll come out a winner more often than not."

19

Murphy drove across the street to the Texaco station, pulled up next to one of the pumps, and turned off the ignition. Exiting the vehicle, he was approached by an attendant who'd come from one of the two garage bays, each with a car on a hoist. He wiped his greasy hands on a rag that he then tucked into his back pocket. He looked to be of high school age, working a summer job.

"What'll it be, mister?" he asked.

"Fill 'er up with the good stuff, son. And check the tires and under the hood. I'm headed out of town."

"Yes, sir."

Murphy spied a payphone next to the office door. Less than a minute later he was talking with Doyle.

"I'd be happy to ride shotgun. You've never been to Vegas, have you?"

"There's always a first time, and I don't expect any heavy lifting. I was toying with the idea of asking Tara if she wanted to ride along."

"You'd choose *her* over me? What kind of a friend are you, anyway?"

They laughed.

Murphy then said, "This guy, Kane, could be the first real break I've gotten on this case. Hayward apparently went out of his way to talk to him. I figure I can't go too far wrong doing the same. But there is something you can do for me."

"Such as...?"

"I'd like you to check with the local hospitals. See if they've had any John Does admitted."

"All right, and I'll go you one better. I'll also check with the regional county morgues."

"With so little time on the case, I've been hesitant to lean in that direction, but I think you're right. We should at least rule it out. On the other hand, given the length of time he's been gone, if he could've made contact with anyone, I'm fairly certain it would've been with the girl from the *Times*—they've got history together. But she said no."

"I'll start calling right away. If I turn up anything, I'll contact you at your hotel. The Flamingo, right?"

"Yeah, that's the plan. Being the middle of the week, I shouldn't need a reservation."

Murphy's next call was to O'Neill's, but Tara wasn't there. The accountant who handled the business had asked for a meeting. She hadn't been gone long; he could probably catch her there. deShazo gave him the phone number.

Tara jumped at the chance to go with him. She said she'd dash home, pack a bag for herself, and throw in fresh underwear and socks for him. By the time he drove back to town, she'd be ready. He could pick her up at the pub.

The young station attendant had just slammed the car hood shut as Murphy walked up.

"I topped off the radiator. Battery, oil, and tires were okay."

"Thanks." Murphy reached for his wallet. "What's the damage?"

The kid read the numbers off the pump: "Eight and a half gallons. That'll be two dollars and fifty cents."

Murphy handed him a five-dollar bill.

"I'll get your change."

"Keep it for yourself. I'm kind of in a hurry."

"You mean it, mister?"

Murphy nodded and said with a straight face, "Just don't blow it on beer and broads." Texaco's motto was: *Service with a Smile*. That was certainly evident as the kid stepped to the driver's door and held it open for Murphy, a wide grin on his lips.

A winding road began at the far end of the San Gabriel Valley and traversed the mountainside to the east. Once it topped the Cajon Pass, it settled into a stark ribbon of asphalt that stretched to the horizon, across expanses of barren high desert. With virtually nothing to command their attention on either side of the road, drivers were often lulled into hypnotic trances by the intermittent lines painted down the center. Single-vehicle rollovers were commonplace as drowsy drivers suddenly realized they were drifting and over-corrected, plunging into the barrow pit or hurtling off the shoulder. Murphy stopped twice to top off the gas tank and get the kinks out, the second time at a truck stop with a crowded café, where they sat down for a cup of coffee and a piece of pie.

Back on the highway, a shiny red Mustang convertible, still with a temporary rear plate, passed them going about ninety miles an hour.

Tara said, "After we're married, I think we should get a convertible. I mean, what's the point of living in a weather paradise if you can't enjoy it?"

"You've lived in LA a lot longer than I have and don't have one. Why not?"

"Oh, in college, I drove a '46 Ford convertible. Black with red leather upholstery. Wide whitewall tires with baby moon hubcaps. A 'woodie' like surfers now dream of owning. I can't begin to tell you all the good times I had in that car."

Murphy glanced over at her. "Front seat or rear?"

"You're not jealous, are you? I figured you knew you weren't the first." She kissed him on the cheek and whispered, "But I want you to be the last."

"So what happened to that car, if you liked it so much?"

100

"My father told me to be practical. I was going to be entering the business world—a man's world—and needed to be taken seriously. He said pretty girls in convertibles didn't inspire confidence. At first, I tried it my way, but in time, I realized he was right. That's when I traded for a Volvo, a no frills, no nonsense vehicle, but one on the cutting edge of automobile technology. My male colleagues were impressed and, out of habit, I've been driving Volvos ever since. But now that I'm in a position to live my own life, I've decided it's too short to worry about what other people think."

"Sounds like you've made up your mind, then, but I'll still need to keep mine. Flashy cars and detective work don't mix. We prefer anonymity when we're on the job."

"Whatever you say, but I can guarantee that the benefits of a convertible will extend to you, as well."

"Oh?"

"You play your cards right, and you'll experience first-hand the kind of maneuvering I previously enjoyed in the backseat of my Ford Sportsman."

Murphy looked over and playfully said, "Do you suppose dealerships in Vegas are open late?"

She laughed. "Down, Romeo!"

"Spoilsport. You get me worked up, then douse me with ice water."

She reached over and stroked his thigh. "Poor baby. How about I make it up to you later?"

"Now we're talking!"

They made good time—considering—and it was just before ten p.m. when they first saw the glow of lights in the distance. But Las Vegas hadn't sprung overnight into glitz and glitter. It had once been nothing more than a dusty crossroad along the Old Spanish Trail. And if artesian springs hadn't been discovered in the vicinity, it would've undoubtedly remained as such. Then during the 1850s, missionaries were sent by Brigham Young to convert the Paiute native population to the Mormon faith, as well as establish stopover facilities for "saints" traveling to and from California's Mormon Colony at

San Bernardino.

A railroad hub followed at the turn of the century, but it wasn't until the building of the Hoover Dam in the 1930s, and the development of atomic weapons during World War II, that a modern city took root. It now had evolved—or devolved, depending on who was speaking—into the gaming mecca of the West, with its casinos financed in large part by Organized Crime figures looking to go "legit." In fact, the Flamingo Hotel, located on the famous Las Vegas Strip, had had undisputed ties to "Bugsy" Siegel, a notorious crime boss with a penchant for temper tantrums that usually ended in someone dying—or at least that was the rumor. It was also rumored that Bugsy, himself, was murdered by someone farther up the food chain when the Flamingo came in substantially over budget and its receipts less than expected. Apparently the adage of there being no honor among thieves was true. Or better yet: *What goes around comes around.*

The Flamingo wasn't hard to find amid the array of dazzling neon, and Murphy turned into the parking lot. After a couple passes through a sea of automobiles, he eased into a spot being vacated by a cowboy, if his wide-brimmed hat and a set of curved longhorns affixed to the truck's hood meant anything.

Unsure of the reciprocity between California and Nevada, Murphy had stowed his hardware in Tara's suitcase before they'd left. He felt naked the whole time they'd been driving and more so now, retrieving his suit coat from the back seat and slinging it over his shoulder. In his other hand, he carried Tara's bag.

As they walked toward the wide entrance, Murphy said, "Man alive, how hot must it have been today for it to still be like this. Who'd want to live here?"

"Sure, there aren't any ocean breezes to cool it down, but there isn't any smog, either. That might be a better bargain."

Once inside, Murphy was taken aback by the noise, flashing lights, and seeming confusion as patrons moved through crowded, smoky isles of gaming tables and slot machines. The scene was a major departure from what he'd experienced in

Europe. Once while on a case, he'd spent a night in Monaco and had subsequently been drawn to its casinos, more out of curiosity than to try his luck. Casually dressed, he'd felt woefully out of place among the tuxedo and evening gown-clad patrons who'd appeared wealthy already—not hoping to become so at the turn of a card or roulette wheel.

At the registration desk, Murphy set down the bag. The clerk, a pretty brunette with an infectious smile, was Johnny-on-the-spot.

"We'd like a room for one night," Murphy said.

"Do you have a reservation, sir?"

"No, I'm afraid we didn't know we'd be coming to Las Vegas until this afternoon. Business, you understand."

"I'm very sorry, but the hotel is booked solid. International Automotive Convention. I'd be surprised if there's a room to be had anywhere in town."

Murphy turned to Tara.

"What do you want to do?" he asked.

"I know what I *don't* want to do, and that's sleep in the car."

He turned back to the clerk.

"Would it be too much trouble for you to call a few of the larger hotels for us? Perhaps there's been a last minute cancellation somewhere."

"Not at all, sir. I'd be happy to."

She opened a drawer under the counter and withdrew a laminated sheet of paper. She ran her finger down the page, noted a phone number, and began to dial. Mid-way through completing the call, she replaced the receiver and looked up at Murphy.

"I don't know why I didn't think of this before, but we actually do have a vacancy: the Bridal Suite."

"We'll take it," Tara exclaimed before Murphy could say anything in response.

After Murphy completed the registration form, the clerk summoned a uniformed bellhop, an elderly gentleman who gave the impression of having catered to guests his entire life.

"Take Mr. and Mrs. Murphy to the Bridal Suite, Henry."

Murphy was about to reach for the suitcase at his feet when Henry snagged it first.

"If you'll follow me." He took the lead.

The suite was on the third floor at the rear of the hotel, down a wide corridor, and situated apart from other sleeping rooms on the floor.

Henry opened one of the double doors at the entrance and stood aside.

Murphy had just taken a step forward, when Henry said, "It's customary to carry the bride over the threshold." He grinned.

"Yes, darling," Tara said. "What could you be thinking about? As if I didn't know. But there *are* rituals that should be observed." She opened wide her arms. "Well, what are you waiting for? Take me; I'm yours."

Murphy played along and cradled her in his arms.

"Maybe you shouldn't have eaten that piece of pie earlier," he chided, pretending to struggle under her weight.

He marched across the room, Henry in tow, and tossed her—rather unceremoniously—onto the heart-shaped bed.

She looked over at the bellhop. "You'll have to excuse him. Normally, he's a perfect gentleman. I think he's getting a little excited about what awaits."

He nodded as if he'd seen this kind of behavior thousands of times—and maybe he had.
Setting the suitcase down, and presenting Murphy the key, he asked, "Will there be anything else?"

"I think not." Murphy pulled a five-dollar bill from his pocket and handed it to him.

"Thank you, sir. And have a *most* enjoyable stay." He then gave Murphy a wink that Tara couldn't have seen.

When the door to the suite had closed, Murphy turned and laughed.

"You made the poor man think I'm a sex-crazed newly-wed. I hope you're satisfied with your little charade."

"Yes, I thought my performance was rather good, actually."

Murphy sighed. "You're incorrigible, do you know that?"

"It's what makes me endearing, and you love it."

"Are you at all hungry? Room service is just a phone call away."

"Not really. That piece of pie *was* gigantic. But don't let me stop you from ordering something."

Murphy shook his head.

"Then I'm going to take a shower." Tara slid off the bed. "You want to join me?"

"No, I think I'll scout out this Gordon Kane. I won't be long."

"You'd better not be. I'd hate to have to start without you."

"Fat chance of that happening," Murphy replied sarcastically over his shoulder as he exited the room.

Murphy rode the elevator back to the casino and looked for one of the floorwalkers whose job it was to circulate and look for potential troublemakers, given the fact there were always substantially more losers than winners: a time-tested formula upon which all gambling is predicated. He spotted one who could've been a professional football player in a former life, his shirt collar straining at what had to be a twenty-inch neck.

Approaching, Murphy said, "Excuse me, but could you point me to the director of security?"

"Is there a problem, sir?"

Murphy flashed his tin and took a similar tone.

"Private investigator. I'm working a missing persons case out of LA."

"LA, huh? Small world. That's where Gordon is from."

"Yes, I know. His name surfaced as someone who likely talked to the guy I'm looking for—before he dropped out of sight."

"Gordon has already left for the day. If it's an emergency, I suppose I could call him at home for you."

"No reason to bother him tonight. I was just looking to set up a meet for tomorrow, anyway. What time does he generally roll in?"

"Nine a.m., give or take half an hour."

"Bankers' hours, huh?"

"I think the expression is: Rank has its privileges." He smiled for the first time. "But no one's complaining. He's a hell of a nice guy."

Murphy held out his hand. "Thanks for your time."

"My pleasure."

Back in the suite, Murphy shrugged out of his coat and draped it across the back of a white brocaded wing chair. The slider to the bathroom was closed, and he could here Tara singing. He'd heard the tune on the radio. "Can't get no satisfaction" was part of the lyrics. He was about to say something to her when there was a knock on the door. He crossed the room and opened it to find Henry standing behind a wheeled cart draped in linen. On it sat a wine bottle sticking out of an ice bucket and two fluted glasses.

"Your champagne, sir." He proceeded to push the cart inside.

Murphy stood aside. "I think there's been a mistake. I didn't order anything."

"Your lovely bride did, sir. And if I might be so bold to say: She certainly knows her sparkling wines. This is a Dom Pérignon 1952, the best we have to offer. Would you like me to pour it?"

"That won't be necessary." Murphy pulled another five-dollar bill from his pocket and handed it over.

"Thank you again, sir. You're most generous." He then beat a hasty retreat, closing the door behind him.

Murphy was wheeling the cart farther into the room when the bathroom door slid open. Tara was wearing a sheer black negligee that left nothing to the imagination.

"Oh, good," she said. "The champagne arrived."

Murphy stopped in his tracks. "Where have you been hiding *that* little number?"

"You like it?"

"Oh, yeah. And so would the bellhop, if you'd have come out a minute sooner. He'd have probably hyperventilated, and I'm not far from it."

"I've been saving it for a special occasion. And when you called, I figured the promise of a night in Vegas would be perfect for its unveiling." She sauntered seductively up to him and put her arms around his neck. "Though to be honest, my thought now is to wear it *only* in case of fire."

20

The next morning in the hotel restaurant, Tara tucked into a plate of bacon and eggs and hash brown potatoes with a side order of pancakes.

"I'm absolutely famished. I feel as if I'd worked out at the gym all night."

"Is that so?" Murphy picked at his own food. "Well, you didn't have any trouble bouncing out of bed this morning. I, on the other hand, was close to needing life support services."

"C'mon, you barely broke a sweat. But are you telling me I'm too much of a woman for your advanced years?" She reached over and patted his hand.

"I'm saying that two nights in a row of championship wrestling finally took its toll on me."

"Do you know what I think? I think a lifetime of smoking has compromised your system. You ditch the demon weed, and you'll be right as rain."

"Easier said than done. That guy I talked to from Northrop had the same experience during the war. When you're scared to death that your next breath might be your last, a cigarette was just what the doctor ordered to keep you sane."

"Yeah, I've heard that sob story before. But you're not in a foxhole anymore, Jack. And any doctor knows that cigarettes will kill you now just as sure as German bullets would have then. Of course, it's your choice—for now. But I don't want you smoking around the children. It sets a bad example. Now eat your french toast before it gets cold."

A half-dozen flippant remarks—most beginning with "Yes, Mommy"—bounced around Murphy's brain, but despite his weakened condition, he chose discretion over foolhardiness.

Twenty minutes, Murphy charged the meal to their room, then checked his watch.

"Time to track down Gordon Kane." He dug two twenties from his wallet and handed them to Tara. "See if you can turn these into a small fortune. I think we're going to need it to pay for our suite, not to mention the champagne you ordered."

Tara folded the bills and put them into her purse.

"But you have to admit that vintage lived up to its reputation," she said.

"Well..."

"And tell me it didn't set the mood for the best night of your life—so far."

Murphy was still short for words.

"That's what I thought." She kissed him tenderly on the lips. "Now go to work, while I try to break the bank."

The hotel registration desk was located adjacent to the restaurant, so Murphy started there. A smartly-dressed young man in thick, dark-rimmed glasses—making him look a bit like Clark Kent, of Superman fame—busied himself behind the counter.

Murphy said, "Excuse me, but I was told last night that the director of security usually comes in by this hour. Have you seen him yet this morning?"

"Yes, sir. He was right here just a few minutes ago. Have you encountered a problem?" He seemed genuinely concerned.

"No, nothing like that. I'd just like to speak with him on a matter."

The clerk came around the counter and stood by Murphy. He surveyed the expansive casino that was nearly dead when compared to the night before.

"Gordon likes to take a tour of the property first thing every morning. Oh, there he is." He pointed. "He's with that group of Japanese guests. He's the one who's about a foot taller."

"And I presume the one who isn't Japanese," Murphy added.

"Oh, yeah, right." The clerk laughed.

By the time he'd crossed the casino, the group had dispersed. Murphy had pictured Kane to be older than the early thirty-something, blue-blazer-clad man headed in his direction. This led Murphy to conclude that, despite his age, Kane had to know his stuff, because casino security—as demanding as it had to be—wasn't a job for amateurs.

Murphy stopped him in the aisle and held out his hand.

"My name is Jack Murphy."

He shook Murphy's hand. "Yes, there was a note on my desk this morning that you were looking for me last night. You're a private detective from Los Angeles, I understand. So how may I be of service?"

"I'd like to talk to you about a missing persons case I'm working."

"And the Flamingo somehow enters in?"

"No, actually it involves you personally. But is there someplace more private where we could talk?"

"Absolutely. You've piqued my interest. My office is inside there." He gestured to a set of double doors marked with a sign that read: PRIVATE, NO ADMITTANCE.

Absent the fact that there were no windows, Murphy couldn't imagine CEOs of major corporations having anything nicer. Clearly, the Flamingo took care of its upper echelon.

"Have a seat, Mr. Murphy," directing him to one of four swivel chairs around a walnut and glass table in the corner. "Can I get you a cup of coffee? It's freshly brewed from the kitchen. Our own special blend. It's really quite good."

"No thanks, I had three cups during breakfast. And you're right; it was excellent."

"I'll just pour myself one, then." He stepped to a credenza

adjacent to his desk and filled a mug from an insulated metal bottle.

While he stirred in a spoonful of sugar, Murphy remarked, "This is some office. I'm a retired military cop, and I've been in a few offices that belonged to generals. None of them came close to what you have here." He scanned the walls from his seat. "I know those Renoir paintings have to be copies—because I've seen the originals at the Louvre—but these are extraordinarily well done. I'm sure as hell not an art critic, but I don't think the average person could tell those from the Real McCoy."

"They're like most everything else in Vegas: illusions of grandeur." He sat down opposite Murphy. "Yes, they're fakes, but they still have a soothing effect on me. Casino security can make you crazy. There's so much money moving from here to there that we're constantly on alert for robbery attempts, not to mention cheating schemes."

"Is there much problem with staff having sticky fingers?"

"Not what you might think. By and large, we're kind of one big family." He then changed the subject. "So are you one of those hard-bitten private eyes we see in the movies?"

"Oh, you mean this?" Murphy touched his cheek. "When I woke up that morning, I had no idea this was going to be in my future. And if I hadn't been outnumbered, I might've been okay. LA isn't just orange blossoms and palm trees."

"You got that right. I used to live there. Aircraft plant security. When I got the chance to trade the LA rat race for Vegas, I jumped at it. At first, even though I'd be making a lot more money, my wife and daughter weren't all that keen on the move. But now you couldn't get them to go back if you beat them with a stick. Sure, it's maybe a little warm at times, but that's why God created air conditioning. Plus, you can take a drive without ever being stuck in traffic. *And* there aren't any chunks in the air to breathe."

"Are you sure you're not secretly working for the Chamber of Commerce?"

"I sound like it, don't I?" He laughed. "Then let me put on

my other hat. So you said you're working a case that might involve me. How so?"

Murphy got right down to it.

"Charles Hayward has disappeared," he said.

A puzzled look. "Am I supposed to know who that is?"

Now it was Murphy who looked puzzled.

"Charles Hayward, the LA *Times* reporter. He was here the first part of June. He even referenced your name when he got back."

"No, I've never met the man or spoken with him."

"This is very strange. Maybe I've jumped to the wrong conclusions. But I'm certain you *do* know his father—Clayton Hayward."

"I'm afraid that name doesn't ring any bells, either."

"Now just a goddam minute!" Murphy shot to his feet. "I know this is Vegas, but what fucking game are you playing, Kane!"

Startled, he looked up at Murphy. "Whoa! Hold on a minute! You've made a mistake."

"Yeah, in thinking I could count on you to help, not stonewall me."

"If you'll sit back down, Mr. Murphy, I'll explain."

Murphy did so—reluctantly. "All right, I'm listening." He glared across the table.

"Simply put: I'm not who you think I am. My name is Campbell. Gordon Campbell." He pulled a business card from the breast pocket of his blazer and handed it over.

Murphy studied it a moment, then shook his head. "What a dope I've been. I'd been told Gordon Kane was the director of security, and I asked for him by title, not by name. The hotel clerk pointed you out, even referring to you as Gordon. Clearly, I made a mistake, but an honest one. I sincerely apologize for my behavior."

"Forget it. No harm done." Campbell got up and refreshed his cup of coffee. "You sure you won't have a cup?" he said over his shoulder.

"Sure, why not? Black, no sugar."

Campbell placed a steaming mug in front of Murphy and sat down again.

"This Charles Hayward of yours may well have spoken to Gordon Kane, but if the topic didn't concern the Flamingo, as Gordon's number two, I wouldn't have been read in."

"So where has Kane gone that you've since taken over his slot? Not too far, I hope. I'm reasonably sure he was one of the last few people to see Hayward before he went missing and I have to get his take on it."

"Well, that's going to be hard to do, given the fact he was murdered."

21

"Shit!" Murphy exclaimed. "When did *that* happen?"

Campbell glanced at the decorative calendar hanging on the wall next to his desk.

"His body was discovered on a dirt road west of town. July ninth. He'd left work here about seven p.m. two days earlier but didn't make it home."

"Who found him?"

"High school kids out for a twilight horseback ride. It wasn't pretty. Two days with temperature above 100 degrees. Plus the vultures and coyotes had had their turns. Two of the kids stayed with the body while the other two rode hell bent for leather to the nearest place they could find a phone to call the police."

"Cause of death?"

"First, he'd been worked over. His wife asked me to go with her to identify him at the morgue. He'd been cleaned up some, but the marks on his body indicated he'd been tortured by people who knew what they were doing. I was reminded of similar victims I'd seen in Korea. The Communists had turned torture into an art form. But that's neither here nor there. He was subsequently shot in the head. Footprints at the scene—

absent those belonging to the kids—showed two people had been involved, and that one of them may've been a woman, based on heel patterns."

"Suspects?"

"None that I know of. Of course, my knowledge is limited to what I've read in the newspaper. The cops came around once asking questions but nothing since. I suspect Gordon's case has already been relegated to the 'Unsolved Murders' cabinet. Rumors have it the file drawers are crammed full."

Murphy was incredulous. "Are you saying dead bodies lying around the desert are commonplace?"

"As an out-of-towner, this would be foreign to you, so let me fill you in a bit. It actually has a bearing on how Gordon and I wound up in Vegas in the first place."

"I've got the time and nothing better to do, so let's hear it."

Campbell offered Murphy a cigarette, which he took without hesitation. They lit up and Campbell began.

"You simply can't underestimate the influence of Organized Crime on the rebirth of Las Vegas after the Second World War. The Mob already had its hooks into the established gambling centers: Atlantic City; Galveston; Hot Springs, Arkansas. It made good 'business sense' to expand its operations. No doubt they would've preferred California, given the population, but the place was too civilized, its state and local authorities too difficult to exploit.

"They settled on Vegas, close enough to draw from the southland but far enough away to be part of the Old West, where a wide-open city could flourish. And flourish it did, in spades. It wasn't New York or Chicago, but the Mob's fingerprints were everywhere: loan-sharking; protection rackets; and contract fixing—predominately in construction—where skimming off the top was elevated to an Olympic sport.

"In time, however, more and more decent people moved into the area to find work. An ad hoc Citizens Committee petitioned the U.S. Attorney's Office and outlined its concerns, requesting a heightened FBI presence. Hoover declined in such a way that would make an honest man question his loyalty to his job. In fact, even now, as strange as it may seem, I don't think fighting Organized Crime is high on his agenda. Nonetheless, crime bosses played it smart and elected to take a backseat approach with regard to their hotel/casino holdings, relying on professional property management firms, instead of muscle, to handle operations.

"Enter Gordon Kane. He'd taken the job as head of security during the time the Flamingo was reshuffling it operations staff. Now Gordon and I had been in Korea together. Grunts. I was eighteen and wet behind the ears. Gordon, a few years older, was my platoon sergeant and took me under his wing. After the war, with the aircraft industry booming, he found work at Northrop with its security department. And he was instrumental in finding me a similar position at McDonnell-Douglas.

"We'd remained close, both professionally and socially, so when Gordon got the Flamingo job, he immediately thought of me as a backup, someone he could trust. He figured there'd be a few 'wise guys' who'd want to hang onto the old ways, where they had free rein."

"And were there?"

"At first, it was as if none of them had gotten the memo. They'd bully their way around and intimidate the staff. And there were more than a few gut-wrenching moments when they had to be backed into a corner and shown the door."

"How is it now?"

"Fairly mellow, as far as the Flamingo is concerned. We drew a line in the sand, so to speak, and the unsavory elements have since, by and large, respected it. Security at other casinos report about the same. But 'Murder Incorporated' is alive and well. You've heard of so-called elephant burial grounds in Africa, where sick and injured animals allegedly go to die. Well, apparently, Vegas serves that role for the Mob. Only in our case, those who show up aren't physically impaired. But they die just the same. Not shoot-outs in broad daylight on Fremont Boulevard like the old days. Now the killings are more discrete. No one sees or hears anything. Corpses are just stumbled upon in out of the way locales."

"Like Kane's."

"So it would appear to the cops. In my mind, that's why they've taken a 'kid glove' approach to the investigation. The Mob's direct influence may've eased back from the gaming industry, but its heavy hand can still be felt in local law enforcement. That's not to say Vegas doesn't have any honest cops, but the attitude seems to be: If they want to kill each other, so be it. And good riddance, as long as innocent bystanders aren't caught in the crossfire."

"Is there any reason to believe Kane had criminal connections?"

"If he'd strayed off the path, I think I'd have sensed it, and I told the cops that, as did his wife. It was more convenient for them to turn a deaf ear."

"But you said he'd been tortured before being killed. How does that fit in?"

"For the cops, it's a moot point. Just another example of Mob justice."

"And that's that, huh? No aggressive pursuit of Kane's killers?"

"No pursuit, aggressive or otherwise. Case closed. They've reset the clock and are simply waiting for the next body to fall."

Murphy shook his head. "This is a hell of a city you've got here. A while back, you almost had me convinced that Vegas was *the* place to live. I see now that you left out some salient details."

Campbell laughed. "Maybe a few. So now what are your thoughts about Gordon and Hayward?"

"I think you already know. Two men arrange to meet. A month later one of them is dead and the other missing. You're in the business. What are the odds of that being coincidental?"

"I'd say pretty slim."

22

A lull in the conversation ensued as Murphy drained the last of his coffee.

He then said, "You mentioned Kane's wife."

"Marjorie. As you might expect, she's taken Gordon's death pretty hard, and even more so since the cops have been insistent on tarnishing his memory."

"Do you think she'd be willing to speak with me? She could have crucial information and not even realize it."

"I'm sure she'd welcome any effort to cast Gordon's death in another light."

"Could you arrange a meeting between us? I'd rather that than simply show up on her doorstep."

"I'll call her and set the scene, then take you out to see her, myself. How soon do you want to go?"

"I guess that depends on Mrs. Kane, but ideally as soon as you can make it happen. I've got a little problem of my own, however, that perhaps you can help me with first. The hotel was full up when we arrived last night."

"We...?"

"If I say 'girlfriend,' will it sound like I'm in high school? In any event, you put us up in the Bridal Suite."

"Well, you're traveling first class, then. It's one of the best rooms in the house."

"I have no problem believing that. But inasmuch as I don't know where the conversation with Mrs. Kane will take me, I think I'd better plan to stay another night—just in case."

"Not a problem. If the Bridal Suite has already been booked, I'll fix you up in one of the VIP rooms. They're always kept in reserve. You never know when Lyndon Johnson might drop in at the last minute to catch a show." He laughed.

While Campbell attempted to get hold of Marjorie Kane, Murphy tracked down Tara in the casino. She was standing at the end of a craps table with a cowboy at each elbow, one of them sporting a bushy mustache that nearly covered his mouth. The three of them seemed to be having a good time, but the cowboys' laughter bordered on maniacal. One of Campbell's floorwalkers, a stocky Mexican, stood off to the side, taking in the action.

The previous night, given the crowd, four croupiers had been required to keep the game running smoothly. This morning, there was but one to deal with the scant players.

As Murphy approached, he heard the croupier announce, "A natural. The little lady wins again." After which the cowboys hooted and hollered, and the croupier pushed a stack of colored chips across the table's green felt toward the large pile that Tara had apparently already accumulated. Like amounts found their way to the cowboys' stashes.

Murphy edged next to the table. "Yes, the 'little lady' appears to be doing *extraordinarily* well."

Tara looked up. "Oh, hi, honey. I'm glad you're here. What do you think?" She glanced down at her chips.

"I'd say that forty-dollar investment has paid off rather well. How much have you got there?"

"I don't really know. These guys," she gestured to the cowboys, "say you don't count your winnings while you're playing."

She placed another bet—as did the cowboys—and the croupier slid the dice to her. She rattled them in her hand and then banked them against the far wall of the table.

"Yo-leven," the croupier said in monotone. "Another winner." And again he pushed chips in each of their directions. The cowboys were betting heavily on her success.

It was then that Campbell showed up and stood next to Murphy.

"Is that...?" Campbell nodded toward the woman at the end of the table.

"None other. You know, I may take you up on moving to Vegas. I could open up a branch office, and Tara could become a professional gambler."

"I've observed first hand that gambling for a living is seldom a wise career move. But from what I see here, she's definitely got a bit of luck on her side this morning. L:isten, I spoke with Marge. She said for me to bring you along. You can follow me in your car, so I can get back here while you talk."

They watched as Tara had two more passes and two more wins, the second time needing to come up with an "acey deucey" on her final try.

Campbell asked, "Were you planning on taking her along?"

"I hadn't been, but now that you mention it, that would make sense. Another woman in the room might ease the conversation."

Murphy glanced back just as the croupier raked in a pile of chips from the three players.

"Tara, I need you to come with me for a while."

The look she gave him was one of relief.

"Now's as good a time as any. My luck just ran out." She started to put her chips in a small plastic container.

Mustache suddenly grabbed it out of her hand, spilling the chips onto the table, then draped his arm over her shoulder, pulling her toward him.

"You ain't goin' *nowhere*. Leastwise till we get our money back."

"Let go of me, you ape!" Tara struggled.

Instinctively, Murphy started forward, but Campbell caught

his elbow.

"We'll handle this." He nodded to the Mexican who looked like there wasn't much he couldn't deal with. But that proved to be a false assumption as he was blindsided by a beer bottle that thudded off his temple. He crumpled to the floor. People nearby either retreated to a safe distance or made for the exits.

Mustache, now using Tara as a shield, smashed his own beer bottle on the edge of the craps table and held the jagged weapon by the neck.

"Get back!" he yelled. "Change o' plan. Buck and me are leavin' and takin' her along."

Like hell! Murphy thought.

He then hurtled into the air, kicking the broken bottle out of Mustache's hand. Tara finally managed to twist out of his grasp and scrambled away. Murphy followed up with a savage right fist to his solar plexus, doubling him over. Then Murphy's knee came up to shatter his jaw. Lights out.

Meanwhile, Campbell had sidestepped a lunge from Buck and had delivered a single Karate chop to his throat. The cowboy was now writhing on the floor, gasping for breath.

Tara rushed to Murphy and threw her arms around him. She was crying.

"I've never been so scared," she said between sobs.

"Well, you're all right now." He kissed the top of her head.

She drew back. "But are you okay?"

"Sure, why wouldn't I be? All in a day's work for a private eye."

"That's what I'm afraid of." She hugged him tightly.

From beginning to end, the incident had happened so fast that Campbell's other security people were just now arriving.

As Campbell knelt by the unconscious Mexican, he barked, "Tracy, call the police and get a couple ambulances here. One for Miguel and one for..." he gestured over his shoulder, "...that scum."

23

Afterward, Tara would indicate in her written statement to the police that she'd felt all along the cowboys had been spoiling for a fight. And that the more they drank—beers followed by whisky chasers—the more worked up they became. She'd been uncomfortable having them at her side at the craps table, not knowing what they might do, but she absolved the casino of any responsibility for not having stepped in earlier, because aside from being loud, the cowboys hadn't done anything to justify intervention.

She had since gone up to their room to change clothes and "fix her face," leaving Murphy and Campbell to finish up with the police in Campbell's office.

After the last of the officers had left, Murphy asked, "Does this kind of thing happen often?"

"We try to nip it in the bud before it gets out of hand. This morning we failed. Tonight awaits. And tomorrow is another day. Money, booze, and a beautiful woman like Tara can lead to tragic consequences. As those cowboys found out."

"Did I hear right? You crushed the guy's windpipe?"

"Army training. Hand-to-hand combat. Never had an occasion to use it in Korea—thank God—but a chop to the back of the neck or throat will put a man down for the count. All my security people have been trained in martial arts. But back to the guy I put down. For all I knew, he might've killed Miguel with that bottle. I figured I owed him a little something special in return. And I noticed you didn't have much trouble with the other one, either." He paused, then, "Oh, and by the way, Jack, this is your lucky day. It's been decided that your money is no good here. In gratitude, the management will be picking up all your expenses during your stay. Also, if you ever need a job, you've got one waiting."

"I appreciate that, Gordon. Thanks. So what do you think they'll be charged with?"

"Aggravated assault, certainly. But I'll push for attempted kidnapping, as well. I want those bastards off the range for a long time. Oh, and I phoned Marjorie Kane again and explained that we'd been detained and would be along shortly."

A few moments later, Tara appeared at the office door and said, "I changed my blouse and put on a skirt instead. Am I presentable enough?"

"You look great," Murphy said.

"'Stunning' would be a better word," Campbell chimed in.

She curtsied. "I'll bet you say that to every woman who's been manhandled by a smelly ranch hand."

They all laughed.

Leaving the air conditioned interior of the hotel was like stepping into a blast furnace.

"Feels like it's going to be rather toasty today," Campbell remarked as they stood momentarily under the canopy.

"'Going to be'?" Murphy replied. "You mean we can expect worse than this later on? How does anyone stand it? I've never been to Death Valley, but Vegas has to be giving it a run for its money."

"Actually, that was my impression, too, when I ran up on my first summer here. It was pointed out to me that Death Valley recorded a temperature of 134 degrees in 1913, I think it was. Las Vegas is balmy by that standard."

"I think you've been out in the sun too long, Gordon.

'Balmy' is a word usually applied to a place like Hawaii."

The DeSoto may've been an engineering marvel under the hood, as pointed out by Clayton Hayward, but the previous owner had failed to add air conditioning as an option. Yesterday's trip from LA to Vegas had been during the evening, and with the windows rolled down, the journey had been tolerable. Today, the car's interior temperature was like an oven, despite open windows.

They followed Campbell's tan Buick Electra north of the city. Along the way, by necessity, Murphy filled Tara in on the elements of the case. At first she was excited about being drawn into his confidences. By the time Murphy got to the details of Gordon Kane's murder, she wasn't so sure. Eventually, Campbell pulled into the driveway of a house at the end of a short cul-de-sac. Murphy parked on the street in front. The name on the mailbox read: KANE.

While the Spanish-influence in architecture resembled that found in many areas of Los Angeles, the landscaping was entirely different. Colored sand and gravel, strategically placed boulders, and a variety of cactus and other desert plants had replaced lush lawns. Murphy didn't know what the water situation was in Vegas but presumed this approach was designed to conserved as much as possible.

They trailed Campbell through a covered, wrought iron-gated courtyard that contained a few pieces of cushioned rattan furniture, grouped for conversation around a rattan and glass coffee table. He knocked on the shellacked wooden door. A dog's barking ensued. A large dog by its tone.

From inside, a woman's voice. "Adolf, that's enough!"

The door then swung inward, revealing a handsome woman in a floral-print sundress and white sandals. Murphy judged her age to be a few years younger than his. Her shoulder length platinum blond hair set off her deeply tanned skin. She held the collar of a Doberman pinscher that seemed more eager to greet the house guests than attack them.

"Come in, Gordon." Then to the dog, "Behave yourself!"

Murphy and Tara followed Campbell into the foyer and

closed the door behind them. The dog, now free of its mistress's restraining hand, nuzzled each of them in turn.

"He's such a baby," she said. "Doesn't have an aggressive bone it his body. So much for protecting the home front."

Campbell then said, "Marge, this is the private detective I phoned you about. Jack Murphy."

She held out her hand which he shook. "Nice to meet you," she said.

Campbell then turned toward Tara. "And this is—"

"Tara O'Neill." She proffered her own hand. "I'm Jack's assistant."

"With a darling accent. Just like my grandmother's—God rest her sainted soul. She'd come from Ireland, too. Bundoran. Along the Atlantic coast."

"Small world. I know the area very well. In fact, my mother's brother and his family lived in Donegal, just to the north. My uncle was a fisherman, I think, or maybe he just worked the docks. I forget. Anyway, that was all before the war. My father and I came to California shortly thereafter."

"And your mother?"

"She had died."

"Oh, I'm so sorry. I ask too many questions." She paused, then, "Where are my manners? Please, let's go into the living room." She turned and led the way, the dog never leaving her side.

The room was furnished and decorated with a southwestern flair. Not entirely cowboy, nor Indian. But something encompassing the best of both cultures. Large multi-color woven rugs complemented the beige tile floor. A rounded fireplace with a tile and plaster façade dominated one corner of the room.

"Make yourselves comfortable," she said.

Murphy and Tara took seats on the rust-colored leather love seat. Campbell remained standing.

"I really need to get back in case there are loose ends to tie up with that little difficulty we had this morning. I left Tracy Wilkes in charge, and you know how Gordon felt about her:

extremely competent and looking for any opportunity to climb the corporate ladder. I'm afraid if I'm gone too long, I'll find her moved into my office and the drapes changed." He added, "If there were any windows." He laughed. Then to Murphy and Tara, "I leave you in good company."

Marjorie Kane accompanied Campbell to the front door where he kissed her on the cheek before leaving.

When she came back into the living room, she said, "Gordon has been a rock for me to hold onto since my husband's..." She left the thought unfinished and wiped the tears from her eyes. "I'm sorry. There are days when I just can't believe he's gone. I expect him to walk in at any moment."

A long moment passed before she was able to regain her composure.

She then said, "It's another of those blistering hot days. Can I get you something to drink?"

Murphy answered, "Anything with ice would be appreciated. Neither of us was prepared for this kind of heat, but I guess you eventually get used to it."

"Yes, though it does make you wonder how the early settlers dealt with the temperatures while trying to scratch out a living. For my part, I'm definitely a modern girl who needs creature comforts. I have lemonade in the refrigerator. Will that do?"

"Perfect," Tara said. "Could you use any help?"

"No, it'll just take a minute."

A few moments later, the sound of ice cubes clinking into glasses could be heard, as Adolph laid at the kitchen entry.

Tara said, "You've got a beautiful home."

"It turned out even better than Gordon and I had hoped," came the reply from the kitchen. "We enjoyed looking for just the right piece of furniture or lamp or painting or knick-knack."

She came back carrying a tray on which were three plastic tumblers and a ceramic pitcher. She placed it on the coffee table, then poured two glasses and handed them out.

"Thank you, Mrs. Kane, you're most kind," Tara said.

"Please call me Marge." She filled a glass for herself and sat in an adjacent matching leather chair.

Murphy took a long sip, then, "Ah, that hits the spot. I can't remember the last time I had some lemonade." He took another draught, then set the glass down. "So what did Gordon Campbell tell you about me?"

"Only that you were working on a case that had led you to my husband. I pressed him for more information, naturally, but he said he didn't know much more and that it would be better if you just explained the matter to me first hand." She set down her glass, as well.

"All right, then perhaps I should start at the beginning. A couple days ago, I was hired to look into the disappearance of Charles Hayward, a reporter for the LA *Times*."

"Dear God!" She buried her face in her hands. "What have I done?"

24

It took a long while for Marjorie Kane to rein in her emotions. When she did, she lit a cigarette with trembling hands and paced the room like a caged animal.

Finally, she stopped and asked Murphy, "Do you think Charles Hayward is dead, too?"

"I can't say for sure, but no one I've talked to has seen or heard from him for some time."

"But you think his disappearance is linked to Gordon's death."

"Since coming to Vegas, my instincts tell me it is, yes."

She sat back down.

"When the police concluded that Gordon's murder was tied to Organized Crime, deep down I knew it wasn't true. But what was I to do? Gordon had played his cards close to his vest. To protect me, he'd said. I figured that no matter what I said, I'd have been dismissed as a grieving widow, in denial of her late husband's questionable connections. Plus, I was scared. So I resigned myself to keep my mouth shut. Then Gordon Campbell called this morning to say there was someone he wanted me to meet. But now that you're here, I'm frightened again."

Tara said, "I'm not a detective; that's Jack's department. But from what he's told me about the circumstances of the murder, it's plain to me that whoever did it was concerned your husband might've confided certain information in others—if only in part. That's why he was tortured. He must've been very brave to not divulge your name.

"And maybe Charles Hayward has met a similar fate—I don't know. Maybe it was through him that they found your husband. But what I do know is that these *bastards*—whoever they are—need to be brought to justice." She paused, then, "I'm sorry for being so emotional about this, but you see my own father was shot to death in LA a few months ago. Behind the pub he'd owned since the '40s. The police say they have nothing to go on. To think that his killer may never be caught is a weight I carry every day."

Tara leaned forward and took one of Marge's hands in hers.

"Don't take on a burden like mine. You can trust Jack. And don't let his bruises fool you. He's the best at what he does. Even when the odds were three to one. But he needs to know whatever you know—no matter how insignificant you may think it is."

Tara sat back and glanced at Murphy, as if to ask, "How did I do?"

Marge crushed out her cigarette in an ashtray and took a sip of lemonade.

"It started months before we moved to Vegas," she began. "As you undoubtedly know, Gordon worked for Northrop, a security job he'd taken after he got back from Korea. He was good at it, and in time was promoted from uniformed duties to plain clothes where he was put in charge of background investigations of prospective employees. Much of what Northrop designs and manufactures are for the Department of Defense. Security—as you might then imagine—is a priority.

"This kept him and his team hopping, given the fact the company was expanding its operations, taking on more and more contracts. Consequently, additional personnel needed to be vetted. Gordon would routinely be gone out of town for

129

days at a time, tracking down references and the like. Then his travels took him to Europe for several weeks. When he came back he was different."

"Different how?" Murphy asked.

Marge thought for a moment. "Distant, I'd say. Pre-occupied. Often, he'd come home late—well into the night. I'm embarrassed to say it, but jealousy got the best of me. I thought there might be another woman and prodded him about it. He told me I needn't worry on that score; that his job had just taken a peculiar turn. He'd found a potential flaw in the background of someone who'd been working at Northrop for many years."

"Did he tell you who it was?"

"Only after I demanded to know who'd stolen his attention, at my expense. Finally, Gordon relented. But he made me swear I'd never reveal the name to anyone. I accused him of melodrama, but agreed. And I've kept that promise until now: The man is Klaus Hoffmann. The name meant nothing to me, so Gordon told me that initially Hoffmann was linked to Werner Von Braun."

"The German rocket designer?" Tara asked.

"Yes. Gordon said that immediately after the war, German scientists were being grabbed by the United States and Russia. Hitler may've been a madman, but German technology was apparently first-rate. They might well have had the atomic bomb before we did if their research facilities hadn't been blown up in bombing raids. At least that's what Gordon told me."

"And what had been Hoffmann's expertise?" Murphy asked. "Did your husband tell you?"

"Only reluctantly. He'd been a mechanical engineer. Jet propulsion was his specialty."

"A perfect match for a cutting edge aircraft company like Northrop."

Marge nodded. "I suppose so."

"But your husband had reservations about Hoffmann."

"That's right."

"Why? What were his concerns?"

She hesitated a moment. "I don't know. Gordon refused to tell me anything more."

Murphy sensed she was lying but chose not to confront her.

Instead, he said, "So whatever misgivings your husband may've had about Hoffmann, did he go to Management with them?"

"No, because at about the same time there was a shakeup in the security department. Gordon sized up the new director as unapproachable, especially since Hoffmann supposedly had a spotless reputation, and his own investigation had been undertaken without authorization."

"Still, if he'd discovered something about Hoffmann that didn't—"

"Well, that's just it. Gordon started to doubt his own conclusions. If Hoffmann had passed scrutiny by the federal government, with all its resources, who was he to question the process? Frustrated, it was then that Gordon started looking around for a job elsewhere."

"Which he found at the Flamingo."

"I wasn't all that excited about the prospects of selling our home in Buena Park to move to Vegas, but Gordon convinced me it would be a very well-paid adventure. That if it turned out not to be our cup of tea, we'd move back. But we actually grew to like it here, despite the heat.

"But Hoffmann began again to weigh on Gordon's mind. He started to second guess himself. Should he have passed his concerns along anyway and let the chips fall wherever? It was like a toothache that wouldn't go away. He started to obsess about it. He'd sit right over there," she pointed to the dining table, "and go over his notes. I was worried he was having a nervous breakdown. Finally, I suggested that if he didn't want to go directly to Northrop, maybe he could contact a television or newspaper reporter. I'm the one who gave him Charles Hayward's name. You can get the LA *Times* in Vegas, too, and we'd often pick up a copy of the Sunday edition just to keep in touch

"Anyway, we'd read Hayward's columns and figured that as an investigative reporter, he might be interested. Gordon talked to him twice. The first time was on the phone just after Memorial Day. That prompted Hayward to come to Vegas a few days later. They met at Hayward's room at the Sands Hotel."

Murphy gave her another chance to come forward. "And you're sure you have no details of what they talked about?"

"No. But afterward, he seemed his old self again. He even talked about taking a vacation and traveling to New England this year to see the fall colors. We'd always wanted to do that but never seemed to find the time." She teared up again.

After a few moments, Murphy said, "You mentioned your husband's notes."

"Yes. Gordon kept them in a locked attaché case."

"Where is that case now?"

"He took it when he met with Hayward. I haven't seen it since, so I assume he gave it to him."

"Did it by any chance have a Mickey Mouse decal on the top right corner of the lid?"

Marge looked at him askance. "How could you know that?"

"I saw it is Hayward's apartment. It was empty. Might your husband have kept copies of whatever he'd compiled?"

"If he did, I don't know where they would be."

Again, Murphy's gut told him she was lying. He sighed, settled back on the loveseat, and drained his glass of lemonade.

"I guess that's that, then," he said at last. "You've been most helpful."

Marge said, "I just remembered. I have a picture of Hoffmann if you'd like to see it. It bothered Gordon to no end that he came to his farewell party." She stood. "I'll just be a minute."

When she returned, she carried an album. Sitting back down, she leafed through the pages until she found the picture. She then passed the album to Murphy.

"Hoffmann is the smiling tall one with the blond crew cut. He's got his arm around Gordon's shoulder as if they were best friends. I don't know the others in the photo. We never socialized with anyone from his work. Gordon said he didn't want those kinds of friendships to cloud his judgment in enforcing security rules."

"I suppose there's wisdom in that, all right, but I recognize another face." He pointed to a laughing man sitting off to the side, a cigarette in one hand and a bottle of Coca Cola in the other. "This is Robert Reed, one of Northrop's engineers. I spoke to him yesterday. Hayward had met with him after returning from seeing your husband. He's responsible for pointing me here. But Hoffmann's name never came up in their meeting."

Murphy handed back the album, and after a couple more minutes of small talk, he and Tara got to their feet and Marjorie Kane walked them to the front door.

Murphy said, "I know Gordon Campbell is a good friend, but I think it would best if you didn't discuss with him what we've talked about."

"Surely, you don't think—"

"No, nothing like that. It's just that until I can figure out what this is all about, the fewer involved the better. My mother had a saying: *Too many cooks spoil the broth.*

25

Back in the sweltering car, returning to the Flamingo, Murphy fell silent.

At last, Tara said, "A penny for your thoughts, honey."

He turned his head toward her. "What? Oh, sorry. I guess I drifted off. Investigations are like solving jigsaw puzzles. The straight edges are the easiest to connect, then you move inward, piecing together more difficult shapes until the picture finally emerges. Only on this case I'm already beginning to detect a picture without having all that many pieces."

"So tell me what you think you see. Is Charles Hayward dead?"

"I'd be shocked if he turned up alive. In fact, I don't think he's going to 'turn up'—period."

"And Klaus Hoffmann?"

"A mystery man."

"Capable of murder?"

"At least indirectly, yes. Let me lay out the sequence of events as I see them."

"Okay, I'm listening."

"First, it went down just as Marjorie Kane explained. But when Hayward got back to LA, he called Robert Reed and arranged a meeting. You see, Hayward wouldn't have known Kane from Adam until being contacted by him. Reed, on the other hand, would've had an opinion on the man, having worked with him at Northrop. Or so Hayward hoped. And, in fact, Reed gave Kane high marks. That was on June seventh."

"Then what?"

"Three weeks went by, during which time Hayward put a fine point on what Kane had given him. And probably meshed it with some of his own research. Regardless, he was tight-lipped about what he was working on. But his editor at the *Times* finally pressed him for details and gave him an ultimatum to produce what he had. Despite his secrecy, though, Hayward must've let something slip along the way."

"Might he have confronted Hoffman directly?"

"Doubtful. The Hayward stories that I've read have always relied on the element of surprise. The targets of those stories woke up to see their names in the headlines. They weren't privy beforehand. In any event, before he could outline his story for his editor, he was taken out of circulation."

"By whom?"

"I don't know. But I think Hayward was taken from his apartment building, because his car was parked in the underground garage when I had a looksee. In fact, my guess is he was jumped in the garage. Even if there'd been a scuffle, the security guard wouldn't have heard it down there. Then they stashed him somewhere and went upstairs to search his apartment. It wouldn't have been much of a problem, either, because I'd been able to go from the apartment to the garage without the guard seeing me. They didn't need to pick the lock, because they had his keys.

"I'm saying 'they,' because the Vegas police said two people were involved with Kane's murder. I could be wrong, but I think we're dealing with the same two. They'd have been looking for anything connected to Hoffmann. I know they found the briefcase that Kane had given Hayward in Vegas. The one I mentioned to Mrs. Kane that I'd seen in Hayward's apartment. It had been broken into. Whatever had been inside was gone.

"Then they went after Kane. He'd been unknown to them before grabbing Hayward. But knowing the methods used on Kane afterward, they would've applied the same kind of screws to Hayward. Both failed to fully appreciate whatever they thought they had on Hoffmann. But one man is confirmed dead and the second is missing in action, and presumed dead. So whatever is in play is lethal."

26

When they arrived at the Flamingo, Murphy sought out
Campbell to thank him for facilitating the meeting with
Marjorie Kane. He followed his own advice and revealed
nothing of their conversation, though Campbell had prodded
him a little. Afterward, Murphy had wanted to head back to
LA, but Tara talked him into staying one more night,
necessitating the purchase of swimming trunks in the hotel
boutique. She'd thought to pack one for herself, a nifty yellow
polka dot two piece that caught the eye of everyone poolside.

Late that afternoon, thoroughly toasted under a blazing
Nevada sun, and having sipped a couple of umbrella drinks a-
piece, they returned to their suite for gymnastic competition.
As usual, Tara received better scores.

The following morning, with their sole bag already stowed
in the trunk of the car, they were just finishing breakfast when
Campbell appeared and slid into the booth beside Tara.

"Good morning, Gordon," she said, scooting over to make
more room for him.

He didn't reply but instead directed a statement to Murphy:
"Marge is dead."

An involuntary "Oh" escaped Tara's lips as she instinctively crossed herself.

"What happened?" Murphy put down his coffee cup and leaned forward.

"The police are just now putting it together, but everything points to suicide."

Before Murphy could respond, Tara said, "When we spoke with her, she shed tears over the memory of her husband, but I never would have guessed *this*." She shook her head in disbelief.

Campbell said to Murphy, "My wife called Marge yesterday afternoon after I told her I'd been to see her that morning. She asked if Marge wanted to go to a movie. Girls' night out. But Marge said she already had plans to have dinner with some friends. Do you suppose she was planning—"

Murphy cut him off. "Who discovered her?"

"I don't know any details except that she was found less than an hour ago—not far from where Gordon was murdered. The police want me to come out and identify her body. I guess because they know I was with her when she had to identify Gordon's. Anyway, I hope you don't mind, but I told them the hotel had brought in a private investigator to look into Gordon's death and that I'd be bringing you with me. They didn't object."

Murphy nodded. "All right." He then said to Tara, "Why don't you wait here while Gordon and I have a look? Maybe you can turn around your losing streak from last night at the blackjack table. Someone recently told me it's best to double down on eleven." He started to reach for his wallet.

She shook her head. "Not on your life. Remember what happened the last time you left me on my own? I'm not letting you out of my sight." She turned to Campbell. "So lead the way; we'll be right behind you."

Campbell's car was being serviced, so they took Murphy's DeSoto. Tara was relegated to the back seat while Campbell rode shotgun, giving directions. Asphalt finally gave way to a rutted dirt road that caused the sedan to violently buck and sway. An overcast sky had significantly dropped the temperature from the day before, making the ride bearable, since the windows were closed to keep out the dust.

A shade under two miles in, and out of sight from the main road they'd left, Murphy stopped the car maybe fifty yards from a knot of two police cars; an ambulance; and a yellow jeep. Adjacent to those vehicles was a red Volkswagen Bug and a group of men, some in police uniforms, some not.

Tara opened her door to exit.

"You're staying put," Murphy said.

"But, Jack..."

"But nothing. Wait here and I *mean* it. I don't know what to expect, but you're better off not seeing what it turns out to be."

She sighed. "Whatever you say." She then pulled the door shut and settled back in her seat.

As they walked up the road, Campbell said, "That's Marge's car, all right. She had a yellow daisy painted over the engine compartment."

A moment later, they were challenged by a pimply-faced cop who didn't look old enough to shave.

Campbell said, "We're expected. Gordon Campbell and Jack Murphy. We'll wait here until you tell your boss."

The young officer walked halfway back to the group and then called, "Captain!" He gestured to Campbell and Murphy.

A man in mirrored aviator glasses looked over, waved them forward, and then broke away from the group to meet them when they neared. With the exception of the shades, he looked as if he'd stepped off the pages of a Louis L'Amour novel: tall and lanky, cowboy hat, a white western-cut shirt with mother of pearl snaps, blue jeans, and boots. A tooled leather holster worn low on his hip cradled an ivory-gripped revolver, and a gold badge was pinned over his left breast pocket. It was hard to assess his age, but one thing was clear: His face was as rugged and creased as an old saddle, no doubt from long hours in the sun. He'd been smoking a cigarette but now crushed it under foot.

"Thanks for comin'." He shook Campbell's hand.

Campbell then gestured to his left. "This is Jack Murphy, the private investigator I told you about."

The cop sized him up and then offered his hand.

"Captain Brandt."

"Nice to meet you, Captain."

"So you're a California shamus, huh? I'll bet the price tag for guy like you is pretty steep."

"Depends on the client. But for the most part, it's just like in the movies: fifty dollars a day, plus expenses."

"Damn! Makes me want to turn in my badge and head west."

"Of course, it's only good money when you're working. That's not always the case. If you want a steady paycheck, I'd suggest you stay put."

Brandt nodded. "Good advice."

Murphy then said, "I want to thank you for letting me tag along this morning. I promise not to get in your way."

"Well, I figured it was the least I could do since you helped take a couple of rustlers off the range for me."

"You mean those two—"

"Yeah," Brandt interrupted. "We were fixin' on roundin' those cowboys up in a day or two when we could get them identified proper. They trucked some stolen cattle into Mexico. Then they tried to run up their score at the Flamingo but ran into you two, instead. They've since confessed their sins."

Brandt studied Murphy's bruised face.

"Were they responsible for any part of *that?*"

"Only in their dreams. They went down like a box of rocks. I got this," touching his cheek, "duking it out with the husband of a client and a couple of his buddies. Must've been the pictures of him tickling the fancy of a stripper that ticked him off. In any event, I put them down for the count."

Brandt chuckled. "I understand you're lookin' into the Kane hit. Gordon here never did cotton to the notion that the Mob killed him, but..."

"But what?" Murphy asked.

"But Vegas is Vegas. It's a shithole, I'm sorry to say, and

livin' here without gettin' any on you can be a real trick."

"I'll keep that in mind. But if anything concrete surfaces that points to a different explanation, you can count on a call."

Brandt nodded. "I'd appreciate that."

Taking the lead, Murphy said, "So what exactly do you have here, Captain?"

He walked toward the Volkswagen but stopped well back, not wanting to contaminate the crime scene. Campbell and Brandt joined him. The driver's side window was splattered and streaked with blood and gunk, obscuring the victim whose head lolled back on the seat. A hole in the window had produced veined cracks rather than shattering it.

Brandt said to Campbell, "We ran the plates. Car's registered to Marjorie Kane. I met her once after her husband was killed, and I'm pretty sure it's her inside, but I want a second opinion."

"I'll need a closer look."

"Sure, go around to the other side. The view's better there."

Murphy followed him, taking a wide berth, and peered in the front passenger window. There was no doubt about who it was. She was even dressed the same as when they'd last seen her.

Campbell glanced up over the roof of the car and said to Brandt, "It's Marjorie Kane, all right." He shook his head in disgust. "Terrible."

Murphy thought so too, but for a different reason, as he surveyed the area around the vehicle.

"It usually is," Brandt replied, "when they blow their brains out. By any chance, do you recognize the pistol in her hand?"

Campbell looked back inside and nodded. "Yeah. It's a .32 caliber Beretta that belonged to her husband. I was with him when he bought it."

When they came back around to where Brandt was standing, Brandt said, "We don't see a suicide note. If there is one, could be it slipped under the seat. We'll check later when we get her out of the car. We're waitin' for the county coroner for a preliminary cause of death. Tracked him down at Lake

Mead on his houseboat. He was takin' a couple days' vacation. Should be here any time now. But it seems pretty open and shut to me. She was depressed over her husband's death, so she shot herself. Wouldn't be the first time somethin' like that has happened. As to why she drove way out here to do it, is anybody's guess. Who knows what she was thinking in her frame of mind? Maybe she thought that by comin' here she'd somehow be closer to him in death."

Murphy asked, "Who found her?"

"One of my off-duty officers." He pointed off to the right. "There's a fishin' hole just beyond that ridge. Requires a four-wheel-drive to get there. Lots of folks park right here and hike in. It was about four-thirty this morning when he drove past. He saw the Volkswagen in the dark but didn't think anything of it. It was when he came back down that he found what you've seen. His jeep has a two-way, so he radioed it in. And here we are. We'll get a sense of how long she's been dead after an autopsy."

"I'd put the time of death around midnight."

Brand gave Murphy a questioning look.

"Retired Army cop," he explained. "I've seen plenty of dead bodies in my career."

"CID?"

Murphy nodded. "Early on, though, I just ducked German bullets like everyone else."

"I dodged a few myself, only they were made in Japan."

"Marine, huh?"

"*Semper Fi.*" Brandt then said to Campbell, "We're obligated to contact the next of kin, if possible. Do you know any of her family? Kids?"

"She didn't have any children. But there's a sister in the Midwest. Iowa, I think. She came out for Gordon's funeral. Helen was her first name. I can't remember her last. Sorry."

Brandt shrugged. "In time, when the sister can't make contact, maybe she'll give us a call."

"I suppose so. In any event, I'm sure I can get the Flamingo to agree to foot the bill on her burial. Just let me know when you're through with her body."

"Will do, and thanks again for comin' out. These things are nasty business." Brandt shook their hands and turned back to the group.

27

At Tara's insistence, Murphy reluctantly described what they'd seen, and as he did, he turned the car around and headed back toward the city. About a mile from the crime scene, they were met by a navy blue sedan headed in the opposite direction. Murphy pulled to the right on the narrow road to let it pass. The white-haired man behind the wheel acknowledged him with a nod of gratitude. A Clark County seal adorned the driver's door.

"Must be the coroner," Campbell said.

"Yeah." Murphy then fell silent as the car bumped and rocked, until at last he asked Campbell, "Did Marge carry that pistol in her purse or maybe keep it in the car?"

"Yes, the glove compartment. Before Gordon's death, she was afraid of guns. Then afterward, she got me to show her how to shoot it. I told her it was illegal to carry a loaded gun in the car without a permit and that she ought to apply for one. She informed me that whoever murdered Gordon wasn't constrained by the law and she wouldn't be, either. She even bought a revolver for the house. Kept it in the nightstand by her bed. She was really unnerved by Gordon's death, and who could blame her?"

Back on the highway, Murphy asked, "When Gordon Kane went missing, was his car found out by his body, like Marge's?"

"No," Campbell said. "It had never left the hotel parking lot. Why?"

"Just curious. I'm trying to wrap my head around all this. When husband and wife both die violently within a month of each other...well..."

"You mean you don't believe Marge's death is a suicide? From what I saw, I think Captain Brandt got this one right. The gun was still in her hand. Plus, you experienced first-hand how fragile she was when talking about Gordon."

"You're probably right," Murphy replied, though he knew for certain that Campbell was dead wrong. "Maybe I'm seeing shadows where there are none. That's the most difficult part about being an investigator: separating light from shadow."

They proceeded to the Flamingo, where Murphy thanked Campbell for his assistance and hospitality, but there was really nothing to be gained by sticking around any longer. They said their goodbyes in the parking lot, and Murphy drove off in the direction of LA. They'd gone but two blocks when Murphy turned onto a side road and doubled back.

"Where are we going?" Tara asked.

"Back to the Kane house."

"Why?"

"Because unless the coroner got his credentials from the Montgomery Ward catalog, he'll conclude what I did: that Marjorie Kane's death wasn't a tragic suicide, like the cops believe; she was murdered."

"Murdered? So what did *you* see that everyone else missed?"

"For starters, the lateral trajectory of the bullet. It entered the right temple and exited the left, then continued on, breaking the driver's side window. Even if the pistol were smaller, it would be unnatural to hold the barrel parallel. More likely, it would've been held in a relaxed position, the barrel pointing slightly upward or placed under the chin. In either instance, the exiting bullet would've missed the window.

"Secondly, the powder burns around the entry wound aren't consistent with a barrel that's held against the skin. There should've been more scorching, as well as a fair amount of blowback. The right side of her face and clothing should've shown blood and tissue splatter. There was none; hence, the weapon was fired at a distance but probably still inside the cab.

"And lastly, after she'd been shot, the pistol was placed in her right hand. But yesterday, when she held on to the dog's collar, she used her left."

"And she poured the lemonade with her left, too. Marge was left-handed. Her killer didn't know that." Tara seemed pleased with herself that she was keeping up with Murphy's narrative.

Murphy said, "At first, I was puzzled. Why had they gone to the trouble of taking her car out there, if their intent all along was to kill her? Wouldn't they have just left it abandoned, as they had with her husband? But then it dawned on me. Marge was a 'horse of a different color.' We're dealing with professionals, not indiscriminate killers. They weren't going to drop the hammer if they didn't have to. So this is what I think may've happened: Marge went to dinner with friends just like Campbell's wife said. Getting into her car afterward, she was jumped. They probably put a hood over her head so she couldn't identify them. Maybe they injected her with a knockout drug to prevent her struggling or calling out. Then they likely stuffed her into the trunk or backseat of their car while one of them drove hers. But once they arrived at the same isolated area where they'd murdered her husband, they were forced to wait until she came to.

"If they determined she posed no risk, the plan might've been to drug her again, and when she woke up they'd be gone. They'd put the fear of God into her and would've figured she'd never report her ordeal to the police. But that's not how it turned out. When she came to, my guess is that she was too terrified to hold anything back. But then her fate was sealed, despite the fact she'd never seen their faces. She would've begged for her life; promised them that she'd keep her mouth shut. The only way they could guarantee that was to shut it for her—permanently."

"My God. The poor woman. But why bother with making her murder look like a suicide?"

Murphy shrugged. "Hard to know. Maybe it only came to them after they found her gun in the glove box."

"Do you suppose she knew more than what she told us?"

"I'm certain she did. But her death begs a much bigger question: Why did she become a target now? She could've been eliminated anytime during the last three weeks since her husband's death. It isn't a coincidence that she was murdered within hours of talking to us. She was targeted *because* I led them to her."

"What are you saying? That we're being followed?" Tara turned in her seat and gave a furtive look behind them.

"Don't worry. They undoubtedly high-tailed it back to LA during the night. But it's all making sense to me now. And it starts with Clayton Hayward, that son of a bitch! I'd come recommended as having a reputation of conducting thorough investigations. Recommended unwittingly by his own daughter, no less. Hayward knew all along his son was dead. Asking me to find him was only a ploy to use me as a bird dog to flush game that may've been overlooked.

"Marjorie Kane blamed herself for her husband's murder, but somehow he'd been savvy enough to shelter her from his killers. And then here I come bumbling along and beat a path to her door for them." He pounded the steering wheel. "Goddammit!"

28

Murphy pulled the car into the Kane driveway and retrieved his pistol from the trunk. He actually believed what he'd told Tara about the killers leaving town, but having the gun tucked in his belt made him feel more comfortable. Less than a minute later, they retraced their steps from the day before, walking through the courtyard.

While Murphy applied his lock picks to the door, he said, "I think we can count Adolph as another casualty in this affair. A barking dog in the middle of the night would draw the attention of neighbors. Their plan was to get inside, find what they came for, and leave before anyone was the wiser."

Murphy felt the locking mechanism release and within a moment they were inside, the door shut behind them. The dog lay in the foyer in a pool of coagulated blood; its throat had been slit.

Murphy said, "I wonder which of them did this—the man or the woman?"

Tara was taken aback. "A woman, Jack?"

They walked around the dog and into the living room.

"Yes, in their line of work, posing as a couple makes them less conspicuous. Campbell told me when Gordon Kane was killed, the police thought that a woman was involved, based on footprints at the scene. The area around Marge's car was fairly well trampled, because, like I said, the cops weren't searching for any clues; they'd already made up their minds they were looking at a suicide." He paused, then "What do you call the kind of women's shoes that don't have high heels but maybe a shorter, broader type?"

"Pumps. Why?"

"At the crime scene today there were those kinds of heel impressions, and there were no women present. The cops also overlooked a set of tire tracks on the passenger side of the VW that looped around the front of the car. The treads weren't from an off-road tire like on the jeep that was there, and the other vehicles were parked well back. I figured the tracks belonged to the killers' vehicle, and when they were finished with Marge, they simply made a U-turn and headed back here. Let's call Adolph: Exhibit A."

On the coffee table was the photo album they'd been shown. Tara rifled through it.

"Jack, that picture of Hoffmann is missing." She handed him the album. The page was blank.

"Exhibit B," he said. "They've cleaned house. But that picture had to be an added bonus for them. They came for Kane's notes."

"Could Hoffmann have known back then that Kane had misgivings about him? Maybe he showed up at the going away party to send a message."

"You mean 'behave yourself, or else'?"

"Something like that."

"No. Too dangerous. Kane would've been disposed of back then, if his investigation had leaked out."

Murphy set the album down and walked to a bank of louvered windows overlooking the patio and swimming pool beyond. The backyard was minimally landscaped much the same as the front. The addition of palm trees, however, when coupled with the sparkling water of the pool, gave the illusion of an oasis.

Opening the French door, he walked outside under the vine-covered pergola. A southwest-style doghouse, complete with tiled roof, was situated near the edge of the flagstone flooring. Adolph had apparently been afforded a life of relative luxury. Then something caught Murphy's eye. As he got down on his haunches for a better look, he was joined by Tara.

"Find something, Jack?"

Murphy looked up over his shoulder and said, "Notice how well-groomed everything is out here. Not a stone out of place. Even the sand has rake marks. Except for right there." He pointed to deep, wide impressions just beyond the opening of the doghouse. "You don't suppose...?"

Murphy crawled half way in.

Backing out, he stood and shook his head. "I'll have to hand it to Gordon Kane. What better place to put something of value than where you have to cozy up to a Doberman to get to it." He took a step back. "Go ahead. Take a look. There's a hinged compartment just beneath the roof. It's empty now, but that's where Kane had hidden a copy of the materials he'd given to Hayward. Exhibit C."

"I'll take your word for it."

They walked back in and took a tour of the rooms but didn't find anything else out of place.

Murphy then said, "There's one thing left to do: I want to wipe down any fingerprints we might've left today or yesterday. Unless they're only reasonable facsimiles of cops, I don't want to complicate matters by having us drawn into their investigation—which will likely go nowhere."

"What about your car, Jack? It's been parked out front twice."

"If Vegas is anything like LA, I'm betting the neighbors are content to mind their own business. Plus, I assume Gordon Kane's murder received a fair amount of press and television coverage, linking it to Organized Crime. Human nature being what it is, the neighbors had probably already distanced themselves from Marge. When the cops get around to declaring her death to be a murder, too, the neighbors will go deaf and blind. No one will come forward as Good Samaritans."

"Jack, I'm scared."

Murphy put his arms around her.

"Remember that speech I gave you on the perils of being married to a private eye? Well, it's come true. But if they think we're going down as easily as Marge and Gordon Kane, they've made a big mistake."

29

Murphy finally snapped off the radio. He'd learned to tolerate the Beach Boys and the Beatles, but he drew the line at country music, and country music seemed to be the only genre being broadcast two hours outside of Vegas. And even then, the static was annoying. Tara couldn't have cared less about the music; she'd fallen asleep almost immediately after they'd left the city.

A jackrabbit, seemingly the size of a kangaroo, suddenly darted in front of the car. Murphy swerved to miss the animal, but it caught the right front tire. The subsequent bump and crunch jostled Tara instantly awake.

"What was that?"

"Apparently having four rabbit's feet didn't account for much luck."

She turned in her seat and looked out the rear window.

Murphy said, "An automobile versus a cute furry creature is always a bad match."

When she turned back, he asked, "Have a nice nap?"

"I was just resting my eyes."

"Well, you could've fooled me. You know that expression about sawing logs...?"

"You're not suggesting I snore, are you?" She seemed a bit

indignant.

"If it wasn't you, there must've been a lumber mill we passed."

"Really? I had no idea. Why haven't you told me before? Now I'm going to be self-conscious."

"Don't be. It doesn't bother me a bit, and it only happens when you're really tired or stressed. Today is the latter."

She nodded. "All that's happened is uncharted water for me."

"What about getting out of Ireland by the skin of your teeth?"

"But I was a kid back then. Even though they'd killed my mother, I knew my father and I were going to be okay. I'm not a kid anymore."

Murphy reached over and took her hand.

"I've noticed." He chuckled. "But if you were even five years younger, there's no way I could keep up."

She laughed. "Don't underestimate yourself, Jack. Even if I *were* younger, you'd still know how to ring my bell."

They'd driven a ways farther when Murphy said, "While you were 'resting your eyes,' I was thinking about our situation. On second consideration, it could be a lot better than we once thought."

"How do you figure that?"

"Think about it. They know we have Hoffmann's name—because Marge would've told them—but without the supporting documentation that Kane and Hayward had on him, what risk are we to them? None."

"I'd like to believe that, but still…"

"Listen, this isn't about eliminating everyone who came into contact with Gordon Kane or Charlie Hayward. If it were, then Bob Reed, the guy from Northrop, would've already bitten the dust. But he's alive and well. Hayward would've confessed what he and Reed talked about, and it was concluded that Reed was in the clear. And so are we, the way I size it up."

"What if Reed's in on it?

"Then Hayward and Kane would've met their ends weeks

earlier. No, Reed is a straight shooter."

Despite his assurance that no one was following them, when he pulled in at a couple of truck stops to top off the tank, he lingered long enough to check out the road behind them. He hadn't detected a tail.

They hadn't burned up the road getting back and arrived at O'Neill's late in the afternoon. The pub was already picking up steam, with the promise of a crowded and boisterous Friday night. While Tara talked business with deShazo, Murphy retreated to the small office and dialed his office.

"Murphy and Doyle. Private Investigations."

"It's nice to know when the cat's away, the mice are still hard at it."

"Jack. You're back. Or are you?"

"Only just. I'm at O'Neill's. Is Matt there by any chance?"

"Yes, just a minute."

A second or two later, Doyle was on the line.

"How was Vegas, buddy? Did you win enough to move us into a swankier office?" He laughed.

"How many nickel jackpots would I have had to win to get us an address on Wilshire Boulevard, do you suppose? Tara, on the other hand, nearly broke the bank at the craps table. But that was yesterday morning. By last night, she'd given it all back, and then some."

"'*Easy come, easy go.*' That's Vegas's motto, isn't it? And if it isn't, it should be. What about showgirls? Did you cast your eyes toward any voluptuous babes?"

"Not a one. Besides, I may be prejudice, but none of them could possibly hold a candle to Tara."

Doyle laughed. "Oh, I get it. She's standing right beside you while you're making this call."

"No, I mean it. I think my running around days have reached their end. But I didn't call to talk about my love life. The Hayward case has decidedly taken a sharp turn."

"How so?"

"I'll fill you in later, but suffice it to say, the guy I went to see was murdered about three weeks ago, about the same time

Hayward went missing. And his wife got the same treatment in the wee small hours of today. Someone is closing loopholes, and Tara and I may be on the agenda. I've downplayed it with her, but there are some serious folks out there who aren't at all squeamish about blood."

"Jesus, Jack!"

"You can say that again. I think I'm going to swear off missing persons cases in the future. And speaking of that, did you find any John Does alias Charles Hayward lying about?"

"I called every hospital and county morgue from here to the Mexican border. Nothing."

"Well, that does it for me. I'm convinced he's as dead as the other two in Vegas."

"You want to call in the police?"

"Not yet. Now wrap your head around this: There's more than a good chance that Clayton Hayward's fingerprints are all over this—figuratively speaking. At least, where you smell smoke, there's usually a fire."

"By the way, he called this morning looking for you."

"Huh. He's trying to throw me off. If I'm right, he knew I was in Vegas, because the people following me would've told him. And that's the real reason I called. I know there are at least two of them on my tail, and I want to know what they look like."

"What have you got in mind?"

Murphy spelled it out.

"Piece of cake," Doyle said when Murphy was finished.

"All right. I'll clue Tara in on the plan. She's insisting on staying at my place for the next little while. She's spooked about being stalked."

"I'd say she has reason to be. Anything else?"

"Just be careful, Matt. These are seasoned pros. And from what I've seen and heard, they love their work."

Murphy disconnected, then fished Clayton Hayward's phone number from his wallet and dialed. After three rings, it was answered by the houseboy.

"Hayward Residence."

"This is Jack Murphy. May I speak with Mr. Hayward?"

"Yes, certainly. One moment, please, and I'll find him for you."

Then, at last, Hayward's voice: "Jack. I was beginning to worry. You said you'd keep me in the loop, and I hadn't heard from you. I called your office, but they said you were out of town."

"Yes. Las Vegas. I was following up a possible lead."

"And?"

"A dead end, or nearly so."

"That's disappointing news."

"And equally disappointing for me to have to tell you. Nonetheless, I'd like to meet—say tomorrow morning around ten, if possible—and go over every step I've taken so far. Charlie's trail may've been cold, but I've managed to discover a few traces."

"Yes, yes, certainly. Tomorrow at ten would be fine. I'll look forward to hearing what you've learned."

"Okay, I'll see you then."

As Murphy hung up the receiver, Tara was standing behind him and asked, "Who were you talking to?"

Murphy turned in his seat. "Clayton Hayward. I'm paying him a visit tomorrow morning."

"What are you going to say to him? Especially since you think he set you up."

"I plan to confirm what he's undoubtedly already been told, although I'll spin it a little differently. I want him to conclude I'm being truthful. At least long enough to take him down. Marjorie Kane's murder has made it personal."

30

Seated at his kitchen table, Murphy scanned the headlines of the LA *Times* from the last four days. There was definitely trouble in paradise, if you understood the undercurrent of the stories. Especially in the Negro sections of the city. Elements of racial unrest were obvious. Like tinder dry grass, only a spark would be necessary to set things ablaze. Murphy wondered what specific event it would be and when.

Across from him, Tara, still in a fuzzy pink robe and matching slippers, sipped her coffee and caught up on the comic strips. Glancing at the clock on the wall, she drained her cup, then got up and rinsed it in the sink.

"I need to put on my face, and then I'll be ready," she said.

Murphy looked up at her. "Don't take too long, okay? I don't want to keep Hayward waiting."

She gave him one of those withering looks.

"Besides," he continued, "I've never truly understood that expression: *putting on one's face*. As far as I could tell, women in the Army didn't even wear lipstick. They rolled out of their bunks, ran a brush through their hair, and fell out for morning formation."

"And you found those women attractive, did you? *Au

naturel, so to speak."

"We weren't running beauty contests."

"No, I suspect not, but don't you think they could've improved their looks with just a little more attention to detail?"

Murphy shrugged. "Sure, I guess so. But that's them. You're perfect just the way you are now. You could be a movie star."

"Like Doris Day, I suppose."

"Well, I—"

"C'mon, I know she's the woman of your dreams. You mention her enough. The quintessential girl next door, with a flawless peaches and cream complexion. Admit it."

"All right. You got me. For my money, Doris Day is every man's dream. But I was trying to give you a compliment. You don't have a need to put on a different face, just like Doris Day doesn't."

Tara sat back down.

"I don't want to burst your bubble, but I actually met Doris Day—twice. During the early 1950s. I was in college then, but I helped my father at the pub when I could. It was in the evening of St. Patrick's Day, and the place was going wild. Then Doris Day, wearing a tailored jacket and skirt, walked in with an entourage of Hollywood types. All attention in the room suddenly shifted to her. She was every bit as beautiful in person as she was on the theater screen.

"Now you have to understand that movie stars often frequent the pub, owing to the proximity of the studios. But this was the first time that my father was smitten. He fell all over himself getting her a table, and he was literally tongued tied as he took her order. It was really quite comical to watch. And, of course, he made sure to introduce me to her. I remember feeling embarrassed, thinking she couldn't care less about the proprietor's daughter. A couple days later, she sent an autographed picture to my father. *Mickey, thank you for a magical night. Love, Doris.* You've probably seen it framed on the wall. It was one of his prized possessions."

"And when was the second time you met her?"

"That summer at Marina Del Rey. My boyfriend's family moored a ketch there. He and I had just returned from a day of sailing the coastline and were on our way to the wharf restaurant for dinner with his parents, when I turned around to say something to him and literally ran headlong into a woman walking on the gangway, nearly knocking her down. 'Oh, I'm terribly sorry,' I said as I attempted to steady her. 'I ought to watch where I'm going.' 'No harm done,' she said. 'I'm sturdier than I look.' But then she followed up with, 'Aren't you Tara O'Neill?' She clearly had the better of me. She apparently knew who I was, but I didn't recognize her, and to my embarrassment, it must have showed. 'Doris Day,' she said, extending her hand. 'Your father introduced us a while back—on St. Patrick's Day.' At that instant, I searched her face for any resemblance to that of the glamorous movie star I'd met and came up wanting. Without makeup and her silver blond hair coiffured to perfection, Doris Day really *was* the girl next door, and her most prominent feature were freckles. Not just a dusting over the bridge of her cute nose, but the serious variety that covered any exposed skin.

"There are reasons why Academy Awards are also given out to makeup artists. They're the ones whose jobs are to turn caterpillars into butterflies. I guess the moral of my story is this: Things aren't always as they seem. And as for Doris Day, I've seen all her pictures and love her to death. And I'm not the least bit jealous that you do to. But I'll tell you something. Doris would kill to spend as little time as I do in front of a makeup mirror." She got up and kissed him on the cheek. "So count your blessings."

Tara's car had been parked behind O'Neill's while they'd been in Vegas. Murphy had followed her to his house last night. She'd stayed in her car as a precaution while he'd gone inside first, pistol in hand. There was no ambush. Afterward, with Tara settled in, he'd gone room by room looking for electronic listening devices. He'd found none, but chalked up the effort to not knowing to what extent he was being surveilled.

This morning, Murphy trailed Tara to her apartment building, a fashionable high-rise on Wilshire Boulevard. They both parked on the street in front, and at her insistence, he rode the elevator with her to her place on the 14th floor. A few minutes later, Murphy got back in his car alone and pulled away from the curb. Down the block on the opposite side of the street he passed a parked black Chevrolet sedan. And as he did so, he acknowledged the man behind the wheel with a nod. Matthew Doyle nodded back.

Weekend morning traffic was usually light in LA, and today was no exception. At the squawk box by the entrance to the Hayward estate, Murphy announced himself. It was two minutes to ten when the tall metal gate slowly swung open. As Murphy drove forward, he couldn't help but feel he was entering a lion's den.

31

Two pickup trucks were parked in front of the house. The signage on the doors identified them respectively as Sunset Pool Service and Manzanita Landscaping. The bed of the latter contained an assortment of mechanized equipment, the most prominent being a riding lawn mower of the variety seen on golf courses. A tailgate extended to the ground, allowing easy unloading and loading.

Murphy maneuvered past both vehicles and parked adjacent to the porch. As he approached the front door, it opened and Clayton Hayward rolled out to meet him. He wore a polo shirt, white trousers, and boat shoes without socks. He gestured to the trucks.

"Saturday morning ritual. Normally, they're gone by now, but for some reason or another they got a late start. Come on in. We'll talk in the library."

Murphy followed him in and closed the door behind them. The library was found off the living room behind wide, sliding knotty pine doors. Floor to ceiling bookshelves of gray barn wood dominated one entire wall. The room was sparsely furnished, but the western artwork and sculptures—a continuation of the living room motif—made it inviting.

Hayward directed Murphy to an overstuffed easy chair, its leather upholstery cracked and worn from years of use.

"Can I get you something to drink, Jack? I've got a superb bourbon. Very smooth."

"No thanks. It's a little early in the day for me."

"I've found it's *never* too early." He reached for a decanter on the desk, poured two fingers of the amber liquid into a crystal tumbler, and gave it a spritz of soda water. "Perhaps some coffee, then?"

"If it wouldn't be too much trouble."

"Not at all."

Hayward called for Alberto, who soon appeared at the doorway.

"A cup of coffee for Mr. Murphy. I believe he takes it black, no sugar." He turned back to Murphy for confirmation.

"You have a good memory."

Hayward rolled his wheelchair in front of Murphy, reached for his drink on the desk, and took a swallow.

He then said, "Yesterday, when Alberto told me you were on the phone, I felt sure you were calling to say you'd found Charlie safe and sound."

"I can assure you, Mr. Hayward that—"

"It's Clay, remember?"

"All right, Clay. As I was saying, I would've liked nothing better. But I'm afraid my investigation, which started out like gangbusters has run into sort of a dead end."

"Alynn led me to believe you weren't the type to be easily put off. I think she said 'especially' when the odds were against you."

"I'm flattered by her assessment, but I can't in good faith take your money when the prospects of—"

"Listen, you're not getting off that easy. I don't give a damn about the money. Results are what I want. Tomorrow's another day, right? You might yet think of something. Someplace you haven't looked. Someone you haven't talked to."

Murphy nodded. "I came here today to discuss my efforts

thus far. Maybe I've missed something that will be obvious to you. If I have, then I hope you'll set me straight."

"That's what I want to hear, Jack. Now, why don't you fill me in."

At that moment, Alberto entered, carrying a steaming mug. He handed it to Murphy.

Hayward said, "Thank you, Alberto. And would you please close the doors on your way out? If anyone calls, just take a message."

"Certainly."

Murphy took a halting sip of the scalding coffee, then placed the mug on the lamp table at his elbow.

"I guess it would be best to start at the beginning," he said. "The day I left here, I went through Charlie's apartment, room by room, looking for anything that might shed light on his disappearance. I came up dry, but I did find a .38 caliber revolver in the nightstand by his bed."

"Charlie has a gun? That surprises me. I own a couple of authentic western revolvers: an 1875 Remington and a Colt Peacemaker. I could never get Charlie to go to a pistol range with me and play with them a little."

"Well, for what it's worth, this one hasn't ever been fired. And he hasn't had it long, because it still has a factory smell to it. A lot of people keep a handgun by the bed for self-defense, to guard against intruders. Seldom does that circumstance materialize, but just having a gun nearby is comforting."

Hayward nodded and sipped at his drink.

Murphy continued. "Now, you mentioned his love for his Corvette."

"Yes, he worships that car."

"Well, wherever he is, he didn't drive there. The Corvette is parked in the apartment garage and has been since the Fourth. I verified that with building security. In any event, Charlie had a holiday gathering at his place that got a little out of hand. One of the tenants complained about the noise. The guard spoke to Charlie about the need to hold it down. That night was the last time the guard saw him."

"Could he have gone off with someone from the party?"

"No, I'm certain he didn't, based on what I learned when I visited the *Times*. First, I spoke with the city editor."

"Morris Klinefelter. We go back a ways."

Murphy nodded. "He said it was you who encouraged him to take a chance on Charlie when he'd graduated from college."

"Morris wasn't all that keen on it at the time, but Charlie managed to pull an impressive rabbit out of his hat. And the rest is history, as they say."

"That's what Klinefelter said. Charlie was the best thing to happen to *Times'* readership in a long time. I say 'was' because the paper has dropped him, or perhaps you already know that."

"Yes, I think I told you I'd talked to Morris. He told me he had no choice under the circumstances. He hadn't wanted to take Charlie back the previous time he'd gone missing. I'd hoped he might see this situation differently. Charlie has been doing so well."

"Klinefelter indicated that, too, but defended his action on the basis that the newspaper wasn't a social welfare agency, or something to that effect. I did find out, however, that Charlie had been working for weeks on a big story."

"What about?"

"No one I talked to at the paper knew anything about it, but Charlie had been scheduled to present an overview of the story on the morning of July sixth. He never showed. The day before, however, he'd called his copy girl and arranged for her to type up the outline that afternoon. He didn't make that appointment, either."

Hayward shook his head and then gulped at his drink.

"I don't like the sound of this, Jack. Charlie has broken stories before that I thought might put him in danger of retaliation. Could this be what's happened? Is this why he had a gun? Was he afraid for his life? Do you suppose the copy girl has an idea of the story's subject matter?"

"She said that normally he shared his storylines with her, but this time she'd been kept in the dark. She did say, however, that Charlie had an appointment last month to speak with a man from Northrop. She assumed the meeting pertained to what he was working on but couldn't be sure."

"Who did he talk to there, did she say?"

"Robert Reed."

"Bob? Bob's a longtime colleague of mine. What would Charlie have wanted to speak with him about?"

"He wanted Reed's take on the credibility of a man who'd once been employed by Northrop but had since moved out of state. Gordon Kane. He worked in Security. I presume you would've known him, too."

Hayward nodded. "But why ask Bob about him when he could've asked me?"

"Reed thought that was odd, as well, and asked him."

"And what did Charlie say?"

"That you and he had had a falling out of late. I found that strange, inasmuch you'd given me the impression that you two had a close relationship."

Hayward sighed deeply, downed the rest of the bourbon, and set the glass aside.

.   "I'm afraid I wasn't entirely honest with you, Jack. It's true we're not getting along. Not since he informed me that he was a...a...*homosexual*." The word was spoken as if it left a bad taste in his mouth.

"So you know about that. I wasn't going to mention it to you, in case you weren't aware. It didn't seem at all germane to the case."

"How did you find out?"

"From the people on the list you gave me, all of whom had had, at one time or another, a sexual relationship with Charlie."

"*Goddam perverts!* That's what they are. And they've seduced Charlie to their twisted way of life. I begged him to see a psychiatrist, but he just scoffed at me. It's all a lot of nonsense, of course, and I told him that one day he'd come to see it as folly. If it turns out that Charlie's disappearance isn't tied to something he was writing, then it wouldn't surprise me if those *animals* are mixed up in this. Maybe he's been kidnapped. He's probably told them I have money."

165

"If that were the case, Clay, you'd have been contacted long before now with a ransom demand. No, despite the fact you disapprove of his lifestyle and friends, they wouldn't do him harm. At least, that was my impression when I went to the Garden of Eden. That's a hangout for homosexuals out on Venice Boulevard. Everyone I spoke to holds Charlie in high regard."

Hayward nodded. "Okay, whatever you say. I'm just grasping at straws, I guess. So let's go back to me knowing Gordon Kane. I saw him around, of course, but we traveled in different circles. It would be more accurate to say that I knew *of* him."

"What do you mean?"

"He had a reputation for being a 'loose cannon,' shall we say. He was notorious for seeing bogeymen hiding behind every potted plant. He was still working for Northrop when I had my accident and took leave of the company."

"Sometime back, Kane got a job at the Flamingo Hotel in Vegas. Prior to talking with Reed, Charlie had met with him. I wanted to find out what they'd spoken about. That's why I went to Vegas."

"And what did Kane say?"

"Well, that's just it. He died about three weeks ago. The police say it was murder. They figure Kane was in cahoots with mobsters; that he'd somehow crossed a line and was killed as a result. Apparently, that kind of lethal behavior goes on quite regularly in Vegas."

"Oh, my God! What if that's the connection? Kane was feeding Charlie information about the Mafia and it cost them both. It seems logical, doesn't it? I mean Kane was killed about the same time that Charlie dropped out of sight. Surely, that can't be just coincidental."

"I jumped to that conclusion, too, until we spoke to Mrs. Kane. Then that scenario looked less promising."

"You said 'we'?" Hayward questioned.

"Oh, right. I took my fiancée along with me. Figured she could lay by the pool while I did my sleuthing. But then when I found out about Gordon Kane, I thought that bringing her along when I spoke to his wife might be a good idea. With another woman present, I reasoned she might feel more comfortable when two strangers showed up at her door."

"Did it pay off?"

"Well, she confirmed her husband and Charlie had spoken twice. Once on the phone. And once in person."

"Does she know what they talked about?"

"Only in part. Seems her husband had been pretty tight-lipped, but it involved something he'd discovered while working at Northrop. She says she doesn't know any specifics other than her husband had concerns about a man named Klaus Hoffmann."

"Klaus? *Goddammit!* This is the kind of crap I was referring to with regard to Kane. He was always hoisting his bullshit theories up the flagpole to see who'd salute. I'm sure, at first, a lot of people at Northrop, me included, had 'concerns' about Klaus. After all, he'd been a player in Hitler's game of world domination. But he was a scientist first. In fact, he was never a political creature. It's well known that he refused to join the Nazi Party. And the security of the United State is much better off since he came our way after the war. Klaus has proved himself to be beyond reproach, a prince among princes, and yet Gordon Kane was apparently poised to gin up old biases against him and drag his good name through the mud. And, presumably, he was using Charlie to do his dirty work. If Charlie had only spoken to me, I could've set him straight about Kane and his dementia. What did Bob say about Hoffmann when Charlie asked?"

"I don't believe Hoffmann's name surfaced. Of course, at the time I met with Reed, I didn't know about Hoffmann. But I pressed him pretty hard about his conversation with Charlie, and he seemed anxious to help me. If Hoffmann had been mentioned, I'm certain Reed would've said something."

Hayward sighed and shook his head. "Just when I'd resigned myself to accept the notion that Charlie may've been killed for something he was going to divulge about the Mob,

167

Klaus Hoffmann is thrown in for good measure. You're the detective, Jack. How do these pieces fit? Because none of this makes sense to me."

"Prior to coming here today, I'd given thought to contacting Hoffmann, but after what you've said about him—and your insight into Gordon Kane—I'm reconsidering."

"Well, I bow to your expertise, of course, but it seems to me that absent anything specific, how could Klaus be expected to respond?"

"True enough. And there is another scenario that we should consider. When I called Alie, she—"

"You don't have to tell me what Alynn said, because she gave me a dose of venom when I called her for advice, and she offered your name. Reluctantly, I might add, because she figured this affair would wind up being nothing more than a wild goose chase, with Charlie eventually being found dead with a needle in his arm. Have I represented her feelings accurately?"

"To a T."

"He's her brother, for chrissakes. I actually think she'd prefer to see him dead, if only to hurt me. Sure, he's a mixed up kid, but he's *my* kid. And I'm nowhere close to giving up on him."

"Then I won't either, Clay. So, if you don't mind, I'd like to hold on to the key you gave me. When I leave here I'll swing by Charlie's place for another look. I could've missed something the first time around. I'll check again with building security. Could be they've seen or heard something this past week. And if all that fails, I'll think of another angle. If Charlie can be found, I'll find him."

Murphy drained his now cold cup of coffee, stood to leave, and said, "I'll have my secretary prepare a typed report of what we've discussed today and get it in the mail to you next week."

"There's no hurry, Jack. I'd rather you spend your time on locating Charlie's whereabouts than wasting it on paperwork."

As the front gate closed behind him, and he began his descent out of Bel Air, what bothered Murphy most was that he hadn't succeeded in being let off the hook. On the contrary, Hayward didn't want him to pull back his investigation one iota, and Murphy didn't think it was window dressing. He'd thought that Marjorie Kane would've closed the loop between her husband and Charlie Hayward. Whatever Gordon Kane had on Klaus Hoffmann was now dead, along with the three people who knew the full story. Did Hayward just *think* that there might be something else for Murphy to discover, or did he *know* there was?

32

Judging by the vehicles in the expansive parking lot, Farmer's Market was doing a brisk business for a Saturday. The number of other than California license plates indicated that tourist trade was well represented.

Murphy found a vacant stall adjacent to the clock tower, itself a Los Angeles landmark, which stood as if on sentry duty, watching over the comings and goings. Tara's teal Volvo occupied a spot three spaces away, but as planned, she'd already entered the warren of vendors' shops and would be waiting for him.

He crossed Fairfax Avenue at the corner light and then Third Street to the apartment building. Of course, he'd lied to Clayton Hayward about maybe finding something he'd missed before, but he needed to go through the motions for his watchers' benefit. Entering the lobby, the security guard seated behind the counter took an interest.

"May I be of service?"

With thinning gray hair, Murphy judged him to be in his late sixties. His belly strained at the buttons of his uniform shirt and lopped over the buckle of his black weave-stamped belt, from which hung a holstered .38 caliber revolver and a matching leather handcuff case. He may've been past his prime, but he carried an air of confident authority. Murphy pegged him as a retired cop. His plastic name plate read: OLSEN.

Murphy displayed his credentials.

"My name is Jack Murphy. I'm a private investigator." He returned the ID case to his coat pocket. "I was here on Tuesday and—"

"Oh, so you're the guy who disarmed Jimmy, huh?"

"Guilty as charged. It was an object lesson more than anything else. He was a nice enough kid but a little cocky. He literally dared me to do it."

"Sounds like Jimmy, all right. Packing a badge and gun kind of goes to his head. Saw that a lot when I was on the force. Youngsters coming out of the Academy. Full of piss and vinegar. Spoiling for action. It was us veterans who had to settle them down before they got in over their heads. I've tried to give Jimmy a few tips on how to handle himself, but he'll have none of it. What does an old has-been like me know, right? But I'll tell you one thing: You damn sure impressed him. He's been walking a little taller since you got to him."

"I've been told I have that effect on people." He paused, then asked, "When you were on the job, did you know Matt Doyle, by any chance?"

"Matt? Sure did. I was sort of on my way out when he was at the top of his game. Homicide detective. And a damn good one."

"Well, he's my partner." Murphy dug a business card from his breast pocket and handed it over.

"Matt finally pulled the plug, too, huh? Well, it's a hell of a loss for the department. And you can tell him that for me." He held out his hand. "Hank Olsen. I assume you're here because you haven't yet located Mr. Hayward."

"Unfortunately."

"Jimmy passed the word that you were looking for him. Said you'd offered a reward for information."

"A hundred bucks. I'd only just taken the case. Thought a

little incentive couldn't hurt. But since then I've become less optimistic."

"For what it's worth, there are five of us assigned here. No one has reported seeing him. And his Corvette hasn't moved from its assigned stall in the garage."

"Thanks, that saves me from checking. But I assured his father this morning that I'd take another gander at the apartment. I've got the key." He pulled it from his pants pocket. "You want to come along? I could use another pair of experienced eyes."

Olsen's face lit up. "Sure. Glad to help out if I can. It'll get the kinks out from sitting all morning."

Two and a half minutes later, they were standing in the living room. Everything seemed just as it had before.

"Musty," Olsen said. "No one's been home for a while."

"Yeah, that's what I thought, too, when I was here last. Walk around a bit. See if anything pops out at you."

Murphy headed to the bedroom. Out of curiosity, he took a closer look at the sprung briefcase in the closet now that he knew it had once contained documentation that Gordon Kane had passed to Hayward.

As he exited the bedroom, Olsen called from the kitchen. "If Hayward had been around in the last little while, he'd have poured this milk down the sink. It's sour."

Murphy heard the refrigerator door close, and then Olsen walked out.

"Anything new from the last time you were here?" Olsen asked.

"To be honest, I didn't expect there would be."

"So where do you suppose he is? You say he hasn't been seen since the 4th?"

"As a matter of fact, Jimmy may've been one of the last people to have laid eyes on him."

"I never had much contact with Hayward, but he seemed like a likable sort. And his newspaper column was always worth reading. You know, if he wasn't a writer, he'd probably make a good cop, because from time to time, his stuff put the cuffs on some pretty important people around town."

"That's what I understand."

Olsen glanced at his watch. "Well, I better get back to my post. Thanks for asking me to tag along. I miss the old times, you know? Life after retirement isn't what it's cracked up to be. Golden Years, my *ass*."

Murphy nodded that he understood. "I'll head down with you."

Back in the lobby, Olsen shook Murphy's hand and said, "It's none of my business, of course, but take it from an old LA cop: In this city, when someone just vanishes, looking for a body is your best bet."

33

Murphy retraced his route and found Tara seated at a wrought-iron table outside the sandwich shop they'd agreed on beforehand. Dressed in white capris and a translucent green blouse, she turned the pages of a magazine while she sipped through a straw protruding from a tall plastic cup. He sat down next to her.

Barely looking up, she asked, "Everything go all right with Hayward?"

"Well, I'm here; that's a good sign. I think he believed I didn't know any more than what I told him. As for calling off the dogs, that's another matter. They're going to be with us awhile longer, because Hayward isn't letting me off the hook. He's convinced I may yet turn up something."

"Like what?"

"Good question. Something incriminating, I suppose. Like what they got from Marjorie Kane. But I'm all out of ideas about where to look. On the brighter side, we're probably safe in the interim. And today, I hope our watchers are somewhere out there in the parking lot, so Matt can nail them with a camera. Knowing who we're dealing with is a preamble to taking them off our backs for good."

"I hope you're right, Jack, because the thought of having them lurking in the shadows is scaring me to death. I wish you'd never taken this case."

If truth be known, Murphy thought, it was unnerving for him, too. What if they just decided to clean the slate and be done with it, rather than debate whether or not his investigation had hit a wall?

Murphy changed the subject. "What are you reading that you find so engrossing?"

She flipped to the front cover and pushed it in his direction.

"*Elle*, huh?" he said. "And in French, no less. You never cease to amaze me. Do you speak French?"

"Two years in high school, and a minor in college. Even then, outside of the classroom, I could only pick up every third word if I heard two Frenchmen talking. But with a little effort, I can read it well enough. Like this magazine. But mostly, I enjoy looking at the pictures. French fashion design has always interested me. Even before I was employed in my previous life by Bullock's Wilshire as women's clothing consultant."

Murphy thumbed through the slick magazine, pausing at a few pages.

"These models have nothing on you, Tara."

She laughed. "Then you'd better get your eyes tested."

"No, I'm serious. They're all so skinny. I like women with a little meat on their bones."

"Well, I've got that all right. *Too* much, as I looked in the mirror this morning. About ten pounds worth. And starting tomorrow, I'm going to do something about it. But for right now, I'm starving."

They ordered BLTs. Tara was still nursing her lemonade, but Murphy got a bottle of beer to wash down his sandwich. They were mid-way through lunch when Matt Doyle—a camera slung over his shoulder—joined them and took a seat directly opposite. His breathing was labored, and beads of sweat dotted his forehead, typical most days when he had to lug his rotund body around.

"I was wondering if you were going to show," Murphy said.

"Looks like you could use something to drink."

"Later, maybe."

"What's that?" Murphy gestured to a manila folder that Doyle had brought with him.

Doyle pushed it across the table.

"The police file you wanted. I told you I had a copy at home. Since we were meeting today, I figured I'd bring it along."

Tara caught a glimpse of the cover that read: MICHAEL O'NEILL MURDER. She turned toward Murphy.

"Why would you—"

Murphy interrupted her. "Matt says the two investigating officers weren't LAPD's finest. I thought maybe I'd see something they didn't. Their notes will be in that file."

Tara reached out for it, but Murphy placed his hand over hers.

"Bad idea," he said.

"Why?"

"There'll be crime scene photos. Murders can be gruesome. You were probably asked to identify your father at the morgue, after he'd been made more presentable."

"But I'm not a child. I want to see all of it. Please, Jack."

"All right. But just remember I warned you." He released her hand, and she pulled the file her way.

Murphy's attention then switched to Doyle. "Did you see anyone? Or am I just overly paranoid?"

"No, you've got a tail, all right. A man and woman just like you thought. Driving a white Lincoln Town Car. But they didn't follow you here. They pulled in a few minutes *before* you did."

"That confirms my suspicions about Clayton Hayward. If they were waiting for me to show up, it's only because he tipped them to where I was going."

Tara then let out a muffled shriek. "Oh, my God!"

They looked over just as she crossed herself. She then scraped her chair back and jumped to her feet.

"I'm going to be sick." Holding her hand over her mouth,

she ran in the direction of the arrow on the sign pointing to the restrooms.

"Poor kid." Doyle opened the folder to the crime scene pictures and displayed them to Murphy. "Whatever memory she once had of her father has now been replaced by this. It's going to be a long while before she gets over it. And head shots are the worst. You and I know first-hand, don't we? There are cases from years ago that I still can't get out of my mind."

Murphy sighed. "That's why I tried to stop her. But what's done is done." He paused a moment, then said, "Oh, before I forget, I ran into a retired cop who knew you on the force. Hank Olsen. He said to say hi."

"Where'd you meet him?"

"He's a security guard at Charlie Hayward's apartment building. I spoke to him today."

"Good ol' Hank Olsen. Could've easily made detective but chose to be a street cop his whole career. Honest people on his beat loved him. And even the dishonest types respected him. Always said he treated everyone the way he'd want to be treated. The force lost a real asset when he retired."

"Funny, that's what he said about you."

"Really? Well that just goes to show you that his judgment is impeccable. I'll swing by one day. Maybe get a beer."

Doyle then got back to the matter at hand.

"The glare off their windshield factored in, but I think I got what you wanted." He patted the camera. "Half a roll of Kodachrome."

"You sure they didn't see you?"

"C'mon, Jack. Do I look like a rookie?"

"Sorry, it's just that—"

"Forget it. I also got the plate number. I'll have it run and see what comes up."

"Worth a try, but my guess is it's a rental procured with phony ID."

"I was going to try to maybe lift some partial prints off the door handles, but they never left the car. They're probably still out there waiting for you."

"Since you got a decent look at them, how about a tentative description until you get the film developed?"

"The driver is a young guy. Maybe late twenties. Short brown hair. Wire-rim glasses. The woman is more our age. Gray blond hair. Attractive."

"Son of a bitch!"

"What? Ring a bell?"

"Yeah. They were sitting right over there," he pointed to a vacant table behind them, "last Tuesday afternoon. I'd come here for a sandwich after searching Hayward's apartment. I had them pegged as foreign tourists by their clothes. Later, when I called the office, Andrea told me she thought she saw a car following me when I'd left our lot. I blew her off. But she was right. And so was your guy in Missing Persons. Clayton Hayward hadn't reported his son's disappearance. Which means that the cops who showed up at the *Times* last week were likely these same two, masquerading. I have to hand it to them; they certainly get around. And it looks like I've been a day late and a dollar short all along."

Doyle looked at his watch, then reached across the table and drained what was left of Murphy's beer. He got to his feet. "I'll get this film into Woo right away. I'll tell him it's a rush job. We should have prints by late afternoon."

Sidney Woo owned and operated a passport photo shop in their building. He was their go-to guy for all their film work. And it happened to be a lot, especially surrounding spousal infidelity, the source of many of their cases. They suspected that Woo kept copies of the more salacious pictures for his own gratification, but what the hell. He worked fast and gave them a "repeat customer" discount.

Moments after Doyle had departed, Tara reappeared, her face pale, despite her tan.

"Matt already gone?" She looked around before taking her seat.

"Yeah, just barely. He got the pictures I was hoping for. He's gone to have the film developed."

"Listen, honey, I'm sorry for what happened. Nothing has

178

ever affected me that way before."

"No need to apologize. In fact, I had the same reaction multiple times in the Army. But I eventually learned to take it in stride."

"Well, if I live to be a hundred, I'll never get over seeing Dad like that." She started to tear up again, then wiped her eyes with her hands and said, "So what's next?"

"I say we go back to my place and take it easy for the rest of the day. I want to go through this in detail." He picked up the police file. "Then maybe later we'll order some Chinese take-out, if your stomach can handle it."

"Nothing sounds good right now, but maybe after a nap. I think it's my nerves. I'm just so tired. But would you mind if we went to my place instead. I need to sleep in my own bed for a change."

34

"Well, good morning, sleepyhead." Murphy looked up from the Sunday *Times* sport section spread on Tara's kitchen table. He was already dressed, and with the exception of a half full coffee mug in hand, his breakfast mess had been cleared away.

Tara shuffled across the linoleum floor in her slippers to the coffee pot on the counter and poured a cup.

"Sorry I wasn't much fun last night." She sat down opposite him. "I was just worn out, emotionally." She stirred in a teaspoon of sugar.

"I'm the one who should apologize. You've been through a lot, all of it my fault. And I certainly didn't expect Matt to bring that police file with him, or for you to have a look at it. Murder scenes are not for the faint of heart."

She took a cautious sip. "Did you finally get hold of Matt after I went to bed? I know you'd tried earlier."

"No, and I've already called this morning. I thought he would've called me by now. He's got both our numbers."

"He's always talking about the possibility of 'getting lucky.' Who knows, maybe he succeeded for once."

"Talk's cheap. The closest Matt's ever come to having a date is drooling over deShazo. At least it's been that way since he and I hooked up. In any event, I was just about to drive over to his place."

"And leave me here alone? I go where you go. Just give me fifteen minutes for a quick shower, a brush through my hair, and some lipstick."

Murphy chuckled. "Are you planning on any clothes?"

"Yes, smart aleck. Unless you'd prefer the alternative." She pulled open her robe for a quick peek, revealing a toned naked body beneath. "If we had a convertible and got stopped, I could always say I was just working on my tan."

Before Murphy could think of a comeback line, she took another gulp of brew and padded out the way she'd come in.

Thirty minutes later they walked out of Tara's apartment building. Murphy took a good look up and down the street as they neared his car parked at the curb. He saw nothing of the white Town Car that Doyle had identified the day before. Nevertheless, he was on constant alert for its presence as they made their way to Doyle's Alhambra apartment on Atlantic Boulevard.

Parking on the street behind, Murphy spotted Doyle's black Chevrolet under one of the complex's carports. They walked past the swimming pool, teaming with screaming kids for the most part, although a few adults sat on the edge dangling their legs in the shimmering water.

Doyle's apartment was on the ground level of the two-story structure. Number 5. The drapes were drawn on the picture window. With Tara at his side, Murphy rapped softly on the door. No response. He knocked louder but couldn't hear any movement from within. Just then, a man in cutoff Levis, t-shirt, and sandals descended the adjacent stairway and approached.

"You're Matt's business partner, aren't you?"

"Yes. Jack Murphy." He offered his hand.

"I thought I recognized you. Matt introduced us awhile back. My name's Ron Anstead. I'm the apartment manager."

"Right. I remember. Ex-Coast Guard. Listen, have you seen Matt around? I tried his phone. There was no answer, and it appears he's not home now."

Anstead's face turned somber. "Well, I've got some bad news: Matt died yesterday."

"*What?*" Murphy and Tara said in unison.

"That was my reaction, too, when the cops came around late yesterday afternoon looking for 'next of kin,' as they put it. I told them I couldn't help much; that he lived alone and what family he talked about had moved to Florida."

Murphy asked, "Did they by any chance give the circumstances of his death?"

"Knowing what Matt did for a living, I asked the same question."

"And what did they say?" Tara chimed in.

"They wouldn't come right out and say, but I got the impression he died of natural causes, although they indicated an autopsy was being done."

Murphy said, "Did they say where his death took place? I noticed his car parked out back."

"Oh, that. Well, the same two cops arranged for it to be towed back here not more than a half hour ago. Apparently they knew Matt was retired LAPD—a member of the club, so to speak—and wanted to save the family, when they turned up, from having to pay impound fees. They gave me the keys, and I put them in the apartment for now. As manager, I have a passkey. Oh, and there was a camera in the car—one of those expensive Voigtländers. I put that inside, too."

"That would be our company camera. I'm going to need to take it with me." He fished a key ring from his pocket and inserted one of the keys into the door lock. Over his shoulder, he said, "Matt gave me a spare for emergencies. I guess this qualifies. Did the police leave you one of their cards? In case you or the family needed to make contact."

"Yes, I've got it up in my place. You want me to get it?"

"If you would. I'll want to talk with the officers about the particulars, as well as point them to Matt's ex-wife and kids in Miami."

"Sure thing. I'll just be a minute." Anstead turned and took the stairs two at a time to the second floor landing.

While he was gone, they entered the apartment, and Murphy took a quick look around. The living room might well have been decorated by Goodwill Industries, not a matching piece of furniture to be seen. The room at the end of the hallway revealed an unmade bed and Doyle's dirty clothes strewn on the carpet. The bathroom was cluttered and in need of a thorough cleaning. In fact, everything that Murphy saw was more or less status quo from the last time he'd been inside the apartment. Doyle hadn't adapted well to the life of a divorcé.

Returning to the living room, he spied the camera and its leather case on the kitchen dinette table. Tara looked on as he worked the film rewind lever. He felt no resistance and open the back to find the metal film canister gone.

"There was film in here yesterday," Murphy said to Tara and then closed the compartment. "Now there isn't."

"You said Matt was having it developed. Couldn't that be where it is?"

"Possibly. I'll know for sure when Woo opens up tomorrow morning." He slung the camera strap over his shoulder and picked up Doyle's car keys that had also been on the table.

Anstead then appeared at the door and entered. He handed the business card to Murphy who jotted down the name of the officer and the division phone number on a small spiral pad he'd pulled from his coat pocket.

When he'd finished, he handed back the card and said, "How about coming out to Matt's car with me? I want to have a look inside."

"Sure, why not? Lead the way."

Murphy first opened the trunk. Spare, tire iron, jack, jumper cables. He closed the lid and moved on. The telltale odor of death—urine and feces—emanating from the large stain on the cloth seat, assaulted his nostrils as he opened the driver's side door. There was little doubt that Doyle had died behind the wheel. Murphy felt under the seat for the missing film canister but came up with only an ancient piece of wrapped hard candy.

He locked the door and walked around the front of the car to the passenger side. On his haunches, he worked the catch on the glove box. Inside were the car's registration, a couple of sharpened pencils, a pad of paper, and a map book for the Greater Los Angeles area. Again he ran his hand under the seat. This time he found a couple of pennies.

"What are you looking for?" Anstead stood at his shoulder. "You think the cops are wrong about how Matt died?"

"They must be convinced that nothing pointed to any funny business, or they'd never have released his car. And there's no doubt that Matt's weight made him a candidate for a heart attack. Still…"

Murphy locked the passenger door and handed the keys back to Anstead. "Matt's ex will probably lay claim to the car. To hear him tell it, it was all he had to his name after the divorce. Even his apartment had come furnished, I believe."

"About half the tenants—including me—are divorced. A furnished apartment, even if it isn't to one's taste, makes life a little simpler."

"I don't expect it'll take too long to probate Matt's estate. But if his rent isn't paid up, I'll be glad to fork over for another month."

"Not necessary. He gave me a rental check last week." He paused, then, "Lots of evenings Matt and I would kill a six-pack, sitting out here by the pool. I'm going to miss him. I guess there's no telling when your time's up, is there?"

They were back on Atlantic Boulevard, headed toward the city, when Tara asked, "Where are we going now?"

"The morgue. I want to follow up on Matt's death."

"You don't believe he died of natural causes, do you?"

"Let's say I need more convincing."

"And if you're not satisfied?"

"We'll cross that bridge when we get there."

But Murphy suspected they were already fast approaching. If there were more to Doyle's death than initially thought, then Murphy's charade with Hayward was out the window. It would be concluded that he'd known a lot more than he'd let on and had, in fact, used Hayward to get the killers into position to have their photographs taken. That would've sealed his and Tara's death warrant, out of precaution, if nothing else. They were probably being sought right now. Instinctively, Murphy checked his rearview mirror.

"Would you mind going alone?" Tara asked. "I don't think I could handle another visit—even for Matt's sake. I still get nauseous remembering how the place smelled when I went there to see my father. How about dropping me off at the pub while you go? I've got work to catch up on. You can pick me up there later when you're through."

As Tara was a softer target, Murphy figured they might simply snatch her as a ploy to get to him. He couldn't let that happen but didn't want to spell out the obvious to her. She was jittery enough.

"What happened to 'I go where you go'? I think it's better if we stick together for the duration of this case. You can wait in the car, if you'd like, while I go inside and try to get some answers."

She sighed. "All right. On second thought, I'd feel better having you around, too."

"Look, I know it's my fault for throwing you into the deep end of the pool and expecting you to swim. But everything is going to work out; you'll see."

Murphy hoped it wasn't a hollow promise.

They drove awhile longer before Tara said, "Maybe now isn't a good time to ask, but did you see anything of interest in my father's file?"

"There was a lot to digest; however, I think there may be a thing or two the investigators should've picked up on. I need to wrestle with it for a while, though; then we'll talk. But let me ask you this: Did you know your father had lung cancer?"

The look on Tara's face indicated that she didn't.

Murphy said, "Yes, that was one of the autopsy findings. Advanced. Inoperable. The conclusion was that he had very little time left to live."

"That would explain his persistent cough. I told him he

should see a doctor. It was those wretched cigarettes. In fact, the afternoon before he was killed he tried to get hold of me at work—he virtually never did that—but I was in San Francisco on business. He told my secretary it was urgent that he talk to me. She left word at my hotel, but I never got the message. He was already dead when I returned the following day. I'll bet he'd actually gotten a medical opinion and knew the score. Maybe that's what he wanted to tell me."

Murphy nodded that she could be right but suspected otherwise.

35

The LA County Coroner building, circa 1912—known colloquially by most Angelenos as "the morgue"—was situated on North Mission Road. Its German/Austrian design, incorporating a red brick exterior with blond stone accents, made it unique to the area, otherwise trending toward the ubiquitous Spanish influence.

Given a county population in the millions, there was never a slow day for services rendered. Although the issuance of death certificates—regardless of circumstances—fell under the purview of the Coroner's Office, its stock and trade was the performance of autopsies to determine specific causes of death. Individuals who died in the care of a physician were generally exempt from these procedures, but those who met their end as a result of violence, or those whose deaths were either suspect or unexpected, were transported here for resolution.

They had to circle the block before finding a parking place, and during that time they saw three ambulances and as many police cruisers enter the gate marked: OFFICIAL VEHICLES ONLY.

"Are you sure you don't want to come with me?" Murphy asked. "I don't know how long I'll be."

"I'll be just fine. I'll just rest my eyes while you're gone."

Murphy withdrew his pistol from its holster and put it in the glove box.

"I don't expect you'll need to use that, but I'll feel better knowing you've got it."

"You're scarring the hell out of me, Jack. You really are. But one thing my father taught me when I was growing up was how to use a gun. Anyone tries to get cute with me, they'll wish they hadn't."

Murphy walked around to the front of the building and stood on the sidewalk, looking up the flight of concrete steps to the stone pillars descending from under the eaves, more for decoration than any structural purpose. He'd been here once before on a case. In fact, Doyle had been with him. But now everything seemed unfamiliar and foreboding.

As he ascended the steps, three women—one older, two in their teens—emerged from the entrance. Each clung to the other, crying. In their grief, they didn't even see him, and he had to sidestep them or risk collision.

Once inside, a placard on the wall displayed the name of Dr. Theodore J. Curphey, identifying him as Los Angeles County Coroner. Most coroners across the country performed their duties with relative anonymity, but given the high profile personalities who lived and died in and around LA, seldom a week went by that Curphey wasn't quoted in the newspaper or interviewed on television with regard to specific cases handled by his office.

And no case had received more public attention than that of Marilyn Monroe in August of 1962. Doyle had been on the force at the time and had since described to Murphy what he referred to as a "cluster fuck." When the nude body of the world's most glamorous sex kitten was found in her bedroom, everyone above the age of puberty wanted to know why.

Media coverage had been relentless even before agents of the Secret Service—at President Kennedy's direction—inserted themselves into the investigation. It was no secret that Marilyn had had a "special" relationship with the President. It was also well known that Robert Kennedy, the President's brother and

U.S. Attorney General, had been waging a relentless war against Organized Crime in all of its many forms. Might Marilyn have been murdered by the Mob and her death made to look like a suicide? A personal message to the President to rein in his brother, or else.

When the investigation had run its lengthy course, Curphey dismissed any conspiracy theories as utter nonsense and ruled that Marilyn's death was the result of "acute barbiturate poisoning," and a "probably suicide," given that no credible evidence to the contrary had been uncovered. However, some seventeen months later, Doyle had explained, the feds reopened Marilyn's case, contending that the "or else" component of their original theory might've been manifested in the assassination of the President, himself.

Curphey angrily fended off allegations that his people had been sloppy with Marilyn's autopsy. Facts were facts, he railed back. He then fired a salvo across their own bow, one that made the headlines of every major newspaper. He admitted he wasn't in a position to speculate as to who might've wanted to see President Kennedy dead, but in speaking with colleagues who'd attended to him that day in Dallas, those investigating the assassination might want to spend less time castigating his office for its handling of a deeply troubled and depressed film star and focus their attention on identifying a second shooter, no matter how inconvenient.

Murphy remembered reading that story in the *International Herald Tribune*. His Army CID detachment had been stationed not far from Paris. And for a time, Curphey's remarks had crept into the conversation of most of the military investigators, some of whom had seen sniper duty during World War II or Korea. The consensus was that a trained sniper, firing from an elevated position could easily put the President down. But a questionable marksman like Lee Harvey Oswald, using a twenty-dollar mail order Italian army surplus rifle, fitted with a cheap Japanese scope? No fucking way. In fact, it was counterintuitive to believe that Oswald missed the President entirely with his first shot but was dead on with the next two. If anything, it should've been the other way around. The kill shot should've been the first fired, when no one in the presidential motorcade perceived any danger and Oswald could've taken his time. Once evasive action was taken after the second shot, it would've have been next to impossible for him to reacquire the target and score the *coup de grâce*. He had to have had help, regardless of the alleged ballistic evidence to the contrary. And yet when the long-awaited Warren Commission Report came out in September of 1964, the conclusion drawn was that Oswald had acted alone, and that there had been no conspiracy—before or after the fact.

The report was meant to put the matter to rest, but it had served to only pour gasoline on people's fears that there was a lot more to JFK's assassination than was being told. And what consequences did that hold for the "land of the free and the home of the brave"?

Murphy walked down a long corridor, following the signs to *Forensic Laboratory*. At the end, an arrow pointed to a set of double doors, through which he made his way.

A matronly receptionist ensconced behind a marble counter smiled and asked if she could be of assistance. Murphy considered her for a brief moment before answering. The last time he'd been here, he and Doyle had encountered a different woman behind the counter, but she'd been even older than this one. It now dawned on him: Who better to calm the nerves of potentially distraught people, summoned to identify the body of a loved one, than a grandmotherly type? *Genius*, he thought.

"I believe the body of Matthew Doyle was transported here yesterday."

She consulted a clipboard on which were attached multiple sheets of lined paper. She found his name on the third page.

"Yes, Mr. Doyle arrived at four fifty-three p.m. Were you contacted by this office?"

"No. I found out about his death through his apartment manager who was notified by..." he took the spiral notebook from his jacket pocket and read the name, "...by Officer Stephen Rose assigned to the Wilshire Division."

"I take it you're not a family member." The same sweet smile.

"I'm his business partner." He handed her his card as well as displaying his badge and credentials.

"Normally, a family member is required to identify the deceased."

"His family lives out of state. But that's not why I'm here. I assume Matt has already been identified through his driver's license or PI license. Plus, he always carried his LAPD retirement badge and ID with him."

She nodded her understanding.

Murphy continued. "If possible, I'd like to speak with the pathologist who performed his autopsy."

Again she consulted her clipboard, then looked up. "That would be Dr. Steiner."

"Is he working today, by any chance?"

This time she opened a drawer under the counter and pulled out a single sheet of paper. She ran her finger down the page and then shook her head.

"No, I'm afraid Dr. Steiner is scheduled off."

"When will he be here again?"

"That would be hard to say. He's doing his residency at UCLA, I believe. We have a lot of medical students who rotate through here to help out. You can imagine how busy we get."

"Might there have been someone he would've consulted with?"

"Oh, my. Now why didn't I think of that? Dr. Noguchi would've reviewed Dr. Steiner's findings and signed off on them before moving the case onward. And you're in luck. I've seen him a couple of times this morning. Why don't I try to locate him for you?"

36

Murphy was informed that it could be as much as an hour before Dr. Noguchi would be able to break away from his duties. In the meantime, Murphy asked the receptionist, whose name he learned was Agnes, to called the LAPD's Wilshire Division and inquire if it was possible for Officer Rose to meet him at the morgue with regard Matthew Doyle's death. The response was affirmative, and Rose, accompanied by his rookie partner, arrived twenty-five minutes later. After introductions, they pulled together three chairs in the corner of the waiting room.

Murphy said, "If you don't mind, perhaps you could give me an overview of how and where Matt's body was found."

Rose said, "We got a radio call yesterday afternoon that someone had reported a possible dead body in a vehicle parked at Farmer's Market."

What the…?

"Who called it in?"

"Some guy, but he didn't give his name, only the location. This is more the rule than the exception in LA: the anonymous phone call."

Rose's partner spoke up. "It took us only three minutes to

get there. The Market is part of our beat. We make a pass through at least twice a shift."

Rose shot a stern look his way, as if to say, "I'll do all the talking, if you don't mind." He then said, "The vehicle was right where the caller said it would be. At first we didn't know if the driver was deceased or not; he was slumped over the wheel. I opened the door for a closer look. He was dead, all right. The stench told me his sphincter had released. His eyes were open and fixed, and his jaw was slack. It was then that I recognized him as Lieutenant Doyle. He'd spoken to my Academy class a few years ago about preserving the crime scene and not contaminating evidence. Plus, I'd seen him around since."

"How long had he been dead, do you suppose?"

"Hard to say."

"C'mon, you see a fair share of bodies."

"Okay. We arrived on scene at about one-fifteen. The body was still warm to the touch. Of course, that may've been partly the result of being in a closed vehicle. It was pretty hot yesterday. Rigor hadn't begun to set in, as far as I could tell. So I'd say, all things being equal, that he'd been dead for no more than two hours."

"And there wasn't anything to make you think that he might've been the victim of foul play."

"We initially checked for any obvious wounds or bruising. Nothing. After we called it in, a team of detectives was dispatched, but they concluded probable heart attack and left. The ambulance guys thought the same, and they see enough of them to know, I guess."

Murphy sat back. "Well, that's that. I appreciate you taking the time to speak with me."

"Sure, not a problem," Rose said.

Murphy then said, "Matt's ex-wife will need to be contacted. She lives in Miami. I don't know the phone number or address, but my secretary does." He extracted a business card from the breast pocket of his suit coat and handed it over. "Every month, she made out Matt's alimony check and sent it off. She doesn't yet know about him, but I'll tell her today. She's bound to take it hard. Matt was sort of the office Teddy Bear."

They all got to their feet.

Murphy said, "Now I just have to wait on the doc who signed off on Matt's autopsy. Noguchi is his name."

Rose nodded. "Well, for what it's worth, he's the best LA has to offer."

"Good to know."

"Handled the Marilyn Monroe case."

"Oh? I was under the impression that Dr. Curphey had taken credit for that."

"Yes, I can understand how someone might arrive at that conclusion. He did the talking on TV, all right, but Noguchi did the heavy lifting. That's become par for the course around here. Curphey is more politician than doctor. Rumor has it he's never dirtied his hands since getting the job. And he's virtually unapproachable. The LAPD doesn't think much of him."

"Yeah," Rose's partner chimed in. "He's lucky to have Noguchi running interference. If you can get past his accent."

37

Murphy had just returned from a trip to the drinking fountain in the main corridor when the door labeled *Visitors Must Be Escorted* swung open and a thin, slight Oriental man stepped into the waiting room. He wore a crisp white laboratory coat over navy blue trousers, a pastel yellow button-down oxford shirt, and a blue/yellow striped tie.

"Mr. Murphy?" he asked, as he neared.

"Yes." Murphy got to his feet.

"Thomas Noguchi." He held out his hand and bowed ever so slightly.

Large-framed glasses with heavy lenses magnified his dark eyes, and his black hair was barely held in place by whatever tonic had been applied.

"I am sorry to have kept you waiting," Noguchi said, and by his tone, meant it. "We have been particularly busy this morning."

Murphy now realized what Officer Rose's partner had meant about understanding Noguchi. He spoke English with a strong Japanese accent. And haltingly, as if he might be thinking in Japanese and then translating it into English.

"It is I who should apologize for assuming I could just walk in here and expect an audience. I promise I won't take much of your time."

"Then please come with me, and we shall speak."

Noguchi led the way back through the door by which he'd come. The pervasive odor of formaldehyde tugged at Murphy's nostrils as they walked. At last, they came to a glassed-in office with wide, ivory colored venetian blinds on the windows. Noguchi stood aside and bade Murphy to enter.

The room was sparsely appointed with respect to furniture, but large, exquisite, original silk-screenings of Japanese landscapes adorned the walls. Noguchi gestured to a glass table and four chairs in the corner.

"Please be seated, Mr. Murphy. I shall just be a moment."

He went to his desk and grabbed a gray folder from on top. Then he sat across from Murphy and spread it open.

"I was told by the receptionist that you have questions regarding the death of," he glanced down at the folder to find the name, "Matthew Doyle."

"Matt and I are—or I should say 'were'—partners in a private detective agency here in Los Angeles. His family lives out of state and has yet to be notified of his death. I've made arrangements with the reporting officers for that to happen. But I guess my concern, Doctor, is that our profession is not without hazards." Then added with a chuckle, "As you can tell by my own bruises."

"And you want to know if his death might have been from other than natural causes. Am I correct?"

"Yes, sir. The police officers on the scene judged Matt's death to be the probable result of a heart attack."

Noguchi grinned. "Maybe those officers should be working here. They could save us a lot of time and effort. And in this case, they were one hundred percent correct. The official medical term being 'coronary thrombosis.'"

"Is it possible that his heart attack could've been induced, rather than caused naturally?"

Noguchi squinted. "Induced?"

"Yes. By a drug of some sort. Something that could be

196

injected."

"There are, indeed, chemical compounds that can stop a heart from beating, but the toxicology screen that was administered revealed only evidence of a blood pressure medication. Do you know if Mr. Doyle was prescribed such medication?"

"Yes, he took a pill twice a day."

"I think we can conclude, then, that the causes of Mr. Doyle's death—though unexpected—are relatively mundane in nature. Whether or not he was aware, he suffered from a degenerative disease of the arteries: atherosclerosis, to be precise."

"Could you explain that in layman's terms?"

Noguchi thought for a moment. "Deposits of fat line the walls of arteries and, in time, build up sufficiently to restrict blood flow. An actual blockage can trigger a heart attack or stroke. It was further concluded that he was diabetic."

"I don't think he knew that, or he'd have said something."

"This is often the case with obese people. They attribute their diabetic symptoms to something less threatening. And, of course, being a smoker—a heavy smoker, by the perceived effects of lung tissue damage—was also a complication to his health. Simply put, Mr. Doyle was a heart attack waiting to happen. And yesterday, his time ran out." He closed the file and got to his feet. "If there's nothing more, Mr. Murphy, I have to get back to work."

Murphy got up, as well, and offered his hand.

"You've been very generous with your time, and I appreciate it. Matt's death took me totally by surprise. I guess I was looking for some other explanation than the obvious."

Noguchi grinned widely. "Like you, I am also a detective in search of truth. But I must discern it from those who cannot speak for themselves."

"I never thought of it that way, but you're right." Murphy then said, "Oh, one more thing. Is there a listing of his personal property items in that file?"

Noguchi reached for the folder and thumbed to the third

page.

"Yes, here it is."

"Is there mention of a film canister, by any chance?"

Noguchi shook his head.

38

Murphy walked slowly down the corridor to the front exit. He had a lot on his mind. There was now no doubt whatsoever as to the status of the film that had been in Doyle's possession. It has been taken from him.

Murphy would've liked to have called into question the official findings of the autopsy. But who was he to disagree with Noguchi? Clogged arteries, diabetes, lack of a healthy lifestyle, and no trace of any toxic substance in his blood translated into just what Noguchi contended: a run of the mill heart attack killed Doyle.

But Murphy knew more of the circumstances, which left him to give a slightly different twist to the story. When confronted in the parking lot by the two killers, Doyle had literally been scared to death. Undoubtedly, they would've liked to have interrogated him, but he'd spoiled their plans. Nonetheless, his presence there with a camera had told them all they really needed to know: Murphy had lied when he'd spoken to Clayton Hayward. And why lie if he didn't suspect Hayward of complicity?

And yet, Murphy thought, they were aware of all that yesterday afternoon. But maybe after dealing with Doyle, they figured there wasn't any rush. They didn't even need to tail him. They could simply dispose of him and Tara later that night. Could he have thrown them a curve by spending the night at her place rather than his? He tried to remember since taking this case if he could've ever led them to her apartment. Yesterday morning, before meeting with Hayward, was the only time, but he was sure he hadn't been followed, because they knew where he was going. As professional as they might be, perhaps they hadn't done their homework. It sounded far-fetched, but they might not have known where she lived. But no matter. For whatever reason, he and Tara had gotten a twenty-four-hour reprieve that surely wasn't going to extend into another day.

As Murphy drove, he laid out the facts of life—and death—as he now understood them. Tara took the bad news like a trooper, albeit a reluctant one.

"What can I say?" Murphy said. "I don't like what's happened any more than you do. Even less, since Matt would still be alive if I hadn't roped him into helping me. But we have to play the hand we've been dealt."

"Easy for you to say. Inside, I feel like I could explode."

"We're going to be okay. I've come out of tougher scrapes than this before. Compared to North Africa during the war, with Rommel breathing down my neck, this is small potatoes. So now we're going to pull a disappearing act. Dropping out of sight will make them nervous. They'll wonder where we are and what we're up to. They'll be looking over *their* shoulders for once." He took her hand in his. "One day this'll be a story we can tell our kids." If he didn't make any more mistakes, he thought. Marjorie Kane's and now Doyle's death weighed heavily on him.

Their destination, Murphy explained, was LA International. He took a circuitous route, constantly scanning for a tail. There wasn't one, even if they'd switched out of the Town Car. Once at the airport, he parked in the long-term lot.

"I could eat something," Murphy said. "How about you?"

"Actually, I feel carsick, but it's probably just nerves.

Maybe fresh air will do me some good."

They exited and made their way through the labyrinth of parked cars to another southern California landmark, a towering structure that dominated the airport skyline. It resembled a flying saucer from a science-fiction movie, resting atop four long. curved legs. They took the elevator to the restaurant that slowly revolved 360 degrees, giving a panoramic view of the world below on days not marred by fog or smog.

Murphy signaled the bartender as they commandeered two vacant stools.

"What's your pleasure?" he asked Murphy but never took his eyes off Tara. This was more often the case than not when they went out together. She was simply drop-dead gorgeous. He could hardly fault other men for admiring her.

"A strawberry daiquiri," Tara said.

"And you, sir'?"

"Scotch and soda. Plenty of ice. Make it a double. And have them taken to our table; we're going to have lunch."

"Not a problem. *Bon appetit.*"

Situated along a continuous bank of windows, every linen-draped table had an unobstructed view. After they were seated, Tara stared toward the ocean.

"Look, you can see Catalina."

Murphy glanced outside and nodded. When he turned back, the waitress set coasters on the table and deposited their drinks on top. She then handed them each a menu and walked away. Tara opened hers, looked inside for a moment, and then set it aside.

"This cat and mouse game has my stomach tied in knots. But maybe that's not a bad thing. Maybe now's the time to get those ten pounds off. Why don't we share something?"

39

Tara's appetite miraculously returned after the first bite of her half of the triple-decker toasted club sandwich. She then finished Murphy's half, leaving him to munch only on the potato chips and wedge of dill pickle that came with it.

When she was done, he said, "Not hungry, huh? You could've fooled me."

"We ordering dessert?"

"Are you serious? You always say it's bad for your figure."

"It's your fault. Stress. How about a piece of apple pie with a scoop of ice cream? We'll share it."

"Like we shared that sandwich? No dice." He laughed.

It didn't take long to polish off two slices à la mode and a cup of coffee each.

Afterward, Murphy settled the bill. Including the drinks from the bar, it totaled nine dollars. He made a mental note that this place was only for tourists with money to burn. The sandwich and pie were good, but not *that* good.

They rode the elevator with a couple of young Frenchmen who talked non-stop to each other in their own language. Most of which was directed toward "la belle" and whether the old guy was her father. When they reached ground level and the door slid open, Murphy took them by surprise by setting the situation straight—in French. His tour of duty in France had made him as fluent as most Army cops found necessary to pursue their investigations and collaborate with foreign police authorities. In this particular instance, he suggested that as visitors to the U.S. they might want to mind their own fucking business.

One of them was about to take exception when Murphy moved his jacket to expose his shoulder holster and pistol. With eyes wide, "Oui, monsieur," was all the Frenchman said before dragging his compatriot along.

"What was that all about?" Tara asked. "I caught some of it, but not all."

"Oh, they just thought you should've had better taste in companionship. I begged to differ, and they saw it my way."

"Men. You're so territorial."

"When it comes to you, I am."

She kissed him. "And I love you for it."

The next stop was the airport terminal and the Hertz counter inside.

"And how long will you require a car, sir?" the female rental agent asked.

"It's hard to say, exactly. Better put me down for about a week."

"I'm sure we can accommodate you." She consulted a clipboard. "I have a midnight blue Chevrolet Malibu available. Four-door. Would that be to your liking?"

"Sounds fine."

Murphy signed the requisite paperwork and wrote her a deposit check. She jotted down information from his driver's license and handed him a set of keys.

"Thank you for driving Hertz."

A mile down Airport Boulevard, between Manchester and Century, Murphy turned into pulled the parking lot of a Super 8 Motel—its large yellow sign towering above—and found one of the stalls marked: REGISTRATION. 15 MINUTES ONLY.

"This is as good a place as any for a base of operations," he said. "It would be a miracle if they found us here."

"How long will we be 'holed up'?"

Murphy chuckled.

"That's the expression, isn't it?" Tara asked.

"Yes. It just sounded funny coming from you. But to answer your question: As little time as necessary. Consider it another mini-vacation. When we get settled in, you can call deShazo and arrange for coverage at the pub. But don't tell her where you are."

"What if there's an emergency of some kind?"

"Then she'll have to handle it. I don't want anyone knowing our location. That'll keep you safe while I concentrate on bringing these assholes down. But I'm going to need some professional help. Or to be more specific: Special Agent Alie Hayward. Once she understands the scope of her father's activities—a father she despises—I doubt anyone could keep her away."

Their room wasn't on par with the Honeymoon Suite at the Flamingo, but it served its purpose and had a "brand new" smell. Tara plopped onto the king sized bed and rolled to her back.

She said, "We're a little shy on changes of clothes, don't you think?"

"It couldn't be helped. In the Army we went into battle what we had, not with what we wished we had. We'll go out later and do some shopping. Make sure you get a swimming suit. That pool looks pretty inviting. No reason you shouldn't enjoy it while we're here."

"And what about you?"

"I'll be busy working."

"*All* the time?" She started to unbutton her blouse. "You know what they say: *All work and no play makes Jack a dull boy.*"

Thirty minutes later, Murphy dressed while Tara, sitting naked on the bed, called the pub and explained to deShazo that she'd be away again for a few days and to take charge. Tara also informed her that she'd be receiving a substantial bonus check this month.

Then, while Tara took a shower, Murphy consulted the small address book in his jacket pocket and found Alie's home number in Atlanta. If there was no answer, he'd try her office at the Bureau. After six rings, he was about to disconnect when she came on the line.

"Hello." Raspy, as if she'd been roused from sleep.

"Alie, it's Jack."

"Jack who?"

"You know a lot of Jacks who call your place on a Sunday afternoon? Jack Murphy. Remember? Your former comrade in arms."

"What time is it?"

Murphy looked at his watch. "About five-thirty your time."

"Yeah, well hold on a sec. I have to pee."

He could hear the phone receiver being dropped on a hard surface. A few moments later a toilet flushed and then she was back.

"Sorry. When a girl's got to go, she's got to go."

"You sound tired. Are you sick?"

"I'm only sick and tired of working graveyards and then being held over to brew coffee and make a donut run. I thought the Army was tough on the fairer sex. The Bureau has it beat by a mile. Despite its policies to the contrary, it's by and large a men's club—female agents only begrudgingly admitted.

"Anyway, I'd only been in bed a couple hours when the phone rang. I was deep in a dream and must've been a little disoriented. But I'm wide awake now. Actually, I've been thinking about you. It's close to a week since we talked. Are you calling to tell me you found Charlie hail and hearty? I'm sure my father will express his gratitude with a hefty check." Her sarcasm was unmistakable.

"No, I haven't found him and doubt I will. But I'm fairly certain what happened to him: He was murdered."

A long silence ensued. Apparently, Alie needed time to process what Murphy had said.

Finally, she asked, "Murdered by whom? Why? When?

205

Where? How?"

"Spoken like a true detective. I'll explain as best I can, but your brother isn't the only casualty in this affair..."

Over the next few minutes Murphy laid out the facts and circumstantial evidence, Alie occasionally interrupting for clarification.

He finished by saying, "The only likely conclusion I can draw is espionage, with Klaus Hoffmann and your father as principal conspirators. And it's been going on for a long time. Whatever information Kane found in Europe that didn't jibe with the accepted story of Hoffmann's conversion to the American dream, it wound up costing him his life and the lives of everyone else he eventually confided in. And guess what? I can't prove a goddam thing. But that won't stop them from trying to silence Tara and me."

"And you thought I might give you a hand, is that it?"

"Our backs are kind of against the wall here, Alie. So, yes, I could use some assistance. We made a good team last year. An encore isn't impossible. Besides, you might say it's your fault that I'm in this jam. If you hadn't referred me to your father..."

"I don't need any coaxing. I'll take a flight out first thing tomorrow. The office will just have to find someone else to make coffee."

40

Murphy was just hanging up the receiver when Tara appeared at the bathroom door, wearing only a towel wrapped like a turban over her hair.

"Who were you talking to?"

"Alie. She agreed to throw in with us. She'll call tomorrow first thing to give me her flight number. I already feel a lot better about our situation."

Tara found her bra and panties on the bed and put them on.

"You really like her, don't you?" she said. "Sometimes I think she's my competitor. I'm looking forward to meeting her. You've referred to her as a Doris Day type, but somehow I can't picture Doris packing a badge and gun."

Murphy laughed. "You sound a bit jealous; you don't have to be. I may've been smitten once, but I only actually worked with her for two days on my last big army assignment. When someone saves your life, you always tend to see them in a special light."

"She was the one who shot you, wasn't she?"

"And I'd have done the same if our roles had been reversed. If she'd hesitated even a fraction of a second, well…I wouldn't have met you."

"When you put it that way, I guess I owe her a lot, too."

Murphy threaded his arms through his shoulder holster and reached for his jacket, draped over the back of a chair.

"Where are we going?" Tara asked.

"You're staying put while I tell Andrea about Matt. I won't be long. She lives close by. I'm going to put her on paid vacation until this mess is cleared up. I don't want them finding her while they're looking for me."

"Okay. I think I'll take a nap, then." She scooted to the head of the bed and dragged a pillow behind her neck. "You kind of wore me out."

"I wore *you* out?" He laughed. "I only wish that were true. It would do wonders for my self-esteem." He bent and kissed her.

Murphy had been to the Duncan's home only once before, but after a couple wrong turns, he found Hazel Street just off Centinela Avenue. It was a quiet working class Inglewood neighborhood of frame homes that has sprouted in the 1920s. He remembered the huge pine trees that marked the front edge of the property and turned into the wide driveway that ran back to a detached garage.

He stopped beside Andrea's four-door red Mercury. Exiting, he ascended the brick steps to a front porch and knocked gently on the paneled oak door. He heard footsteps nearing from inside and then the door opened.

"Jack? What are you—" She stopped short of finishing her thought.

Murphy saw Andrea's face and knew what had happened—again.

He stepped in past her. "Where is he?"

"Jack, don't," she pleaded. "It was my fault. I should've stayed out of his way."

He cautiously turned her face to the light and winced.

"I don't like the looks of this. Your cheekbone may be broken."

"Maybe that explains why I couldn't sleep, even with an

icepack and a handful of aspirin."

"You need to go to a hospital, Andrea."

"I would've yesterday, but I was afraid they'd ask questions. I didn't want the police involved. Johnny's actually a good husband and father when he isn't drinking."

"A good husband right up to the point where he kills you or one of your kids. And where *are* your kids?"

"In their rooms. They're a little smarter than I am. From experience, they've figured out when to make themselves scarce."

"Where were they when it happened?"

"At the beach with the neighbor kids and then a sleepover. They'd left mid-morning before Johnny got on a tear. He's been putting in long hours at the shop, because they've been short-handed. It must've finally gotten to him. He hasn't been this out of control for a while.

"I could see there was no use reasoning with him, so I left and went to the office. I finished typing one of Matt's reports and then tidied up your desk a little. There was a pocket calendar that I accidently knocked on the floor. And when I picked it up a key fell out. It looked like it had been taped to the inside of the back cover."

"It must've been the appointment book I got from Hayward's copy girl. What sort of key was it?"

"You can decide for yourself." Her purse was hanging on the door knob to the coat closet near the front door. She dug through it for a moment and returned with a small brass key that she handed to him.

Murphy examined it closely.

Andrea said, "I thought it might be connected with the case you're on, so I called your house, but there was no answer. Then I decided to take it to you. Even if it wasn't important, it would give me an excuse to delay coming back here. Then I noticed the gas gauge on my car read nearly empty, and I'd left without any money. I had no choice but to return home. Johnny was waiting for me behind the door. He grabbed me and threw me to the floor. Accused me of being a slut and sleeping with *you*. I told him he was crazy and tried to get up. He kicked me in the face. I blacked out. When I came to, I looked like this."

Murphy pocketed the key.

"Well, this is the last time," he said.

"What are you going to do?"

"What I should've done the first time you came to work, trying to hide a bruise with makeup. Now where is he?"

"Out back. Grilling hamburgers."

"Like a Sunday afternoon picnic? As if nothing has happened? Well, if that doesn't take the cake." He paused, then, "Listen, your parents live somewhere around here, don't they?"

"Yes, in Lennox."

"Pack a bag for you and the kids. You're leaving. This is the end of a once beautiful romance. Have you got money?"

She nodded. "I put some aside for emergencies. Johnny doesn't know about it. It's hidden in the hall closet."

"All right. Get your stuff together while I have a 'Come to Jesus' meeting with Johnny. Then we're out of here."

"You're not going to hurt him, are you?"

"You're worried about *him*—after all he's done to you? You're a good person, Andrea. And far better than he ever deserved. But he's not the same man you married. He's become a predator that needs to be eliminated. I promise I won't go that far, but he's going to remember today for the rest of his life. Now get going."

41

The back kitchen door opened onto a covered concrete patio. At the edge, near the lawn that made up the backyard, Johnny Duncan, metal spatula in hand, stood over the smoldering coals of a barbeque grill. The secondary screen door banged shut after Murphy stepped through it.

Without turning around, Duncan bellowed, "It's about time! I've been callin' for five minutes. Bring me another beer and be quick about it!"

"I think you've had enough."

Duncan whirled at the voice. "I might've figured the bitch would tattle to you." His speech was slurred. "You're all she talks about. It's Jack this and Jack that. Well, take her. My gift. But the next time you fuck her, you'll have to put a paper sack over her head. She ain't so pretty *now*."

Murphy stalked forward.

"You sorry bastard," he hissed. "There's never been anything between Andrea and me. It's all in your head, and she told you that."

"She's a lyin' whore."

"She begged you not to hurt her, didn't she?"

"She got what she deserved. Now get the fuck outta here

before I give you a dose of the same medicine. You don't scare me. Or maybe I should just call the call the cops and have you arrested for trespassin'."

"That's a good idea, Johnny. Maybe I'll save you the trouble and call them, myself. And when they get here, I'll do all the explaining, because you won't be able to."

"What are you talkin' about?"

"Just this: I'll tell them I had come over to talk with Andrea about an office matter. That's when I saw she'd been beaten up. I'll make sure they know this wasn't the first time, and that they might want to talk to your kids about what you've done to them. I'll say I came out here to try to convince you to get some kind of therapy before you killed somebody."

Duncan just stood there, seemingly transfixed by Murphy's calm tone.

Murphy then reached for the asbestos cooking glove that hung on the grill. Putting it on, he picked up one of the empty beer bottles littering the ground. He held it by the neck and smashed it on the side of the grill.

Duncan jumped back, unsure of Murphy's intentions.

"But I'll tell them you wouldn't listen to reason; that you became angry and defensive. That's when you broke this bottle and tried to cut me with it. Instinctively, I backed up onto the lawn. That's when I saw the baseball bat." He reached down and hefted it. "It must've been left there by your kids, I'll say. Then, when you came at me again, I jabbed the end of the bat into your chest."

Murphy aimed for the solar plexus, and Duncan staggered backward, dropping the spatula. He gasped for air but remained upright.

"But this only seemed to make you even madder. You screamed you were going to kill me and came at me again. I had no choice but to defend myself."

He savagely rammed the end of the bat into Duncan's nose and felt cartilage give way. Blood gushed over his lips and down his chin.

"But you were like a man possessed, and the only way I

could stop you was by doing *this!*"

Murphy swung the bat up as hard as he could and caught Duncan in the crotch. He crumpled to the ground.

With Duncan now moaning and writhing, Murphy bent over him and whispered into his ear. "So who do you suppose the cops are going to believe? A private detective and ex-Army investigator with a spotless record, or an asshole who preys on women and children? And also think about this: If I find out you've come anywhere near Andrea, I'll find you and finish what I started."

Back inside the house, Murphy gathered up Andrea and her two sons, neither of whom were yet in their teens. He didn't know what she'd told them, but there was no mention of their father, nor did she ask about him.

Murphy stowed the two suitcases in the trunk of Andrea's car while the boys climbed into the backseat. It was then that Andrea took note of the Malibu.

"You get a new car?"

"It's a rental. Mine was a little hot."

"You're in danger, aren't you? I can tell."

"I've got a long history of taking care of myself." He paused a moment, then asked, "Off hand, do you know the phone number or address of Matt's ex-wife?"

"The address, yes. 1201 Ocean Boulevard, Miami. I've got her phone number at the office. But why not just ask Matt?"

"That's the reason I came to see you. Matt had a heart attack yesterday."

"Is he all right?"

Murphy shook his head. "He didn't make it." Andrea had enough to deal with without going in the questionable circumstances of Matt's death.

"Oh, no." Her eyes filled with tears.

He put his arm around her shoulders. "I'll see that his ex is notified," he said.

"I can do it if you'd rather. I've talked to her a couple of times on the phone. I'll call first thing tomorrow when I get to the office."

"In your condition, I think not. Besides, I'm closing the office until the Hayward Case is resolved. It's gotten a bit out of hand."

"What does that mean?"

"I can't explain now. In any event, consider yourself on paid leave for the next week."

"But what about our clients? What happens when they call and no one answers?"

"I thought about that, as well, but I don't recall anything too pressing on my plate or Matt's. We'll just have to sort it all out when the time comes."

"Okay, if you say so."

"Now listen, after you and kids settle in with your folks, have your dad take you to an emergency room. You need attending to."

"I will. I promise." She kissed him on the cheek.

"And find a divorce lawyer. He'll help get your husband out of the house and a restraining order to keep him away."

"But—"

"No buts, Andrea. Think of it this way: He'll be saved from dying in the gas chamber for killing *you*."

42

Murphy sat in the waiting area opposite the gate where Alie Hayward's flight was scheduled to off-load its passengers. He was glad Tara wasn't with him, because he'd been chain smoking, lighting a new cigarette with the butt of the last. The arrival board showed the plane's ETA to be 1:47. He glanced at his watch. It was twenty past the hour. Alie had called him from the Atlanta terminal at four-thirty a.m. his time to give her flight number and approximate time of arrival. She hadn't been able to get a direct flight, having to settle on short notice for what she called a "milk run." If she'd told him the stops along the way, he'd been too groggy at that hour to remember them, but TWA Flight 1456 was concluding its last leg coming from Denver.

To stretch his legs, Murphy walked to the bank of windows that overlooked miles of crisscrossing tarmac runways. He counted a dozen aircraft in various stages of either coming or going. As he stood there watching, he thought about Tara. It was obvious after he'd returned from Andrea's yesterday that the events of the past week had taken their toll on her. As if Vegas hadn't been enough, what with Marjorie Kane's murder, now Matt Doyle was dead, as well, and their own future was in question. She tied her best to put on a game face, but beneath the surface, she was terrified.

They had talked through their situation after he'd called and left a message for Officer Rose, giving him the address of Doyle's ex-wife. He'd apologized for not having a phone number but figured the Miami police could track her down with the news.

But by the time their discussion had run its course, they opted for dinner over finding a clothing store. A greasy spoon was within walking distance of the motel. The fare wasn't half bad, and they made the same trek this morning for breakfast. Afterward, they found the nearest Kmart and bought a couple days of make-do clothes. Murphy regretted he wasn't going to be around much to see Tara in the skimpy swimming suit she found, but maybe lying poolside in the sun would calm her nerves while he and Alie found a way to save the day and their lives.

Standing at the window, he also gave a thought to Johnny Duncan. What had he done when he'd been able to stagger into the house? Put a bag of ice on his balls? Pop the cap on another bottle of beer? Call the police and report he'd been assaulted? If the latter, Murphy wondered if the cops were now looking for him, too. Well, they'd have to take a number if they were, because two killers were likely already on the job.

Murphy checked the arrival board again to find that Flight 1456 was on approach. Back at the window he saw it touch down and taxi to the gate. He recognized the distinctive dolphin-shaped fuselage and triple tail as a Constellation—Lockheed, if he remembered right. These four-prop aircraft had been around for a while. He'd even seen a few in Europe. This one was silver with red TWA lettering and striping. With jet engine aircraft already the standard for intercontinental flights, it would only be a matter of time before they took over the skies in the States, as well.

Alie must've been seated near the rear of the plane, because most of the passengers had passed through the arrival gate before he spotted her. The last time he'd seen her—the previous summer in Germany—she'd been wearing a navy blue skirt and matching jacket. She wore a similar outfit now, but one better tailored. A black leather purse on a long strap hung from her shoulder. And she looked just as adorable as he remembered. She smiled and quickened her pace when she saw him. Then face to face, she threw her arms around him and held on. The scent of her perfume was intoxicating.

When at last she stepped back, she wiped a tear from her cheek and said, "With the exception of that shiner, I'd say California has been good to you, Jack. Must be all that sunshine and sea air."

"Thanks. I do feel like a new man since I shed all the extra pounds I'd been carrying around in the Army. And you, well, you must have to beat those other agents off with a stick."

She blushed. "Even if that were true—which it isn't—I don't have time for a private life. I'm devoting everything to being the best agent—female or male—that the Bureau has ever had, but I'll tell you something: It isn't easy being a woman. You have to work twice as hard for half the credit. But I'm not here to bore you with my grievances. Let's find my suitcase and then mount up."

Murphy stowed Alie's bag in the Malibu's trunk.

"I'm impressed," she said. "Business must be booming to drive a brand new car."

"It's a rental. Mine's out there somewhere." He gestured to the ocean of parked cars.

"So it's like that, huh?"

"Afraid so. I figure I've been followed since I took this case. We should be anonymous in this one. Plus, it's got air conditioning. Mine doesn't."

Once in the car, Murphy said, "You want to go to the motel? I've booked a room for you next to ours."

"Later. Unless the well has gone dry with regard to any leads."

Murphy extracted a key from his trouser pocket and held it out for her to take.

"This was concealed in an appointment book belonging to

your brother that I got from his copy girl at the *Times*. My secretary found it yesterday quite by accident. At first, I thought it might be to a desk drawer or file cabinet. But there's a number stamped into it which makes me think it's a locker key. I'd planned to call her first thing this morning to see if she knew what it opened, but Tara and I got caught up in buying some clothes. We kind of left town in a hurry when I figured she and I might be in the crosshairs." He paused, then, "Oh, by the way, this girl and Charlie were an item back in high school."

"Oh? What's her name?"

"Shannon Rigby."

"Right. Shannon. I remember her. She wasn't typical of Charlie's high school friends. Nice girl from a good family. They lived in the newer section of Bel Air. Her father owned a string of dry cleaning stores. If Charlie had had any sense, he'd have married her."

"Those were her sentiments, too, except for a minor detail: Charlie was homosexual."

"*What?* Are you sure?"

Murphy nodded. "Shannon confirmed it, though that hasn't stopped her from carrying a torch for him all these years."

"Does my father know?"

"Yeah. Said he tried unsuccessfully to get Charlie into therapy."

Alie laughed. "When I was growing up, my father had no tolerance for homosexuals. Referred to them as degenerates who needed to be disposed of. Discovering that his own son was one of them must've been tough to swallow."

"So what do you make of the key?"

Alie read the number on one side: "1206. Wait a minute. My father bought memberships at the LA Athletic Club for Charlie and himself right after Charlie went to live with him. This could be Charlie's locker key. You said Charlie's office at the *Times* had been searched. Maybe they were looking for this key?"

"No. I don't think they knew about it anymore than they

knew about Marjorie Kane. The question is: Why didn't they? I've talked with former American POWs from the Second World War and Korea. That name, rank, and serial number crap is good for about twenty seconds. You may think you're John Wayne when the interrogation begins, but you leave like Minnie Mouse. Whatever they want to know, you're eventually going to tell them.

"But that's not what happened with Gordon Kane and your brother. I know Kane was tortured, yet he didn't give up his wife. Something similar surely happened to Charlie and he didn't divulge the whereabouts of this key, assuming it has relevance, that is."

"Why else would Charlie stash it at the office rather than just carry it with him? It must be important. But that aside, you've brought up an interesting point: Why didn't they crack under interrogation?"

"I think there were basically two reasons. First, this was a quick and dirty operation to bury what Gordon Kane had uncovered. There wasn't time for lengthy drug-supported questioning; hence, the use of torture. Secondly, it's my guess they were clumsy. They pushed too hard, too fast. They may be proficient killers, but suitable interrogation techniques are not their forte. The result was that Kane and your brother died during the ordeal before they could reveal everything they knew.

"I now think that's why I was hired. To find anything incriminating. Marjorie Kane being one example. And maybe this key being another."

43

As Murphy drove away from the airport, Alie plucked the cigarette from his lips and took a long drag.

"You back on the weed?" he asked.

"No, I haven't had one since the last time we worked together. It must be an omen."

"Well, the 'last time' had a happy ending, with the exception of me winding up in the hospital, a little worse for wear."

She took another pull on the cigarette and then returned it to him.

"So what excuse did you give the Bureau about needing time off?" Murphy asked.

"The truth—of sorts. I said I had a family matter to attend to in California. Though I'm hoping not to be too exposed. The Bureau takes a decidedly dim view of 'rogue agents,' even if their intentions are pure."

"I'm sorry to have put your career at risk. It's just that I had nowhere else to—"

"Forget it. I'm the one who should be sorry. If it hadn't been for me, you'd be living the good life and working on your tan. Your partner would also still be alive. And I'd have been none the wiser that I actually had skin in the game. No, Jack, we're in this together—just like old times—no matter how the chips fall.

"And don't forget that you weren't the first choice to track down my brother—I was. What if I'd consented, and what if I'd followed his trail and come up with the conclusions you have? I can only assume I'd have been marked for termination, too. Seems like my father must've missed a few parenting classes along the way, don't you think?"

They laughed.

Located downtown on 7th Street, the Los Angeles Athletic Club was established in the 1880s as the first private club in the city, catering to the influential rich. In time, the "men only" criterion was abolished to allow free association of the sexes. Now, eighty-five years after its inception, it maintained a bar, restaurant, and hotel accommodations, in addition to traditional athletic facilities. It also hosted weddings, receptions, and other gala events. It was said that more business deals were consummated here than on southland golf courses.

Murphy headed for Pershing Square and its underground parking, rather than gamble on finding a metered spot on the street.

Now on foot, nearing the club's entrance, Murphy said, "I've passed this place dozens of time and never paid any attention to the signage. I certainly wouldn't have pegged it as a sports club. Looks more like a five-star hotel."

"Wait till we get inside. I had a boyfriend in college whose family belonged. If I remember right, the lobby resembles the foyer of the Louvre."

Once through the revolving door, Murphy took in the plush trappings and exclaimed, "Wow! You were right. This is definitely *not* the YMCA. What do you suppose the dues are?"

"Trust me. You can't afford them."

They traversed the thick Persian carpet toward a richly paneled counter topped with polished brown granite. Behind, sat a tan young man with a blond crew cut. Muscles strained the white polo shirt he wore. The embroidered name over the

221

pocket identified him as Mike. He concluded his phone call and watched as they approached.

Apparently recognizing neither of them as members, he asked, "May I help you?"

Murphy flashed his badge. "We'd like to ask you a few questions."

Mike gave Alie a lazy once-over from top to bottom, as if imagining what she looked like naked. Murphy broke the spell by stepping in front of her. For two cents he'd have popped the guy.

"Questions, huh? Okay, but make it snappy. There's a handball tourney starting in an hour, and I'm kind of busy with the details."

Murphy could no longer contain himself. "You got issues with authority?"

"Just fuzz, in general."

"Is that so? Well let me give you a reason not to like *me*, in particular."

Murphy reached over the counter and grabbed him by the shirt collar.

"Get your ass off that fucking stool!" Murphy yanked him to his feet. "And show some goddam respect when you speak to us."

A trickle of arriving patrons, undoubtedly noticing the altercation at the front desk, but not wishing to get involved, gave wide berth and simply held up their photo membership cards before disappearing into the facility.

Mike shrugged out of Murphy's grasp.

"What do you think you're doing? You can't come in here and jerk me around."

"I must be dreaming then, because I thought I just had. And if I don't detect an attitude adjustment damn quick, I'm going to rearrange your pretty-boy face and claim self-defense. Your choice."

Mike ground his teeth. "Okay. I apologize."

"That's more like it. Now, we'd like to know if Charles Hayward is a member."

"If you're referring to Hayward, the newspaper reporter: Yes, he is."

"When was he here last?"

"The club doesn't officially keep track of stuff like that. But he usually comes in two or three times a week to swim laps, though I haven't seen him in a while. Of course, that doesn't mean he hasn't been around. I don't always work the front desk where I might see him come in."

Murphy fished the key in question out of his pocket. "Could this key be to his locker?"

Mike examined it briefly, then handed it back.

"Nope. Ours are similar though."

"You couldn't be mistaken?" Alie asked. "Maybe you should take another look."

"Don't need to, for the simple reason that the key you have is stamped with the number 1206. For whatever reason, our lockers and keys begin with the number 2000 and increase accordingly.

Murphy shot Alie a look of disappointment.

She then said, "I assume the club maintains a master key for emergencies."

Mike nodded.

"Good, because we need to look in Hayward's locker, nonetheless."

"Listen, now don't get me wrong, and it's probably none of my business, but don't you people talk to each other?"

"What are you getting at?" Murphy asked.

"Only that a cop already searched Hayward's locker."

"When was that?" Alie asked.

He consulted the desk calendar. "The evening of Monday, July fifth. I specifically remember that because the mayor was hosting a holiday black tie and tails affair, and the athletic facilities were closed. The club had some of us dressed up, as well, checking invitations here in the lobby. Anyway, this guy comes in and shows me a badge. Said he was there to search Charles Hayward's locker and produced a key. I told him to knock himself out and pointed the way. I didn't see him again, what with everything else that was going on."

"Can you give us a description of him?" Murphy asked. "Short, skinny, fat, bald, young, old?"

Mike thought a moment. "Average height, I guess. About my age. Brown hair cut short. Wire-rim glasses. And he spoke with a foreign accent. German I think. We've got some German members, and he sounded like they do."

Alie then said, "Grab the master and let's take a look at that locker for ourselves."

"Sure thing. I just need to call someone to spell me."

After replacing the phone receiver, he extracted a small ring of keys from a drawer below the counter, and consulted one of several Rolodexes. He removed a two-by-three card.

"Locker 2467 is assigned to Charles Hayward." He showed the card to Murphy.

They couldn't see the pool, but a heavy odor of chlorine hung in the air. The men's locker room was situated behind a set of double doors, and those in various stages of nakedness scrambled to cover up when they noticed a woman had entered. Their verbal protests were met by Mike loudly saying, "Police business!" as he continued to lead the way through the maze of ventilated six-foot lockers. A metal bench ran down the middle of each aisle. Number 2467 was located near the end of a row.

"Have at it," Murphy said.

Mike stepped forward and worked the master key in the lock. He stood aside as he swung open the door.

Another disappointment. There were only three items inside: a pair of rubber shower shoes and a can of athlete's foot powder.

They both knew what the other was thinking: Either there was never anything of consequence in the locker, or the man with the German accent had beaten them to it.

44

"You haven't changed a bit, have you, Jack?" They were strolling back to Pershing Square.

"What do you mean?"

"Still a hard ass, just like your Army reputation."

"But with one exception: I now have a heart of gold. It must be those bean sprouts that Tara has me eating."

"Well, you'd never know it the way you manhandled that guy back there."

"I needed to get his attention, that's all. If I'd let him give us the brush off, we wouldn't have found out about the German being there. That actually fits with the chain of events I'd come up with. Charlie was taken sometime after he made that phone call to Shannon Rigby the morning of the fifth. That gave them whatever notes he was going to have her type up for him, and whatever else was in his apartment."

"He must've had the club locker key on him at the time. They drew the same conclusion we did and came looking. But the big question is: Did they find anything?"

"I wondered that, too, when I saw the contents. Now that I've thought about it further, I think the German found just what we did: nothing. But by that time, Gordon Kane was a known quantity, and presumably with Charlie dead, they went to Vegas to terminate him. Then the following week, after a long enough interval had passed to support the story that Charlie had been reported missing, they posed as cops and went through his office, searching for any additional damning evidence."

"And they came up empty."

"Correct. But even then, their paranoia wouldn't let them conclude they were in the clear. And that's where you would've come into the picture, if your father had been successful in talking you into it. But you declined and recommended me. I understand now that finding your brother was never part of the equation. I was hired to stir through the coals for any embers they'd missed."

"And you found Marjorie Kane for them."

"Don't remind me. I feel as responsible for her murder as they are. But even after they had the documentation her husband had squirreled away, they weren't satisfied. They know there's something else to find. That's why as of Saturday morning they still wanted me looking. Now, I figure they just want me dead and are willing to take their chances that what they fear won't surface." He held the key in his palm. "And my gut tells me this is the 'key' to the whole affair." He returned it to his pocket. "But right now, I could use a drink. How about you? I know a place we can walk to from here."

The Rum Runner had been Matthew Doyle's favorite watering hole, and Murphy's, too, before finding O'Neill's. Even afterward, he'd taken Tara there a couple times when she'd come into town. It was owned and run by a crusty old salt— Samuel Carter—who'd seen naval action in the First World War. And he was always eager to recount the events leading to the sinking of his last ship—the USS San Diego—to anyone with the patience to listen. In fact, the story was of some historical significance, inasmuch as the San Diego was the only major American warship lost during the war, although the cause was in dispute. Initially, it had been thought that she'd been sunk by a German U-boat torpedo. Later, evidence pointed to

226

the cruiser more likely having been struck by a floating mine. In any case, it was the high note of Carter's otherwise mundane life.

A weathered model of a mahogany speed boat hung over an equally weathered door which might've come from an ancient frigate. And the nautical motif continued once inside.

"Well, as I live and breathe." Carter was standing behind the bar when they entered. "Jack Murphy. Long time no see."

"I guess it's been a while, hasn't it?" Murphy then asked Alie, "What's your pleasure these days?"

"Vodka tonic with a twist of lime. Plenty of ice."

Murphy surveyed the darkened room and spotted the booth closest to an overhead porthole that let in a minimum of light. There were as yet no other patrons, but he knew this would change around four o'clock.

He pointed. "How about over there? I'll get our drinks."

When she walked out of earshot, Carter winked at Murphy. "You trade up to a newer model, Jack? And here I thought you and that Irish babe made a perfect couple."

"You got it all wrong, Sammy. We're still together and getting serious about tying the knot."

"So who's that?" Carter gestured with his head. "She is one fine looking woman. And familiar, too. She ever been in here before?"

"No, but I know what you mean. Think Doris Day."

Carter squinted across the room. "It's kind of uncanny, isn't it?"

"She's an ex-Army cop. Same as me."

Carter shook his head. "The police never looked like that when I was a sailor."

"I didn't know they *had* cops on Noah's Ark." Murphy chuckled.

"I'll have you know I was once quite a ladies' man."

"Just kidding. Now how about that vodka tonic? I'll have a double Scotch and soda, also with ice.

A minute later, Murphy handed Alie her drink and sat down with his. He took a half empty pack of cigarettes from his

227

pocket and offered one to her.

She waved him off. "No thanks. Those drags I had in the car made me realize how much I miss them. I'm afraid if I start up again, I'll be a goner."

"Tara's been after me to quit. Maybe I will after this case. Of course, that's what I said when I was on my last case." He extracted one from the pack and lit up.

Ice cubes rattled the sides of their glasses as they caught up on each other's lives. Alie's take on the Bureau surprised him.

"I'm serious, Jack. From what I've experience thus far, it's full of political climbers. Prima donnas focused only on promotion. Few want to dig in and get their hands dirty. And as far as those of us who do are concerned, no one has our backs."

"We had our share of rank-happy types in the Army, too, remember?"

"Sure I do. But I always figured if I was in shit up to my neck, the cavalry would show up to pull me out. The Bureau boys would turn away if they saw me twisting in the wind. I'd just be one less woman in the ranks. I guess what I'm saying is that I'm disappointed. Not in being expected to prove myself but that they're inclined not to let me succeed, simply because I'm a woman. We're not valued. There were five of us in my Academy class. Since graduation, I'm the only one left.

"But you know what? They're not going to beat me down. My time's coming, whether they know it or not, whether they *want* it or not. And when it does, they're going to sit up and take notice. And that includes Hoover, if he's really the man he wants us to believe he is."

They finished their drinks and headed for the front door. A couple regulars—if judged by Carter's banter—had taken stools at the bar.

"Be seeing you, Sammy," Murphy said as they passed.

"Don't be a stranger, Jack. And when you see Matt, tell him I got his winnings."

"Winnings?"

"We made a bet on the Friday night TV fights. My guy

went down and out in the third round. Glass jaw. I thought he would've been around by now to collect."

Murphy motioned Carter over to the end of the bar where he and Alie stood.

"I've got some sad news," Murphy began in a hushed tone. "Matt had a heart attack on Saturday."

"Oh, no. What hospital is he in? I'll go see him."

"I'm sorry, Sammy, but he didn't make it."

"Sweet Jesus!" He crossed himself.

"I didn't know you were Catholic, Sammy."

"Comes with tending bar. I might as well be a priest for all the confessions that come my way."

"Well, you can hear mine, then. The coroner said it was natural causes. But there's more to it than meets the eye."

"What do you mean?"

"Matt and I were working a case that involves some nasty characters. I think they grabbed him, and that's what triggered the attack."

"The *hell* you say."

"And I plan to take those bastards down hard—no matter what it takes."

45

They were halfway back to the car when Alie said, "You'd intended to call Shannon Rigby about that key." She looked at her watch. "Unless she's working bankers' hours, she should still be at the newspaper. There's a phone booth up ahead."

She stood at the open door while Murphy consulted the white pages directory that hung suspended from a chain beneath a small metal shelf. Committing the number to memory, he deposited a dime and dialed.

A woman's voice: "*Los Angeles Times.* How may I direct your call?"

"Shannon Rigby, please."

"One moment." Click.

"City Desk." Another woman, but not Shannon.

"May I speak with Shannon Rigby?"

A pause. "She's not at her desk right now, but I'd be happy to give her your name and number where you can be reached."

"Tell her Jack Murphy called. I'm at a payphone right now and can't hang around. I'll just have to try again later."

"I'll make sure she gets the message. No, wait. She just came in. Hold a moment while I transfer you."

Then a voice that Murphy recognized. "This is Shannon."

"Shannon. Jack Murphy."

"Have you found Charlie?" A hopeful tone.

"I wish I could say I had, but I'm afraid not. I'm calling because I think you may be able to help me."

"Certainly. Anything."

"Well, when I was there last, I took Charlie's appointment book, remember?"

"Yes."

"As it turns out, inside was a key imprinted with the number 1206. Looks like it might be to a locker. Have you ever seen that key before?"

"Yes, but it isn't a locker key, per se. It opens Charlie's mailbox at the post office. He often kept it in his top desk drawer rather than on his key chain. When he was too busy to go himself, I'd pick up his mail for him. His official work mail came directly to the *Times*. But he preferred the security of the post office box to the mailbox at his apartment for his personal mail. In any event, I didn't find the key when I cleaned out his desk, so I assumed he'd taken it."

Murphy could hardly contain himself. "Which post office?"

Alie had only heard Murphy's side of the conversation. He filled her in as they hoofed it to 5th and Spring, the location of the branch where Hayward had rented a box.

Murphy finally said, "We could be on another wild goose chase, but I'm clinging onto a positive attitude. Charlie must've concluded this wasn't just another of his exposés. What better place to send stuff for safekeeping than the post office?"

A score of people stood in lines, cradling packages and large envelops to be weighed and stamped by the three counter clerks who went through their routines as if they were robots. Banks of bronze mailboxes were located on interior walls of the lobby where postal workers could access them from behind. It must've also been rush hour for patrons to pick up their mail, because Murphy and Alie had to muscle their way to box number 1206.

Murphy slipped the key into the lock and opened the flap

231

door. It was crammed, owing to the fact that it hadn't been emptied in weeks. It took two handfuls to deplete the contents which he gave to Alie. They then found a wooden bench in the corner of the room and went through the stack, piece by piece.

When they'd finished, Alie sighed. "There's nothing here but bills and bulk mailings—junk."

"Shit!" Murphy said under his breath. Then a little louder. "*Shit!*"

A couple of nearby biddies with silver-blue hair turned and glared their disapproval.

One of them said, "What language! If I were your mother, I'd wash your mouth out with soap."

"I apologize ma'am. A slip of the tongue in the heat of the moment."

"Well, see that it doesn't happen again, young man," the other one said.

"No, ma'am," a sheepish Murphy said.

When they left, Alie chuckled. "Two old ladies putting you in your place? I never would've believed it, if I hadn't seen it."

"It's what I get for thinking out loud. I was just so certain that we were onto something. And yet another blind alley. Maybe this California sun has dulled my senses. Tara wants me to dump the private eye gig and manage her pub while she tends the kids she's anxious to have. I'm beginning to think I should take her up on the offer."

"For my money, Jack, you're the best investigator I ever encountered in the Army. And I haven't met anyone who comes even close to having your instincts since."

"I appreciate the vote of confidence, but my 'instincts' have gotten two people killed in the past week and put Tara's life in jeopardy."

"But you've uncovered something worth killing *for*. We just have to find out what that something is and put a stop to it. And we can't do that sitting here licking our wounds."

As they walked toward the exit, Alie tossed the pile of mail into a trash can near the door.

Murphy asked jokingly, "Isn't that a federal offense?"

"So arrest me. Charlie's creditors will just have to wait and bill his estate."

The pedestrian traffic had picked up, and the sidewalk was crowded. As they waited for a green light to cross the street, Alie said, "So where to now?"

Murphy didn't answer. Instead his attention was focused on the opposite corner newsstand.

"What's the matter, Jack?" She followed his gaze.

He finally looked at her. "Magazines," he said cryptically.

"What?"

"When I first went to Charlie's apartment, I noticed he had magazine subscriptions on the coffee table. And at least one of them was a weekly. But there were no magazines in his mailbox. There should have been." He turned. "C'mon. We're going back."

Once in the post office, Murphy got the attention of one of the uniformed workers behind the counter and waved her over.

"I've been out of town for a while, but when I checked my box, none of my magazines were there."

"They're probably in overflow, sir. I'll get them for you. Box number?" She seemed harried as she made for the backroom door.

"1206," Murphy called after her.

When she emerged, she carried a stack bound with a thick rubber band. She passed it over the counter.

"Thank you," Murphy said.

"My pleasure." She then turned away.

Again seated at the wooden bench, they quickly discarded the magazines. What remained was a large manila envelope made out in longhand to Charles Hayward. Alie tore it open at the top and dumped the contents into her lap.

Murphy looked over. "Those cassettes are the same variety that fit the tape recorder I saw at Charlie's office. Shannon said he liked to record his interviews for accuracy." He picked one up. "Charlie's interview of Gordon Kane must've been a long one. This is tape number three of that conversation."

He handed it back.

Alie rifled through the accompanying pages of written material, then said, "The mother lode, Jack."

Murphy got to his feet. "We passed an office supply store just up the street. Let's hope they have a recorder that'll play those tapes. Finally we catch a break."

"Not 'we,' Jack. You. It's seizing on the little things that make a great investigator. If you hadn't remembered seeing those magazines in Charlie's apartment, we'd have missed all this." She paused and then said, "If you decide to manage a bar, that's your business. But don't think for a second that you've slowed down one bit."

"If I'd known at the beginning that this case was actually a deadly scavenger hunt, I might've paid attention to the mailing labels on those magazines at Charlie's place. It would've saved a lot of grief."

46

They picked up a pizza and a carton of beer before going back to the motel. Tara was laying poolside on a chaise lounge as they approached.

Resplendent in an orange bikini, she shielded her eyes against the late afternoon sun, when Murphy said, "Tara, this is Alie Hayward. Alie, Tara."

Tara swung her feet to the ground and stood. She draped a pool towel over her shoulders, then offered her hand to Alie.

"Nice to meet you. Jack has spoken of you often. You've made quite an impression on him, it seems. And I can now see what he means about your resemblance to Doris Day."

"I've been told that since I was in college, but when I look in the mirror, I just don't see it."

Murphy then said, "Well, I'm starving. How about we go upstairs before this pizza gets as cold as the beer?"

Alie detoured to the adjoining room that Murphy had arranged for. When she emerged, she'd traded her business attire for jeans, a t-shirt, and tennis shoes.

"Bring a chair," Murphy said to her.

A minute later, they were sitting at the small table in Murphy's room.

Lifting a bottle from the carton, Alie said, "Imported from Germany. This really *is* like old times, Jack."

"I've become a Guinness man, now, thanks to Tara. But ounce for ounce, nobody brews a better beer than the Krauts."

With that, they dug in.

In time, Alie said to Tara, "I'm sorry that you've been dragged into this mess. If only I hadn't recommended Jack for the job of allegedly finding my missing brother, neither of you would be 'hiding out,' so to speak."

Before Tara could respond, Murphy said, "And if only I'd known ahead of time, maybe I'd have approached this case differently. But second guessing ourselves doesn't get us anywhere. I may've worked us into a corner, but somewhere in that stuff on the coffee table," he gestured with a nod, "is information that will give us a ticket out." He placed his hand over Tara's. "Just wait and see."

She smiled. "I know better than to doubt you. So why don't I make myself scarce, and you two can get to work." She took a long draught on her bottle, draining it, and grabbed another out of the carton. Getting to her feet, she said, "I'll be down by the pool, watching the sun set."

As Tara passed, she put a hand on Alie's shoulder. "I'm really glad you're here. And I know Jack is, too."

After Tara had closed the door behind her, Alie said, "You hit the jackpot when you let her into your life. And I'm a little jealous. When we first met, I sized you up as a man's man, the kind every woman dreams of finding. If only our paths had crossed earlier, Jack, who knows what might've come of it?"

"Two cops living under the same roof?" Murphy shook his head. "No doubt a recipe for marital discord. Tara doesn't even want *one* cop—albeit private—living under *her* roof. But I appreciate knowing that you saw something positive in me then. Let's face it; I'd pretty much gone to seed. It took Tara to turn me into the man I once had been: the guy you'd never known; the guy who'd been fit enough to go three rounds with Joe Louis during the war in North Africa as a publicity stunt for the *Stars and Stripes*."

"Really, Jack?"

"Scout's honor. Look at my nose. It lists to the right, complements of a right hook by the Brown Bomber. Army docs offered to fix it for me, but I chose to wear it as a badge of distinction. I mean, how often do you get the chance to have the heavyweight champion of the world alter your face?"

"Well okay, champ, let's see if we can dance around Charlie's material and come up with a knockout punch of our own."

They sat on the couch beside the coffee table and spread out the various items.

"How about we start at the beginning?" Alie reached for the folder marked *Germany 1945*. Opening it, she said, "Comes with a photograph." She looked at it and passed it to Murphy.

"It's a picture of Klaus Hoffmann," he said. "Obviously a lot younger, but the same man who Marjorie Kane identified as Hoffmann from a photograph of him at her husband's going away party at Northrop." He put the photo down. "What's in the file?"

"Looks to be a copy of the original vetting document completed by our State Department. Times have changed; there isn't much here by today's standards." She read from the report: "Klaus Aldous Hoffmann. Born October 4, 1913 in Karlovy, Czechoslovakia. Only child. Parents killed during the First World War. Raised by father's sister, subsequently killed during Second World War. Studied mechanical engineering at Technical University in Prague. Graduated 1937. Married Marta Luckowitz in 1934."

"Luckowitz? A Jewish girl, do you suppose?"

"They had two children: Richart and Freida. Wife and children eventually died in the extermination camp at Treblinka, Poland."

"That answers the Jewish question. Go on."

"In March of 1939, Hoffmann was sent to work at the Genshagen Plant operated by Daimler-Benz."

"Makes sense. Benz had to branch out during the war. In

addition to producing automobiles, it also designed and manufactured engines for tanks, submarines, and aircraft. It's well known that these plants were run with forced labor made up of concentration camp detainees and civilians pressed into service. Hoffmann probably fell into the latter category. He may've been born in Czechoslovakia, but his actual place of birth, Karlovy—it's now Karlsbad—was located in the Sudetenland, Czech border areas that had been populated by ethnic Germans for hundreds of years.

"With England and France's blessing, those areas were annexed by the Nazis in '38. 'Peace for our time,' though if memory serves, representatives of the Czech government weren't invited to the negotiations. In any event, after the pact was signed, Nazi tanks rolled into the Sudetenland to liberate the German-speaking citizens from 'Czech oppression.' A few months later, the Reich invaded Czechoslovakia proper."

"Jack, you simply amaze me. How do you know all that stuff? I mean, you're a walking encyclopedia."

"After the war, I made it my business to study up on the causes. I was too busy dodging lead before then. But back to Hoffmann's file: His wife and kids may've been expendable, but as a mechanical engineer, he would've been viewed as potentially valuable to the German war effort."

Murphy picked up Hoffmann's photograph. Inscribed across the bottom was a date: August 4, 1945.

"I had occasion to see what people looked like who'd worked as slave laborers. And they damned sure didn't look like this. Hoffmann would've been thirty-two in this picture. Doesn't appear to have missed too many meals, does he?"

He handed the picture to Alie who gave it a more thorough look.

"Could be he figured he had to make the most of a terrible situation," she said. "The instinct to survive is strong, no matter the circumstances. Maybe it was the old 'if you can't beat them, join them' mentality that took hold. There was plenty evidence of that in the camps. To live another day, detainees helped with the unthinkable."

"Sad but true." Murphy took a long drag on his cigarette, then ground it out in the ceramic ashtray. "Okay, we're not in a position to judge Hoffmann's motives. So how did he come to our attention back then?"

Alie again consulted document.

"It says he just approached an American Army officer and offered his services."

"When was that?"

"A day before that picture was taken: August 3rd."

"And when was he transported to the States?"

"The following month: September 25th."

"They must've been in a hurry to grab Hoffmann before the Soviets did. It's my understanding that Von Braun and his rocket scientists were treated similarly. We wanted them working for us more than we wanted them tried for war crimes. It's weird how things work out. Von Braun's V-2 rockets rain death and destruction on London during the war, and now he's an American hero, working to put a man on the moon for us."

"Ours not to wonder why..."

"I guess not. But did you notice anything odd about Hoffmann's background information?"

"Such as?"

"It had to have been self-reported. Europe was in shambles. There wouldn't have been any way to verify what's in that report. Hell, Hoffmann couldn't have produced his own birth certificate. That explains why there's no supportive documentation."

"Are you suggesting Hoffmann might not be the person he claimed to be?"

"I don't know. But Gordon Kane thought there was something about him that wasn't kosher."

They had just finished listening to the last of Charlie's tape recordings when Tara entered the room.

"Still at it, huh?" she said. "The fog's rolling in. It was getting damp and chilly."

Murphy said, "Why don't you stay here? Alie and I can go to her room and finish up. We shouldn't be too much longer."

239

"I don't want to run you off," Tara said, "but I got too much sun today. I'm nearly dead on my feet. I think I'll read in bed for a while and then call it quits."

"I'm actually getting a bit tired, myself," Alie confided. "It's been an exhausting day, what with a transcontinental flight thrown in for good measure. We've gone through most everything, Jack. Why don't we just sleep on it and regroup tomorrow?"

47

Murphy lay in bed, staring at the ceiling, his fingers laced behind his neck. It had only been a week ago today that he'd first set eyes on Clayton Hayward. It seemed a lot longer. But after what he'd read and listened to last night, there was a distinct possibility of turning this affair around within the next twenty-four hours; however, the plan fomenting in his brain was not without risk.

Beside him, breathing softly, Tara was experiencing the "sleep of angels" as his mother had called it. He rose up enough to look across her to the clock on the bedside table. Seven minutes after five. Careful not to wake her, he slipped out of bed, gathered his clothes from the couch, and made for the bathroom.

Within twenty minutes, he emerged showered, shaved, teeth brushed, and dressed. Tara had turned onto her back and was now snoring loudly. He tiptoed to the adjoining door to Alie's room. While in the bathroom, he'd heard her stirring around. He knocked lightly.

A moment later, the door began to open.

"You decent?" he asked.

"If by that you mean: Am I dressed?" The door was now

open wide. "The answer is yes. Come in."

Murphy stepped inside but left the door ajar behind him.

Alie said, "I've been up since four. Couldn't sleep. I've been going over all of it in my mind. Where does my father fit in? He's nowhere to be found in the narrative."

"That's because Kane had never considered that Hoffmann might've had an accomplice, and apparently the thought hadn't occurred to Charlie, either. In any event, this is where Charlie logically made his one and only misstep. He phoned your father on July second, to be precise."

"How do you know that?"

"The first day I met your father, he told me the last time he'd spoken with Charlie was that evening, and that he had called from his apartment. He was very specific as to the date and time. I think he wanted me to find that call, if I ever got hold of Charlie's phone records. I didn't think much about it then. I'll bet those records would show that call to be the only one to your father going back for some time."

"Why would you say that?"

"I got the sense from Charlie's friends that they'd had a major falling out over the homosexuality revelation. In any event, I think Charlie had the idea of using this story to break the ice with your father. They had their disagreement, but Charlie wanted his acceptance."

"How much would he have divulged, do you suppose?"

"Enough for your father to go into damage control mode. Now, I don't know shit from Shinola about espionage, other than what I read about in novels, but eliminating the threat of discovery would've been logical. Hoffmann, the imposter, was to be kept in place at all costs. But they hedged their bets a little."

"What do you mean?"

"On a hunch, I called Northrop yesterday morning while I was waiting for your plane to arrive. I asked for Hoffmann, pretending to be his stock broker with a hot tip. His secretary said he was on extended vacation in Mexico. Didn't know exactly when he'd be back. Said he'd been gone since around the Fourth."

"So if they managed to keep a lid on this, he'd come back as if nothing had happened. And if they couldn't, then he was gone forever."

"That's the way I see it. Once Charlie called, your father was forced to make contact up the food chain, and subsequent events took on lives of their own. Including Charlie's murder."

"My father betraying his country *and* sacrificing his own son? It defies understanding." She paused a moment, then, "No, maybe not. He often spoke of the time he'd spent in England in the twenties, early thirties. His parents thought a little time abroad would broaden his perspective. He was a student at Trinity College, Cambridge."

"How is that significant?"

"Kim Philby, the British double agent. He was a student there at the same time. I didn't know that until I read a newspaper story a couple years ago about his defection to Moscow. I wondered at the time if my father and he had ever crossed paths. He'd said the political discussions that students had were unlike anything he'd ever experienced. 'Exhilarating' is how he'd described them. What if the Communists recruited him then, just like they had with Philby?"

"If that's true, then your father was already at Northrop, spying for the Soviets, long before Hoffmann got there. Which would make Hoffmann *his* accomplice. But regardless, I don't think he had an inkling that his politics would cause the death of one of his children. He wound up being caught in his own web of deceit."

"You sound like you feel sorry for the son of a bitch. Well, don't. He's a monster. If I'd taken the job of supposedly locating my brother instead of you, I'd have been fair game, too. A clean sweep."

"It was a risk to use either one of us, but after searching Charlie's apartment and his office at the *Times*, they knew they didn't have all the documentation, because they hadn't been able to come up with the tape recordings. Charlie had either alluded to them in passing, or your father already knew he regularly taped his interviews for stories. Then it was someone's idea to concoct a story about Charlie being missing and have someone brought in who'd maybe stumble onto those tapes. That someone would then be terminated."

Alie shook her head. "No doubt with my dear sweet father looking on."

48

"Can you hold it down in here?"

The comment startled them. Tara stood in the doorway wearing the red pajamas she's bought the day before.

"A girl has to get all the beauty rest she can."

Alie replied, "I don't think you have anything to worry about on that account."

"I wish Jack had said that." She glared at him.

"So do I," Murphy responded sheepishly, then, "We're about done for the moment. You feeling like breakfast?"

"When have I ever not? Give me a few. I have to transform myself into something more presentable. You two go on plotting and planning. As nice as this place is, there's nothing like sleeping in your own bed."

With that Tara turned back into her room, and moments later they heard the toilet flush, followed by the running of the shower.

Murphy returned Hayward's documentation to the manila envelope.

Alie then said, "You're already way ahead of me, aren't you, Jack?"

"Only because I've been walking their tightrope for a week

now."

"So clue me in."

"All right, but keep an open mind. In army combat, we were taught to concentrate our efforts on reducing the greatest risk. Priority One was to knock out the enemy's big stuff: tanks, artillery, mortars, and machine guns. Once that was accomplished, the odds of survival improved dramatically for the average GI."

"What are you getting at?"

"Just this: The hired guns that have been brought in for a search and destroy mission need to be neutralized."

"So your plan is what? To coax them into the open and…kill them?"

"'Kill' sounds a little crass, but yes. With them out of the way, we'll have some breathing room to arrange your father's future, and Hoffmann's, if the feds can somehow get their hands on him."

"Assuming I'm okay with taking out the trash—and being a federal agent, I'm not sure that I am—how do we get them to where we want them?"

"Not 'we,' just me. But before I answer that question let me try to allay your hesitation by putting what I'm proposing into perspective, at least from where I stand. Hoffmann and your father are Soviet spies; this seems indisputable. Hoffmann for the last twenty years, and I assume your father—from what you've said—for much longer. Once the feds have evaluated what we'll give them, they'll dig deeper to make sure their case is airtight. And if your father hasn't skipped by then, they'll make an arrest. But despite his espionage activities, he's likely only an accessory to murder; he hasn't actually killed anyone, as far as we know. Those who did will have vanished into the shadows with impunity. They've killed before, and they'll go on killing, because that's what they're paid to do. Maybe not in the States anytime soon, but wherever else Soviet interests dictate.

"Now, I know as well as you do that Uncle Sam employs similar men and women for like duties. I actually met a few of them while in the Army. They'd honed their skills in the Office of Strategic Services—the old OSS—and continued on when the CIA was established. I'm sure their official job description was something other than 'assassin,' but a rose by any other name... I doubt they'd have the slightest compunction to target these killers—Charlie's killers—and neither should we."

"You make it sound like we'll be candidates for public service awards." It was obvious that she'd warmed to the idea.

"Almost every day, someone stumbles onto a body in LA and calls the cops. By tomorrow, if I'm lucky, there'll be two more to find. Now, as to your question about how to get them within reach..."

Murphy concentrated on keeping the breakfast conversation light and away from what lay ahead. Tara seemed particularly interested in his contact with Alie while in the Army.

Alie said, "Though we were both CID agents, our paths crossed only once. Just a few months before Jack retired and my enlistment was up, after which I joined the FBI."

"That much I already know. I'm curious about the circumstances that brought you together."

"Well, I'm afraid the details are classified, but I'd be safe to say it involved a serious breach of security at one of the NATO bases in Germany."

Tara turned to Murphy. "But weren't you stationed in France?"

"Yes, but the case I was working led my partner and me to Germany. Our commanding officer contacted the MP battalion there, and they sent Alie—their best investigator—to assist us. Like I've told you before, as it turned out, I wouldn't be alive now, if it hadn't been for Alie's quick thinking and dead aim."

Alie laughed.

"No, seriously," Murphy said. "Few would've had the foresight—and guts—to take that shot."

"It seemed like a good idea at the time. But don't be modest. I understand you encountered the same circumstances with one of your own partners."

Tara looked shocked. "You never told me that, Jack."

"It's not a secret; the subject just never came up. It was a gun smuggling case. We were about to slap the cuffs on the Greek mastermind when Heber—that was my partner—made a misstep. Next thing I know, he had a gun to his head. I couldn't let him be used as a shield, so I took him out of the equation."

Tara said, "You mean you shot him?"

"Like Alie said. It seemed like a good idea at the time, and I saved his life in the process. But Heber wouldn't work with me after that. Requested a transfer back to the States. Danny Burke was my partner when Alie threw in with us." He turned to Alie. "It was Danny who told you about Heber, wasn't it?"

"Yes, but only *after* I'd shot you. He thought it was funny."

Conversation lingered over a third cup of coffee, then they retraced their steps to the motel. The marine layer, almost a daily occurrence, had been replaced by low-hanging dark clouds, the sign of an approaching summer storm. Though for now, the temperature was a pleasant seventy-something.

Back at the motel, Murphy took Tara aside.

"I'll be playing hardball from now on. It's the only way to resolve our potentially fatal problem."

"What are you planning to do, or don't I want to know?"

"I'm going to get the opposition off our backs—once and for all."

"Does that mean what I think?"

"Let's call it self-defense. They're responsible for four deaths, thus far. I'm not going to let them rack up you and me and then disappear. I'm going to fight fire with fire."

She hugged him. "What if it doesn't work out like you think? I don't know how much more of this I can take. I'm so scared."

"I know what I'm doing." He held her at arm's length. "I've been trained to play rough when necessary, and in this instance, failure isn't an option."

"How will you find them?"

"They'll come to me, once I rattle the cage."

49

"Are you sure you don't want to stick around while I set events into motion?" Murphy asked Tara.

"No thanks. I'd just be a fifth wheel, if I stayed. You and Alie can do without the distraction. I'll just head downstairs and watch the kids playing in the pool."

After Tara was gone, they roughed out what Murphy was going to say to Clayton Hayward. As for Alie's part, she was as distant as if her father had been a total stranger. The tape recorder they'd bought the day before came with a small devise for recording phone conversation. Murphy attached it to the receiver and popped in a blank cassette. Then he placed a call to Information and activated the recorder for a trial run. Everything worked fine. He erased and rewound the tape.

While Murphy pawed through his wallet for Hayward's number, Alie simply handed him the receiver and dialed.

"Same number I had growing up." She then cozied up on the couch where she could hear what her father had to say as Murphy attempted to work his magic.

After seven rings, Murphy was about to hang up when Alberto answered, "Hayward Residence."

"Get your boss on the line," Murphy growled. "Tell him

it's Jack Murphy."

A few moments passed. Alberto must've had his hand loosely over the mouthpiece, because only muffled words could be heard.

At last, Hayward spoke, "Jack, where have you been keeping yourself? I've been trying to find you the last couple of days."

"I'll bet you have. No doubt you're more than a little worried."

"Worried...?"

"*Cut the crap, Hayward!* You know goddam well this has been a farce from the beginning."

"I have no idea what you're talking about, Jack, but I find your tone most curious."

"My *tone?*" Murphy chuckled. "Well, I guess I'm just a little cranky about being used. You hired me to find your missing son when you knew he'd already been murdered to keep your secret world from unraveling."

"I really—"

"Save your breath, because I've got what your goons missed: Charlie's complete backup documentation for the story he was pursuing—tape recordings and all. That's really what you paid me to find, wasn't it? So let me give you your money's worth—a synopsis along with some conjecture on my part: It all began when Gordon Kane phoned Charlie at the *Times*, explaining that he'd once worked security at Northrop Aircraft and had reason to believe one of the engineers was a foreign agent. Of course, this piqued Charlie's interest, and they agreed to talk face to face. Charlie arranged a time and Kane, having since moved to Nevada, chose the location.

"It was in Charlie's room at the Sands Hotel that Kane unfolded his story, identifying the man in question as Klaus Hoffmann, who'd been brought to the States after the war along with a host of other German scientists. Hoffmann was already well entrenched at Northrop when Kane started working there after an Army stint in Korea. Kane admitted that he'd never been a fan of welcoming our enemies with open arms. This nagged at him until one night while working a graveyard shift, he took a look at Hoffmann's personnel file. Inside, he found a copy of the original vetting document, completed by the State Department in the months following the war. He jotted down a few notes.

"Then an unexpected opportunity arose. Kane was sent to Europe to do background investigations on a handful of prospective employees. It was while there that he decided to satisfy his curiosity about Hoffmann. What he dug up was someone who claimed to have been Hoffmann's lover the last two years of his life. She swore that he'd been killed when the factory they worked in was targeted in an Allied bombing raid. She even produced a photograph of them together.

"This was a staggering piece of news for Kane: The Klaus Hoffmann he knew was not the man in the photo. Wheels started to turn, and when they ground to a halt, the only conclusion he could draw was that an imposter had been given access to industry secrets for twenty years. But by the time he got back to the States, his exuberance had waned some. After all, the man claiming to be Hoffmann was now a nationally respected scientist, and Kane's evidence—that photograph— was anything but ironclad.

"Long story short: Kane left Northrop for greener pastures in Las Vegas. Months passed, but the prospect of Hoffmann being a spy weighed heavily on him; hence, his call to Charlie. The thought being that as an investigative reporter, he might be willing to run with it. Which he did. But no one at the *Times* had any idea what he was working on. He became secretive, as he tried to connect all the dots. Kane's paranoia had become contagious. Charlie even bought a gun, recognizing that he was playing with fire. However, he never envisioned that the danger of uncovering a clandestine operation lay closer to home. Neither he nor Kane had considered that Hoffmann might have an accomplice. A fatal oversight. But even if they'd pursued that line of reasoning, they'd have come up short, because Hoffmann didn't have an accomplice. Hoffmann *was* the accomplice. The Soviets already had an agent in place

251

when he arrived. And that agent was you, Hayward. It wasn't until after your accident and retirement from Northrop that Hoffmann became their primary asset."

50

"What have you been smoking, Jack? Dutch Cleanser? You've missed your calling. You should be writing scripts for movies."

"Bear with me, then, while I wrap it up. Now, Charlie wasn't new to the game. He would've realized that a story of this magnitude would require investigation beyond his capabilities. He also would've concluded that the paper's legal eagles would certainly weigh in. They'd reason he might well have uncovered decades of espionage, but the prudent thing to do would be for him to turn over what he had to federal authorities. And for that eventuality, Charlie had gathered up everything he had compiled and sent it to his post office box for safekeeping. Then he hid the key that only just recently came into my possession.

"But now getting back to you. Charlie was so frustrated by the thought that the story of his career was slipping through his fingers, that he broke his silence and phoned you to commiserate. Now, it's my guess he didn't share Hoffmann's name, only that there was a foreign agent working at Northrop. But he didn't have to confide a name for the alarm to sound. Aside from Hoffmann, your own self-preservation had been thrust front and center. Once you hung up from Charlie, you contacted your superiors. I'd like to think you did so *reluctantly*, since you'd have had some idea of what would follow. First, Hoffmann was spirited out of the country—a supposed well-deserved extended vacation. There was presumably no connection to you, so you remained in place to orchestrate the proceedings. But Charlie had to be taken out of circulation ASAP. Under torture by the 'clean-up' team, he gave up Gordon Kane, the other person who knew about Hoffmann. As to why he didn't tell them about his post office box and the location of the key, I can only assume his interrogators got too extreme in their technique, and he died prematurely. Just like they went overboard with Gordon Kane before he could divulge that his wife had also been read into the Hoffmann affair. But they eventually remedied that when they started tailing me, and I inadvertently led them to her door. She became the third murder victim. And then there was my partner. He would've undoubtedly experienced the same treatment if his heart hadn't given out first."

Murphy paused for Hayward's response.

"As I said before, Jack, you have a fertile imagination."

"I'm just a penny-ante private eye. I know I can't *prove* any of this. I'm like Charlie; I don't have the resources. But the FBI does. And when Hoffmann doesn't return to work, they're going to dig deep, and they're going to find you. But listen, I don't want to turn this stuff over to the feds. The only thing I'd get out of it would be a pat on the back. 'Atta boy, Murphy. Good job. We'll take it from here.'"

"What exactly are you saying?" Hayward's tone was one of caution.

"That what's done is done. You and Hoffmann passed secrets to the Russkies over a long period of time. Whatever damage you inflicted would only be a matter of record. Hoffmann's flown the coop, and your apprehension—although fodder for front page headlines—would be like closing barn doors after the horses have fled. Of course, you're an accessory to four murders—if I count my partner—but what the hell. Your arrest won't bring them back, either. So what I'm suggesting is that you and I make a deal."

"Such as...?"

"Quid pro quo. First, you call off your dogs. Being a candidate for murder number five doesn't set well with me. Then I'll turn over to you everything Charlie had on Hoffmann in exchange for a lifestyle more befitting my station. You see, my Army pension barely keeps me in cigarettes, and the gumshoe gig has its limitations. I don't aspire to a life like yours, but I'd like to have enough dough to live comfortably. We'll treat this whole sordid affair as if it never happened, with the exception of your bank account being a little lighter."

Silence on Hayward's end.

"The no-haggle amount is a cool one million dollars. Chump change to someone like you. But if it'll make you feel any better, it's not all for me. I'll be giving my late partner's kids a chunk so they can go to college. It's only fair, considering I roped him into helping me with this case."

More silence.

"You can't seriously be thinking of turning me down. You've been running a shell game for years without detection, but when the FBI gets wind... Look, I'm giving you a way out—for Alie's sake, if nothing else. I'm even willing to take a down payment to seal the agreement. We can work out the details on the balance later. C'mon, don't be stupid. Hoffmann's gone, and you're left holding the bag. Take my offer."

Hayward finally said, "And what guarantee do I have that you won't continue to bleed me?"

"Experience has taught me there are no guarantees in life, except death. But from where I stand now, I can't foresee a circumstance where I'd renege on the arrangement."

"The quintessential honest man, huh? That's how Alynn described you when she recommended your services." Hayward chuckled. "I'd say her judgment was flawed. By the way, what are you going to tell her? She's bound to ask about her brother."

"I'm going to tell her the truth: You hired me to find him,

and I struck out. It's the nature of the business. You win some; you lose some. Besides, she doesn't give a shit about him, anyway. Of course, if she ever found out about the lie you've been living for her entire life, she'd slip the noose around your neck and spring the trapdoor, herself. And I doubt she'd shed any tears."

"No, I presume not. In any event, how much of a 'down payment,' as you say, do you require?"

"Let's say ten percent as a show of good faith. That shouldn't pose much of a burden. You've probably got that much cash just lying around."

Hayward laughed. "You overestimate the liquidity of the rich, Jack, but I think I can come up with that amount all right. When do you want it?"

"Today. Or, rather, this evening."

"Will you be coming here for it?"

Murphy laughed. "I was born at night, Hayward, but I wasn't born *last* night. No, I'll let you know where to take it, so stick close to the phone."

"And in return you'll give me Charlie's documentation."

"Yep. Every bit of it. But don't think about stiffing me on the rest of my money."

"How could I? You've got me over a barrel."

"And don't you forget it."

51

Murphy returned the phone receiver to its cradle, then snapped off the tape recorder and removed the cassette. He jotted the time and date on the label and tossed it onto the coffee table.

"That's that." He sat back on the couch and laced his hands behind his neck.

"Did you detect any remorse in his tone?" Alie asked. "Because I certainly didn't."

"No, his responses were very measured."

"Well, so much for your idea of my father as a tragic figure, 'caught between a rock and a hard place,' as they say. No, he threw everyone away who once loved him. Charlie is just an extreme example. The man is to be loathed, not pitied. And his treason will seal his fate." She paused, then asked, "Do you think he believed you about 'quid pro quo' and letting bygones be bygones?"

Murphy sat upright. "Not for a second. He hasn't lasted this long by being stupid. In his mind, I'm the one who's naïve enough to think I can run with the big boys and finish out in front. He's probably on the phone right now with whomever. And he's being told to play along until they can get me in their sights. Which means I've got to figure a way to give myself an edge."

"You mean give *us* an edge. I've changed my mind about letting you do this alone. We're a team, remember?"

"Listen, Alie, if what I'm planning goes sour, Tara will likely be their next target—just to wipe the slate clean. I need you to make sure that doesn't happen."

"I understand, but I don't like the thought of you being outnumbered *and* presumably outgunned. But okay. What do you want me to do? Stay here with her?"

"No need. We came here when I figured they were searching for us. Now they know I intend to make an appearance. They'll hang close to your father to find out where. So, I'm thinking the coast is clear. We'll check out of here. You and Tara take the rental. Set up shop at her pub. I'll retrieve my own car from the airport and get on about throwing a monkey wrench into what they have planned for me."

While Murphy settled the motel bill, Alie and Tara stowed the bags in the trunk of the rental car. Tara had been told of the plan, after which she'd broken down.

"I already lost my father to violence," she'd said between sobs. "I couldn't bear losing you the same way. You don't have to be a hero on my account."

"I'm no hero, Tara. I just can't let them disappear into the shadows. Call it justice. Call it revenge. Call it whatever you like, but this won't be a showdown like you see in cowboy movies, where the good guy faces the desperados in the middle of a dusty street and the fastest draw wins. I have no intention of giving them a fair chance."

With Alie behind the wheel, Murphy exited the backseat at the airport. He came around to the open passenger window and leaned in.

"Wish me luck."

Tara grabbed him around the neck and kissed him.

"Come back safe, darling. There's a lot more where that came from."

52

Murphy watched the car as it melted into traffic and was gone. He then found his own, paid the parking fee, and headed into Inglewood. Doyle had told him that Charlie Hayward had bought his gun at Mel's Sporting Goods near the corner of Crenshaw and Imperial. It wasn't that far away. He found a spot up the street and walked back. It had started to drizzle since leaving the airport, and he hurried.

On the inside of the display window, a painted sign proclaimed a summer sale, with 20%-30% off selected items. A bell jingled above the door as he entered. Business must've been slow, because he was the only customer. A stout, red-haired man, sporting a neatly trimmed beard and wearing a plaid shirt, looked up and greeted him jovially from behind the sales counter that ran the length of one wall.

"What can I do you for, or are you just dodging the rain?"

"I'm looking to buy a rifle." Murphy approached.

"I've got a pretty good selection. What are you planning to use it for? Hunting?"

"Yeah."

"Big game or small?"

"Never know what I might run into. What've you got that'll

do double duty?"

The man turned to survey the wall rack of rifles and shotguns. Murphy noticed he was missing two fingers from his right hand and three from his left. An angry-looking scar began above his hairline and disappeared beneath his shirt collar.

"That leaves out the .22 calibers," he said over his shoulder. "They're more suited for plinking at birds and varmints. Maybe a lever-action Winchester." He took it down. "This is the rifle that won the West. And it can be fitted with a scope for more accuracy at long distances."

"I don't think so." Murphy had taken stock of the display, as well. "What about that M1 carbine over there?" He pointed to the used section on the end.

"Ah, a man who knows his weapons, I see." He replaced the Winchester, took down the carbine, and gave it to Murphy to examine. "I got this just the other day at an estate sale. I've been through it. Excellent condition. My guess is the former owner picked it up after the war—they were a dime-a-dozen then—and it never left the closet."

Murphy extracted the magazine, locked back the operating slide, turned the breach toward the light, and peered down the barrel.

"Clean as a whistle, all right." He snapped the magazine back in and placed the rifle on the counter.

"You know, I haven't seen anyone do that move since my Army training days." He gestured over his shoulder to a black and white photograph on the wall. It showed a group of soldiers in battle gear and parachutes. "That's me in the middle. Twenty years old, full of piss and vinegar, and shit for brains."

"Airborne infantry, huh?"

"505th." He briefly held up his mangled hands. "Bailed out over Sicily in '42. Hit the ground okay, but then the Krauts and Eyeties lobbed a few mortar rounds in our general direction. Shrapnel. But I got no complaints. As it turned out, I missed the rest of the war." He shrugged. "Who knows? Maybe something worse might've happened."

260

He offered his right hand for Murphy to shake. His grip was surprisingly powerful, despite his injuries.

"Name's Mel Osborne. I own the place."

"Jack Murphy. Lifer. Enlisted after Pearl Harbor. Retired last year from CID."

"I had you figured as ex-military the moment you walked in the door. So what are you doing now, if you don't mind me asking, or are you just living off that generous army pension?" He laughed.

"Don't I wish, but no. I'm a private investigator." Murphy dug a card out of his wallet and gave it to him.

Osborne studied it. "Downtown address. So what brings you out this far to buy a rifle? "

"I happened to be out this way on a case." Then he embellished the story a little. "Plus, you were recommended by a friend of mine."

"Oh, who's that?"

"Charles Hayward."

Osborne thought for a moment. "Hayward…Hayward..."

"Reporter for the *Times*," Murphy prompted.

"Oh, right. I remember now. When he first came in, I thought he looked familiar. It turned out it was from his picture in the paper. Nice guy. Real personable. Said he needed a gun for personal protection but didn't want anything complicated. He settled for a .38 snubby. I told him if he ever got in a situation where his life was in jeopardy, he should just keep pulling the trigger until it went *click*. The Golden Rule: *Do unto them before they do unto you.*"

"Good advice. I think I'll take it to heart, myself. Now about this carbine. I noticed your sign says you've got an indoor range. Would it be possible for me to fire a couple rounds to zero it in?"

"Sure, that's the whole purpose." He then called to the teenager who was straitening shelf merchandise. "Billy, I'll be out back. Try not to give away the store while I'm gone."

"I'll do my best, Uncle Mel." He didn't even look up from his work.

"My sister's boy," Osborne explained.

He then grabbed the carbine in one hand and reached under the counter with the other for a box of ammunition.

"This way," he said.

The well-lighted concrete bunker extending behind the store was maybe twelve feet wide and seventy-five deep. Double stacks of sandbags lined the walls. There was a single shooting station. And at the far end, a red and black bull's-eye target hung suspended from a ceiling-installed pulley system.

Osborne ejected the ten-round magazine and laid the rifle down. With some dexterity difficulty, he fed in three cartridges. Then he snapped the magazine back into its housing and released the operating slide, sending a cartridge into the breach. He engaged the safety and laid the rifle on the shooting stand, the barrel pointing down range.

"Locked and loaded. Ready when you are. It should be like riding a bicycle. You never forget how."

Murphy shrugged out of his jacket and shoulder holster and laid them aside. It had been a *very* long time since he'd even touched an M1, and he tried to remember his experiences with it—not all of them good, though insightful.

Lighter and more compact, the semi-automatic M1 carbine was welcomed by U.S. troops as a replacement for its larger predecessor, the M1 Garand, referred to by General George Patton as "the greatest battle implement ever devised." But then *he* didn't have to lug it around. The smaller carbine version, however, had a serious flaw: inadequate penetration and stopping power. A .45 caliber round fired from the proven Thompson sub-machine gun put a man down. Period. But with a .30 caliber carbine, frontline troops often complained of the enemy advancing and returning fire despite taking a slug.

Murphy slid a pair of supplied ear protectors onto his head, then leaned over the stand and threaded his left arm through the rifle's canvas sling affixed for shoulder carry. It fit tight against his forearm and elbow. He was encouraged that it felt natural. Maybe Osborne was right. Maybe it *was* like riding a bike.

The undercarriage of the rifle partially rested on a rolled up woolen Army blanket bound with duct tape at the ends. Levering off the safety with his right thumb, he squinted through the rear peep sight and lined up the bottom of the small red circle with the top of the barrel's front blades. He took a breath, let part of it out slowly, and squeezed off a round. The rifle bucked in his hands but not as much as he remembered from his combat days. He reengaged the safety, disentangled from the sling and stood up, leaving the rifle leaning on the blanket support.

Pulling the protectors from his ears, he said, "Reel in the target, would you? I'd like to see just how rusty I am after all these years."

Osborne activated the pulley motor and the target approached until it was a foot away from the stand. There was a hole three inches immediately to the left of the X in the bull's-eye.

Osborne said, "I assume you aimed dead center."

"Yep."

Osborne hefted the rifle and rotated the right windage knob adjacent to the rear sight. He stopped after three clicks.

"That should do it." He handed it back to Murphy. "Give it another try. Fire both remaining rounds this time."

Osborne reset the target and stood by, looking down range, fingers in his ears. Murphy again assumed the firing position and unleashed two rounds in rapid succession, after which he stepped back from the stand and waited for the results as the target again neared. Not quite in the center of the red circle but close enough. And both telltale holes could've been covered with a nickel.

"Well..." Osborne mused. "Looks to me like you've still got the touch. Nice shooting. You shouldn't have to adjust the elevation for any target less than 100 yards."

"I'll keep that in mind."

Murphy put his shoulder holster back on and then his jacket.

"So what's the price for this fine piece of military hardware?"

Osborne didn't hesitate. "$29.95. And you won't find a

better price anywhere else."

"Sold."

"I'll even throw in a new box of shells."

"No need. I'll just take what's left of this one. Should be plenty."

Back inside the store, Osborne wrapped the rifle in brown butcher paper and put the box of ammunition in a bag. Murphy paid for it, then slid two additional fifty-dollar bills across the counter.

"What's that for?" Osborne looked confused.

"A little extra for your time and trouble and expertise."

"A hundred bucks? I couldn't possibly—"

"Nonsense. It's not really my money. Accept it in recognition of service to your country from a wealthy client of mine. I hear he lights his cigars with them. You'll put them to better use, I'm sure."

Osborne beamed. "I'll say. I've got a daughter enrolling at Cal-State in the fall. This'll about cover her first year's tuition and books."

"Money well spent, then." Murphy extended his hand which Osborne shook. "Thanks again for your help."

"And good hunting to you."

53

During the time that Murphy was inside, the drizzle had turned into a downpour—just shy of cats and dogs—which was driven by gale force winds. Head down, leaning into the resistance, he dashed to his car and deposited the rifle and ammunition in the trunk and was thoroughly soaked by the time he got in behind the wheel. He took a folded handkerchief from his trouser pocket and blotted dry his face and neck as he watched water cascade down the windshield. Los Angeles needed the rain. The television weathermen had been saying it was a dryer than usual summer, and that the fire danger in the surrounding foothills had reached critical levels. But getting a season's worth in one day caused other problems, most notably erosion and flooding where previous years' fires had destroyed vegetation.

Murphy first fired up a cigarette, then the car's engine, and merged into traffic. He'd told Tara that he'd need an edge, because he'd be going up against a well-trained opposition at the top of their game. The rifle would ostensibly allow him to confront them from a distance, but he still required a location where he wouldn't be set upon by cops even before the gun smoke cleared. If he'd lived in LA longer, a perfect spot might've come to mind. As it was, he could think of only two possibilities. He'd never actually visited either one, but he'd driven by both while pursuing other cases.

Griffith Park was situated above Los Feliz Boulevard in Hollywood. A popular destination for locals and tourists, its three thousand acres were home to golf courses, hiking and equestrian trails, picnic spots, and a zoo. And at the southernmost end, the Greek Theater could seat over five thousand for performances under the stars, which could be seen in their own right from the adjacent observatory on the slopes of Mount Hollywood.

Murphy circumvented the park and entered from the north, crossing the Los Angeles River via Victory Boulevard. Due to the rain that hadn't let up since he'd left Inglewood, the place was deserted with the exception of a few parked cars at the zoo, which he assumed belonged to personnel. But even if the entrance sign hadn't indicated that the park closed at ten p.m., and was routinely patrolled by rangers during the day and after hours, Murphy saw immediately that it didn't suit his needs. The terrain was simply too open, owing to large expanses of grass. And what cover there was would've been too far off the beaten path to entice his targets. He left by the south exit and headed toward his next destination.

The Hollywood Reservoir, located high in the hills above the iconic intersection of Hollywood and Vine was one of the best kept secrets in LA. Most Angelenos were even oblivious to its existence, despite the fact that the dam had been around since the mid-1920s, having been constructed by William Mulholland, then LA's visionary water commissioner.

After a couple false turns, Murphy found the parking area on the south end overlooking the dam. A single car occupied a stall closest to the entrance. Murphy pulled in next to it and switched off the ignition. From where he sat, the pedestrian entrance looked to be part of a wider vehicular gate topped with barbed wire. Beyond was a garage structure with its overhead door open. Inside, Murphy could make out the back end of an Army Jeep still painted olive-drab green. He assumed the car he'd parked beside belonged to staff, but he saw no one walking about.

Adjacent to the gate was a covered payphone kiosk, and next to it, beneath a sheet of plastic or glass, appeared to be an outline of the lake. Taking advantage of a lull in the rain, he hustled over for a closer look. The map identified the asphalt trail that skirted the banks of the lake and numerous proscribed picnic spots. Two other access points to the fenced area were also noted. One was on the north end, and the other farther to the east, each with a payphone, according to the symbols on the drawing.

A metal sign affixed over the walk-in gate indicated that only pedestrian and bicycle traffic were allowed; dogs were forbidden; fishing was permitted without a license; and users were expected to carry out whatever they carried in. Summer hours were shown as 8:00 a.m. to 10:00 p.m. Unlike Griffith Park, however, there was no indication that the area was patrolled after closing. From what Murphy had seen so far, the heavily wooded terrain seemed okay, although he decided the two other access points were better suited because they appeared—at least in the drawing—to be more remote.

Now back in the car, he took a circular northwestern route past Forest Lawn Cemetery and onto Lake Hollywood Drive. From there, roadside signs pointed the way to the north and east gates. All along that stretch, parking was limited to the shoulders of the road, and due to the rain which had started up again with a vengeance, there wasn't a car in sight.

Murphy pulled over just prior to the east gate and surveyed the area. Beyond the chain link fence, the reservoir was clearly visible to the south, as was the reverse side of the Mulholland Dam. He surmised that had it not been for the low cloud cover, he might've had a spectacular view of the LA Basin.

He listened to the radio while he smoked another cigarette, hoping the rain would subside long enough for him to get a better sense of the terrain. When it didn't, he cursed under his breath and left the shelter of the car. Immediately, he could feel the rain run down the back of his neck and under his collar.

The setup for the payphone and map of the lake duplicated that of the south gate. He stepped under the covered kiosk and checked for a dial tone. Then to make sure it was fully operational, he dialed the operator. He hung up when a woman's voice came on the line. Despite the effects of the rain, he could make out deep-tread tire tracks across the dirt shoulder to the gate and figured they'd come from the Jeep he'd seen earlier. He reasoned that the routine was to drive the Jeep up the trail in the morning, unlock the east and north gates, and then repeat the process to lock them at night.

The vehicular gate was hinged to swing inward but was now held in place by a length of chain wrapped around the frame and secured by a padlock. The gate for foot traffic was spring loaded, designed to close on its own after passing through. A shorter chain and lock hung from one of the gate's crossbars.

Murphy entered and walked down the paved path. Maybe fifty yards from the gate a grove of eucalyptus trees sheltered three clusters of concrete tables and benches. On a warm, sunny day, virtually on the banks of the lake, it must've been an inviting picnic site. Today, it was just sodden and dreary.

Murphy slowly turned 360 degrees, studying the terrain. He then walked another hundred feet or so farther on and again looked in all directions. Along the embankment were adequate prospects of cover and concealment. The Army had taught him that no operation ever proceeded as planned, because the enemy was under no obligation to cooperate. Still, how did that adage go about "failing to prepare"?

54

Murphy was shivering by the time he trudged back to the car, bent against the wind and rain. What he wanted most was to shrug out of his soaked clothing and stand under a hot shower. But that would have to wait until after he visited a hardware store. He cranked up the heater full blast and headed back into the city. He'd thought any hardware store would stock what he needed but was mistaken. Third time was the charm. He stashed it in the trunk with the rifle and ammunition. Holing up for the rest of the day was the next order of business.

He parked a street away and approached his house via the alley that bordered the rear of his property. As he neared the back steps to his kitchen, he could see that the window pane in the door had been broken out. He withdrew his .45 and tried the knob. The door was unlocked. He entered cautiously but found no one. The rooms, however, had been tossed; that was obvious. No doubt they'd come looking for him after Matt's death but stayed long enough to search the house. They'd come away with nothing, because there wasn't anything to find. And they wouldn't waste their time looking for him now, knowing he was planning to come out of hiding anyway.

Minutes later, he'd stripped out of this clothes—now lying

in a damp pile on the bathroom floor—and was being pelted with the hottest water he could stand. Chilled to the bone, he vowed to remain there in the steam until the water heater drained. Afterward, he pulled on a pair of jeans and made himself a sandwich, washing it down with a bottle of beer. He'd given a thought to calling Tara, just to hear her voice—Damn! He really was in love—but decided against it. She was already worried about him. Why fan the flames with a phone call? He'd see her soon enough. If he came out of this alive.

Plenty of "iffy" missions had come his way as an Army cop, but he'd always had backup. For what lay ahead, he would've liked to have had Alie at his side, but he couldn't leave Tara exposed. He cursed himself for involving her in the first place. Taking her to Vegas had been a colossal mistake.

So today, he was going solo: judge, jury, and executioner rolled into one. And in the end, there'd be no remorse. They'd be like squashed bugs on the sole of his shoe, easy to scrap off on a doormat and forget.

Murphy hadn't slept well the night before, and running around wet and cold had only dulled his senses more. He needed as much rest as he could get before going into action. Setting the bedside alarm for eight p.m., he laid back and closed his eyes. But he needn't have bothered with the clock. He awoke every half hour or so to check the time. The Army had a name for it: operational jitters. Maybe pilots were well-rested when they flew into battle, but the grunts on the ground were nearly always sleep-deprived and groggy. At the sound of the first shot, however, the adrenaline kicked in. In fact, combat soldiers were adrenaline junkies. And Murphy figured that before this day was over he'd be hopped up, too.

By seven-thirty he was already sitting on the edge of the bed, his throbbing head cradled in his hands. He downed a half-dozen aspirin from a bottle in the bathroom medicine cabinet and then returned to the bedroom for the warmest long sleeve shirt he could find. A pair of athletic socks followed before he visited the closet again. When he'd mustered out of the Army, he'd taken only three clothing items of GI issue: his pair of combat boots, the toes still spit shined beneath the dust; a field jacket; and a matching color knit watch cap.

Suited up, he stood in front of the full length mirror affixed to the rear of the bedroom door. With the exception of the jeans, he might've passed for the same soldier he'd once been about a million years ago, or so it felt. Then as per his daily ritual, he checked the magazine in his .45. Full. He eased back the slide a bit to see a shell in the chamber and stowed the weapon in an outer pocket of the jacket. Out of habit, he stashed his PI credentials in another pocket along with a full pack of cigarettes and his Zippo lighter. This wasn't going to be the night he gave up smoking.

Murphy hurriedly retraced his route back through the alley to his car. The rain continued to fall in biblical proportions, and once back on the road it was obvious the storm drains were having difficulty keeping up. Standing water clogged every intersection, slowing his progress, but he knew he had plenty of time to reach his destination and mentally prepare himself.

That morning, he'd noticed a dirt road traversing the hillside north of the reservoir. Little more than tire tracks through parched sheep grass. He supposed it was used to service the telephone lines that paralleled the winding highway below. The car fishtailed a hundred yards through the mud to a spot where he could see the east gate but wouldn't be noticed by passing traffic—specifically any itinerant cops on patrol. He figured he'd be hard-pressed to come up with a plausible explanation for being parked in the rain, dressed for combat, with an M1 carbine in the trunk. And even less likely telling the story face down in the mud with a cop's knee in his back, slapping on the cuffs.

He had to remind himself to think about what was going right, and not dwell on what could turn to shit in a heartbeat. He focused on what he could see outside. On a different night, this would be a perfect spot for teenagers to watch the sun set and make out. This evening, however, there was absolutely nothing romantic about the view. Obscured by the rain, the reservoir and dam were growing dimmer by the minute, and it wouldn't be long before the area was plunged into darkness.

Cracking his window open just enough to let in some fresh air, he lit a cigarette, then took a long drag and sat back in reflection: The wild goose chase that Clayton Hayward had sent him on would be coming to an end very shortly. Murphy smiled inwardly at the thought of Hayward and his associates huddled up, wondering why he hadn't called to set up the meet, wondering if maybe he'd changed his mind or lost his nerve. But Murphy knew exactly what he was doing. He was keeping them off balance, preventing them from developing a reasoned action plan of their own.

He'd chain-smoked through half a pack when he saw a covered Jeep below, presumably from the north gate, inasmuch as it turned off the highway opposite the east gate, its headlights illuminating the area beyond. There were two occupants. The passenger exited, worked the lock, readjusted the chain, and swung the gate inward. The Jeep drove inside, after which the man on the ground walked the gate back into position, reattached the lock and chain, and secured the pedestrian gate the same way. Then he got back in and the vehicle continued down the path, its taillights finally disappearing in the rain.

Murphy looked at his watch. Nine-thirty. Apparently the patrol had jumped the gun by a half hour, no doubt aware that the place was deserted due to the rain. Now exiting his car, as well, he walked to the rear and unlocked the trunk. He loaded the carbine's magazine with
ten cartridges. He snapped the magazine back into the undercarriage, worked the slide to chamber a round, then again removed the magazine, inserted another cartridge and rammed the magazine home again. One more round probably wouldn't make a difference. On the other hand, he'd hate to come up short in this contest for want of a single bullet.

He left the loaded rifle in the trunk, closed the lid, then backed the car around and headed down the muddy path to the highway.

Showtime.

55

Murphy parked opposite the payphone. Exiting the car, he dug Hayward's number from his wallet. Then depositing a dime in the coin slot, he dialed.

"It's about time, Jack," Hayward answered.

"How did you know it would be me? I'm impressed. I didn't even hear it ring on my end. You must've been sitting with your hand on the receiver. That means you're taking this seriously. As well you should."

"Believe me, I've thought of nothing else since your call this morning."

"Did you get the money?"

"Yes, just as you demanded. One hundred thousand. The balance to be delivered whenever and wherever you prefer."

"Very good. I knew this sordid affair could have an amicable ending. Now here's where you'll take the money tonight."

"Really, Jack, can't we dispense with this cloak and dagger nonsense. Whether you believe me or not, you'd be safe here. Think of us a business partners."

"I'm sure someone in your chain of command would like nothing better than to turn me into a 'silent' partner."

"Undoubtedly, but you and I have an arrangement. My superiors don't like it, but they'll honor it. You can trust me on that score."

"Nevertheless, we'll do this my way."

"Whatever you say. Where do you want to meet?"

"The Hollywood Reservoir. It's deserted this time of night. Go to the east gate. It's normally locked, but I'll have taken care of that by the time you arrive. About fifty yards down the asphalt path are some picnic tables. I'll meet you there after I'm certain you've come alone."

"Sure, sure, but when you say 'alone' I hope you're not expecting me to leave Alberto in the car. He goes where I go."

"I hadn't thought about that, but okay. And remember this: I'll consider any trickery to mean that our agreement is null and void. Which means by sunup the feds will be crawling up your ass."

"Indelicately put, but yes, I understand completely."

"I'm curious. What excuse are you giving your houseboy for this nocturnal behavior?"

When Hayward hesitated, Murphy said, "Oh, I guess I'm a little slow. Alberto is a player. Of course, he'd have to be. You said he was a Cuban exile. I'll bet with a Communist flair. It's been all one big happy family, hasn't it?"

"And even more so since my accident. Alberto has been more like a son to me than a comrade in arms."

"Undoubtedly closer to you than Charlie was, but that's none of my business. What is my business is you getting here ASAP with my money."

"Certainly, but there's no telling how long it'll take to get where you are in this weather. We'll do our best not to keep you waiting, but you'll probably need to cut us some slack."

"You'll find I'm a reasonable man, one with a bright future, thanks to your generous donation. I'm not looking to queer the deal. But let me reiterate one thing: Now that you know where I'll be waiting, don't think about double-crossing me by unleashing those two piss-ant Krauts from Murder Incorporated. Up till now, they've only gone up against targets

274

that didn't shoot back. They'd have to bring their A-game if they came for me. During the war, I killed Germans for sport. I'd like nothing better than to run up my score." The gauntlet had been thrown. "Now get going and don't dawdle."

Of course, Murphy knew Hayward wouldn't be coming. It had never been his intention to keep his end of the bargain. He'd only played the charade to learn Murphy's whereabouts before loosing the hounds. In fact, they were no doubt already on their way.

Murphy walked to the trunk of his car. Opening it, he reached for the bolt cutter he'd bought at the hardware store. Then with the heavy tool in hand, he paused and stared through the chain link fence, as if in a trance.

"Fuck it!" He tossed the cutter back into the trunk and slammed the lid shut. Then he wiped the rain from his eyes, went back to the phone, and dialed the operator.

"Get me the police," he demanded. "Hollywood Division."

A pause, then, "Sir, that number is—"

"This is an emergency. Just put me through."

A click. "Desk Sergeant Baker."

"Let me speak with the Watch Commander."

"Sir, why don't you just talk to me first? Then if—"

"Trust me, you're going to kick this upstairs anyway, and I don't have the luxury of repeating myself. People have been murdered, and I don't want to be next. Now transfer my call."

The line went dead, and Murphy wondered if he'd been disconnected.

Then, "Lieutenant Snyder. Who am I talking to, and what's this about murder?" He came across as more annoyed than concerned.

"My name is jack Murphy. I'm a private investigator here in LA and—"

"Murphy, huh? Do I know you? Name's familiar."

"I have no idea, but I get around."

"You work alone?"

"Not usually. Listen, I'll give you my life's story later. Right now I'm in a jam that could be fatal if I don't get some reinforcements PDQ."

"Wait a minute. I remember now. Jack Murphy. Matt Doyle's partner in crime. I ran into him just the other day at the Criminal Courts Building. He gave me a business card and identified his partner as Jack Murphy."

"You planning on talking me to death before the bad guys arrive? Because if you are, it'll be less painful for me."

"All right, all right. So what have you and Matt gotten yourselves into that you need the LAPD to resolve?"

"Four murders, one of them being his."

"What? Matt's dead?"

"Saturday afternoon. We were working a case that turned out to be something neither of us had bargained on—espionage. Matt came up short."

"Espionage?"

"Yeah, complete with foreign agents and assassins. Look, I can explain all this later, but for now, those responsible for Matt's death are headed my way. I need a reception committee."

"Where are you?"

"Hollywood Reservoir. I'm parked at the east gate."

"How long have we got?"

"That'll depend on road conditions in this rain, but I'd say no longer than an hour."

"Okay. Stay put. I'll divert some units to your location. They'll undoubtedly get there before I do. For Matt's sake, I'm going to oversee this operation *personally*."

Murphy got back into his car, this time on the passenger side. If forced into a shootout before the cops arrived, he could roll out and use the car for cover. He transferred his pistol from his pocket to his lap, then lit another cigarette and watched the rain pelt the windshield.

He'd come prepared to solve this problem himself. Why had he suddenly changed course and brought in the police? Alie had had more sense than he. She'd balked at the notion of 'vigilante justice,' despite his argument for it. Yes, he'd killed men before, but he'd never lain in wait to do it, except in battle, and this wasn't war.

Instead, he'd let the police pull triggers on the Germans, because he was sure they wouldn't go down without a fight. Then he'd identify Hayward and Alberto as accomplices. He was pretty sure that on his say so the cops would hold them long enough to go through the evidence. After all, Hayward had all but confessed on tape and had agreed to pay a bribe to keep the affair in the closet.

But for now, it was a waiting game.

56

Only two cars had passed since Murphy had gotten off the phone with Snyder. Both times he'd slouched in his seat, and his index finger tightened involuntarily on the trigger of his pistol.

He checked his watch again. Barely a minute had ticked by since the last time he'd looked. Slow motion. Where were the cops? Being alone didn't give him the warm fuzzies. He was about to retrieve the rifle from the trunk, just in case the Germans arrived before the cops did, when the first of the black and whites rounded the curve of the road to the east, its headlights illuminating the diagonally driven rain. It was followed by two others, caravan-style. Murphy put the .45 back in the pocket of his jacket, exited the car, and stood by the left front fender. The lead patrol car stopped opposite him, and the driver rolled down the window. He wore a yellow rain slicker, and his cap was covered in plastic.

"You Jack Murphy?"

Yeah." He stepped closer and displayed his badge and ID.

"I'm Sergeant Wilson. The Lieutenant's not far behind. We'll figure the best way to deploy when he gets here. Hop in the backseat with us for now."

With that, the other two cruisers followed his lead, pulling to the side of the road and idling their engines.

The similarly dressed patrolman riding shotgun turned in his seat. "So you're a private eye, huh? Anything like Mickey Spillane writes about?"

"If you mean sleek cars and beautiful women clients who fall into your arms, then I'm afraid not. For the most part, being a private investigator is short on action and long on paperwork. This case is more the exception than the rule, and I appreciate you guys coming to the rescue."

"'*to protect and to serve*.' That's our motto," the patrolman said. "But you know what? I've been on the force two years, and I've never taken my service revolver out of the holster except on the firing range and to clean it."

Murphy was about to tell him he should consider himself lucky when Wilson checked his side view mirror.

"Lieutenant's here," he said over his shoulder, then opened his door and got out. His partner did the same, and Murphy followed suit. The cops in the other cars emptied out, as well, and came forward.

Snyder's unmarked car pulled alongside. He was the only occupant. He left it idling and crossed in front. Like the others, he wore a yellow slicker over his uniform. Murphy judged him to be in his early thirties, and by his bearing, a take charge kind of guy.

He held out his hand. "Lieutenant Snyder."

"Jack Murphy."

Snyder then said, "I thought over what you told me on the phone. I don't much give a shit about foreign spies—let the feds deal with them; they're making the big bucks. We're going to treat this as a cop killer response, as if Matt Doyle had still been on the job." He then addressed the men who'd gathered around. "Are we clear about what that means?"
They all nodded they understood.

Murphy was pretty sure what Snyder meant: Shoot at the slightest provocation and fill in the holes afterward. Army cops had the same credo when one of their own had been taken out by the opposition.

Snyder turned back to Murphy. "If they're coming here, there's only two ways in: The way we came or up ahead. What's your guess?"

"Unless there's something I haven't considered, they'll have started out from Bel Air..." he looked at his watch, "...about forty minutes ago. Matt got a look at what they were driving as of Saturday: a white Lincoln Town Car. I doubt they've seen a need to swap vehicles since."

Snyder nodded. "You've been here awhile. What's the traffic been like?"

"Two guys in a Jeep came to lock the gate to the reservoir about nine-thirty. Since then, only a couple cars have passed by. Both westbound."

"I like that, because we're going to concentrate on what comes from up ahead. That's the logical route from Bel Air. Nevertheless, we'll isolate this place from the east by putting up a roadblock back down the way we got here. Anybody shows, they'll be told there's a landslide blocking the road."

Snyder surveyed the line of police cruisers. "Whoever's in the last unit, take care of that roadblock. Set your radio for operational communication. Go."

Two men peeled off and sprinted back to their car.

"We'll set up another right here." Snyder then looked at the two men who had spoken with Murphy. "Wilson, Zimmerman. You take my car. Find a vantage point to monitor the road without being seen."

Murphy said, "There's a muddy utility access road down a ways on the right. It's got a decent view."

"You heard him," Snyder said. "Sing out when you see anyone coming. If it's the Lincoln, swing in behind. We'll have them bottled up between us. Now get going."

They sped off. Snyder and the remaining two men positioned the two cars across both lanes, roof-mounted lights flashing. Everyone stood behind the vehicles, using them as shields. Snyder took the shotgun from the cab of Wilson's car and racked in a shell. One of the other officers did the same.

"Always more intimidating this way," Snyder said to Murphy. "Makes people think twice about running a blockade."

Those at the roadblock to the east radioed that they were in position but that the area seemed deserted, undoubtedly because of the storm.

Snyder glanced over at Murphy. "You armed?"

"Yeah, an Army Colt." He decided not to mention the rifle in his trunk. It would only complicate matters by prompting questions he'd prefer not answering.

"Well, there's no better time, wouldn't you say? Follow my lead if the situation heats up."

Murphy extracted the .45 from his jacket pocket and checked that the safety catch was disengaged.

No more than a minute later, Wilson's voice came on the radio.

"Headlights coming up the road. Can't make out the...yes, it's a white Lincoln. Two occupants in the front seat."

Snyder keyed the mike. "Close the back door."

57

Shafts of light cut through the rain as the Lincoln rounded the bend in the road and swerved to a stop on the wet asphalt. Snyder's car, its portable roof light flashing red, white and blue, pulled into view maybe thirty yards behind and straddled the road. Both officers exited and drew their weapons, using the car for cover.

Murphy and the others squinted and shielded their eyes against the headlights that suddenly went to high beam. The Lincoln remained motionless.

Snyder said to man next to him, "Anderson, pass me the bull horn."

Anderson reached into the backseat for it and held it out for Snyder to take.

Snyder put it to his lips and bellowed, "Step out of the vehicle, your hands above your heads."

If it hadn't been raining, and if the Lincoln hadn't been facing them head on, they might've seen the passenger window lower, a prelude to what would happen over the next fifteen seconds.

Snyder was about to make encore demands when the Lincoln lurched forward, its rear tires struggling to gain traction as the driver gunned the engine. At the same time, muzzle flashes erupted from the passenger side. A barrage of bullets thudded into the police cruisers, shattering windows and blowing tires. Anderson caught a slug that ripped through his yellow slicker and threw him to the ground as if he'd been jerked by a tether from behind. Braving the continued onslaught, Snyder and the other officer blasted away.

Murphy held his fire. The effective range for a .45 caliber pistol was under twenty-five yards, and he'd be wasting rounds if he squeezed off any now.

The shotguns appeared to have had no effect as the Lincoln now barreled toward the hillside, attempting to make an end run.

Then the automatic weapons fire died—maybe for the shooter to change magazines. Murphy went into action. Bracing himself against the doorframe, and using both hands to steady the heavy pistol, he fired all eight rounds in rapid succession, the last followed by a *click!* as the slide locked back. The car jacked sharply in front of the blockade and crashed through the chain link fence of the reservoir perimeter.

Officers Wilson and Zimmerman were immediately on the scene. On Snyder's orders Zimmerman radioed the other roadblock with what had happened, telling then to remain in place to isolate the area from that location. Anderson's partner had already called for paramedics and was working to staunch the flow of blood from the severe shoulder wound.

Wilson held a flashlight as he and Snyder approached the crash site with revolvers drawn. They needn't have bothered. Murphy knew he'd headshot both of them—twice. He joined them at the bottom of the embankment. The Lincoln had rolled and come to rest on its roof, the two occupants entangled in what could've been construed as a macabre bloody embrace.

The engine was still running and the rear wheels spinning. Wilson reached inside the cabin and switched off the ignition.

Snyder asked Murphy, "Were you expecting one of them to be a woman?"

"Yeah, but only Matt actually saw her. They got to him

only minutes after he gave me a rough description."

Wilson crawled half inside the passenger window and went through the pockets of the man, looking for identification. He had something in his hand when he withdrew.

"The guy had this on him." He handed it to Snyder. "German passport."

Snyder turned to the front inside page. Wilson focused the flashlight on it.

"Helmut Stoltz," Snyder said. "A Heidelberg address."

"The woman should have one similar," Murphy said. "They're bound to be forgeries. People like this don't travel under their real names. When you get around to taking fingerprints, the FBI or Interpol may have something on file. Given the woman's age, I doubt this was her maiden voyage."

Wilson said, "I don't see the weapon they used."

"Well, it's got to be around somewhere," Snyder replied. "We didn't imagine it; just ask Anderson. It probably ejected when the car rolled."

Wilson slowly painted the area around the vehicle with the flashlight.

"There," he finally said. The weapon was lodged in a clump of scrub oak. He retrieved it by the trigger guard. "I've never seen one like this." He held it out.

"I have," Murphy said. "It's a Skorpion submachine gun. The Czechs developed it a few years back. It has a pistol grip but can be shoulder fired by flicking back this metal stock assembly." He pointed to it. "A little like the Sten 'grease guns' that we and the British used during the war. In any event, it's designed to inflict a lot of damage in a very short period of time. On full automatic, they'd go through that twenty-round magazine in the blink of an eye. That's why they fired in short bursts to conserve ammunition. And they had the upper hand until they stopped to swap out magazines."

Snyder and Murphy were halfway back up the slope when Wilson stopped them.

"Lieutenant, you better come look at this."

Flashlight in hand, Wilson was on his haunches at the rear

of the car. The trunk lid was slightly ajar. Snyder and Murphy joined him and bent down to see what he'd found.

"What the…" Snyder started, then, "Let's get it open."

Murphy jumped up on the car and kicked at the underside of the lid's edge with the heel of his combat boot. At last, the damaged locking mechanism gave way and two lifeless bodies tumbled out.

Murphy jumped down.

Snyder crouched over the corpses. Both had been shot at close range, as evidenced by powder burns around the bullet hole in each of their foreheads.

"What do you make of this, Murphy?" Snyder asked. "Any idea who they are?"

It suddenly dawned on Murphy what was at stake for Alie if he answered truthfully. But once he started down the path that came to mind, there'd be no going back for either of them.

"The older man is Clayton Hayward; the younger is his houseboy. This case began with Hayward hiring me to find his missing son. Once I'd concluded that he'd been murdered and why, Hayward was insistent on helping to bring the killers to justice." Murphy shook his head. "Sadly, I can see now that I never should've accepted his offer."

Snyder sighed. "Listen, Murphy, this mess is going to take the rest of the night to clean up, and I need to oversee it. There's nothing more you can do here, but I want you in my office at ten a.m. sharp with a complete account of everything. You said espionage, so the Chief will surely want the feds invited."

"Good idea, especially since Hayward's daughter is an FBI agent in Atlanta. She and I were both Army CID agents. I phoned about her brother's death, and she flew out yesterday afternoon."

"Where is she now?"

"I figured if these two bozos somehow got by us, they'd make a play for my fiancée, because she knows what I know. Alie—that's Hayward's daughter—stayed behind to protect her. Apparently, it was her father who was in greater need. In any event, that's where I'm headed now. She'll be devastated when I give her yet more bad news."

Snyder shook his head. "I certainly don't envy you. Good luck."

Murphy said, "I'll see you in the morning then. Put on a pot of coffee. It'll be a long session." He turned to go, then turned back. He held out his pistol by the barrel. "You'll need this for ballistics."

"Oh...yeah... thanks." Snyder stowed it in the pocket of his slicker. "Maybe *you* ought to be running this crime scene instead of me." He smiled for the first time since arriving.

Murphy patted him on the shoulder. "No, I've just had more practice, that's all."

58

Alie met Murphy at the back door of O'Neill's with a .38 caliber revolver in her hand.

"Don't shoot! I'm unarmed." He put his arms in the air in mock surrender.

Tara pushed past her and embraced him.

"Oh, darling." She kissed him long on the lips, then stepped back. "I've been praying all day. I even promised to start going to mass again, if you came back safe."

"Well, here I am. Drenched, but none the worse for wear."

"Mission accomplished?" Ale asked.

"Yeah, but there's been a wrinkle."

She had a quizzical look on her face.

"I'll explain everything, but first I need a drink."

He shed his wet field jacket, draped it over the back of a wooden chair, and sat down with Alie as Tara drew three glasses of Guinness from the tap.

"I closed up early," Tara said. "I wasn't in a mingling mood, and it was a slow night, anyway. Most of the regulars had even stayed away rather than brave the rain, I guess."

Murphy detailed where he'd gone and what he'd done since they'd parted that morning at the motel, culminating with the shootout at Hollywood Reservoir. For all the animosity toward her father, Alie broke down when he got to that part. He had the feeling she was surprised by her own emotions.

When she regained her composure, she said, "But why? He was one of them."

"I don't think we'll ever know definitively, but I'll take a stab at it. They'd gotten their main man—Hoffmann—out, presumably ferried to somewhere safe while your father tried to put things back in order. But the Kremlin—or wherever he got his marching orders—may've concluded that he posed a liability. After all, he'd been in their employ for a long time. If he were arrested, what might he divulge about the Soviet apparatus in the United States, and elsewhere, as part of any deal he'd surely be offered? And that went for Alberto, too, his trusted sidekick. It was just easier for the Reds to cut their losses and call it a day."

"So then why did the Germans come after you? And why carry around two bodies in the trunk?"

"Good question. I think their intention was to dispose of those bodies—and presumably mine—the same way they'd taken care of Charlie's. Never to be found. They'd been flying high throughout this operation but were frustrated when Tara and I dropped out of sight. When I surfaced and provoked them, they couldn't resist. Maybe it's part of the Assassins' Code not to leave a job undone."

"So did you inform the police of my father's role in all this?"

Murphy took a long draught of his drink before answering.

"Not exactly. I…uh…said he was...uh…working with me."

Alie sprang to her feet. "You told them *what?*" She was as mad as she was incredulous. "Have you lost your mind, Jack? We're talking about murder and espionage, here. Not jaywalking."

"Now just calm down a minute. I did this for you. There's no good reason for your father to take you down with him."

"But—"

"But nothing. From the moment I phoned you on Sunday

288

with the news that he was a spy, you knew your days with the FBI were numbered. Let's face the facts. That spiel you gave me about vowing to prove your worth to the Bureau was nothing more than a smokescreen for my benefit. You knew the score. Hoover would never overlook a family flaw as big as yours. He'd put you in front of a firing squad for even being acquainted with a Communist, let alone calling this one 'Dad.'

"Now put your scruples aside, sit back down, and hear me out. We've got a date with the cops at ten in the morning, and we need to be on the same page when we get there."

Murphy waited to flesh out the skeleton of the "official" story he planned to tell to the authorities until Tara had returned from the kitchen with a pile of sandwiches on a platter.

When at last they were all seated at the table, Alie grabbed a half sandwich, took a bite, and said while chewing, "I can hardly wait to hear how you're going to spin this, Jack."

"Well, first and foremost, the only thing implicating your father is the tape recording I made. Gordon Kane never suspected him, and Charlie certainly didn't. For the cops' benefit, I've already painted him as a victim. A man who lost his life by putting himself at risk for a good cause."

"You turned him into a *hero?*" Alie blurted. "Do you suppose there could there be something wrong with this corned beef? Because I'm getting sick to my stomach."

59

They didn't call it a night—or morning—until shortly before three a.m., after which Tara took Alie home with her, and Murphy drove back to his place. Six hours later they met for breakfast at a diner off Hollywood Boulevard. They found a booth in the rear. None had slept well, but a couple cups of coffee brought them back to life. They went over the story one last time. The plan was for Murphy to do most of the talking. They recognized potential holes in the narrative, but he felt sure he could plug them if pressed.

Alie made it known that she had serious doubts about the subterfuge. Giving false or misleading statements was a crime. Murphy then asked her how she'd like to change her name and sell shoes for a living, because being the daughter of a Soviet spy carried with it distinct baggage. Why throw away a career when a little imagination would save it? And who would be hurt? No one. The man posing as Klaus Hoffmann had fled the country. The feds would have enough on their hands trying to determine just how much damage he'd done over the past twenty years. As for the deaths of Gordon and Marjorie Kane, and Matt Doyle, the official causes would be set right, not doubt a comfort to their relatives. Unfortunately, her brother, who began this case as an alleged missing person would, without a corpse, only be presumed dead. But he would be credited for his role in exposing acts of espionage. Whatever useful information Clayton Hayward might've given up had he not been murdered, as well, was now a moot issue. Dead men told no tales.

Alie glanced at her watch and gulped the last of her coffee.

"All right, Jack, you've convinced me. Let's get it over with. And pray that no one calls your bluff."

When they arrived at LAPD's Hollywood Division, they learned that the meeting would be chaired by none other than Chief of Police, William Parker, a gruff, bespectacled man of about sixty who had the reputation of having been around the block a few times. Nothing was likely to faze him. A violent shootout, four corpses, and an officer wounded no doubt demanded his presence, if for no other reason than self-defense. Local petty politicians took delight in criticizing his tenure— Parker had been LA's top cop since 1950—and calls for his ouster were seemingly daily occurrences. It was always thus for big city police executives. Too much policing brought accusations of heavy handedness and being out of touch with the communities being served. Too little and the dialog changed to being soft on crime. But a police-involved gunfight in the sleepy Hollywood Hills would command front page headlines when the details were finally released. As of this morning, however, Parker had ordered a blackout of the event, much to the consternation of reporters beating down his door for information.

Milling about the conference room were: Lieutenant Snyder, whose bloodshot eyes and rumpled uniform proved he'd been up all night; Snyder's boss and desk jockey, Captain Eugene Morse, all spit and polished for the visiting Parker. Next, there was Russell Simpson, Special Agent in Charge of the FBI's Los Angeles Field Office. He was fiftyish, balding, and squat, with the blotchy cheeks of a heavy drinker. Due to malfunctioning air conditioning, he'd already taken off his suit coat and hung on a rack in the corner. Sweat stains bloomed around each armpit of his white button-down shirt. A .38 caliber snub-nosed revolver—standard Bureau issue—rode high on his right hip.

A second FBI man, by the name of Stoddard, also in shirtsleeves, was a good ten years younger, blond, well-tanned, and obviously in much better physical condition than his boss. He, too, sported a snubby, but in a cross-draw holster.

Bureau protocol required Alie to present herself to Simpson before the meeting began. He grunted an acknowledgment without even making eye contact, took his seat, and poured himself another cup of coffee from one of two plastic carafes on the table. Murphy had watched the interchange and figured that beyond his obvious dismissal of female agents, his rudeness might also stem from knowing he'd be on the hook for whatever arose from evidence of espionage. Stoddard, on the other hand, introducing himself as Simpson's assistant, took Alie's hands in his and told her how sorry he was that she was required to be here under such trying circumstances. Murphy liked him immediately.

At last, Captain Morse closed the door, and Parker called the group to order. After everyone was seated, he instructed Murphy to start at the beginning.

Flanked by Tara and Alie, Murphy walked the group through his involvement, most of it exactly as it had transpired: How his services had come to be recommended to Clayton Hayward in the first place. Details of their initial meeting. A father's concern for his son's well-being. The ensuing investigation into Charlie Hayward's disappearance.

"It wasn't until interviewing Marjorie Kane that Klaus Hoffmann's name surfaced. She indicated that her late husband had been suspicious of Hoffmann for some time before leaving Northrop. He'd even compiled a file on him, which was subsequently given to Charlie Hayward to pursue.

"I asked if her husband had retained a copy of that file. She said he hadn't, but I sensed she was lying. However, her future wouldn't have been altered by telling the truth and handing it over to me. The next morning her body was found in her car not far from where her husband had been murdered. The police concluded suicide; a sappy idea that she'd fallen into despondency over her husband's death.

"I came to a different conclusion: She and her husband, as well as Charlie Hayward, had been eliminated. The common thread had to be Hoffmann, but the whys and wherefores remained a mystery. Then I suspected something else; that I was being followed. Though at that point, I didn't know by whom. And I'd led them to Marjorie Kane's door. She was dead because I hadn't fathomed what I was really dealing with."

At this point, Chief Parker called a halt to the proceedings.

"Let's take a five minute break. This morning's coffee has finally caught up with me."

60

Murphy saw that with the exception of Special Agent Simpson, those in the room had simply sat back and listened with interest. Simpson had seldom taken his eyes off the legal-sized yellow pad in front of him, doodling more than taking notes. And when he did look up, his expression registered his skepticism. Was he going to be the proverbial "fly in the ointment" as the story moved into its more inventive phase?

When the group reconvened, Murphy picked up the narrative where it had left off.

"When Tara and I returned from Las Vegas last Friday, I made two phone calls: The first to Clayton Hayward to set up a meeting for the next morning. I wanted to lay out my investigation so far, and my conclusions. Then I called my partner, Matt Doyle. If I was being followed as I thought, I figured maybe he could get photographs of who it was. I chose the Farmer's Market to set up the stakeout. I told him I'd be there sometime around noon—hopefully being tailed."

Murphy then recounted his second—and last—face to face meeting with Hayward, the details largely fictitious to insure that the puzzle pieces would subsequently fit.

"He was waiting alone on the front porch when I drove up.

He gave the impression of someone who'd have been pacing anxiously, if he hadn't been confined to a wheelchair. He told me he'd discovered something disturbing; that his phones had been bugged. While making a call that morning, he'd noted static in the connection. After hanging up, he'd screwed off the mouthpiece cover—an engineer's curiosity to find the source of the problem. That's when he found it. He then checked his other phone. Same thing. He'd left them in place and waited for me to arrive.

"I took a look. Sure enough, there was a gadget in each phone that shouldn't have been there. I had a thought that if someone had gained access to the phones, maybe that same someone had planted listening devices elsewhere in the house. We didn't speak while I gave the place a once-over. Electronic surveillance is out of my line of expertise, so I wasn't surprised that I didn't find anything, although it might've been staring me in the face. But I proceeded on the assumption that our conversations—phone or otherwise—had been monitored all along. And that meant I'd likely picked up a tail right after leaving Hayward's place the first time.

"If you're wondering why his phones would be bugged, I asked myself that question at the time. I believe the reason rests with Charlie Hayward. There was a saying during the war: *Loose lips sink ships.* As careful as he might've thought he was, I think he let something slip along the way. That inadvertent lapse—directly or indirectly—brought him to the attention of those handling Hoffmann. Charlie's phone was probably the first to be tapped. Then maybe the paranoia spread to Clayton Hayward, after Charlie was silenced. They would've wanted to know where Hayward would next turn, when he realized his son was missing. And as it happened, he turned to Alie—and through her to me.

"In any event, now that I knew about the eavesdropping, I decided to keep Hayward in the dark as much as possible. I'd intended to pick his brain about Hoffmann's tenure at Northrop, inasmuch as they would've been colleagues. Now I was afraid that even mentioning Hoffmann would put Hayward's life at risk, as well. So I danced around my trip to Vegas—leaving out Marjorie Kane's death—and wound up telling him only that I'd more or less struck out, except that I was fairly certain Charlie's disappearance involved a story he was pursuing for the *Times*. The specific subject, however, was unknown to me or his co-workers at the newspaper. So I'd drawn a blank there, too. I did tell him, however, that I suspected Charlie had been the victim of foul play.

"He confided that he'd feared that from the beginning. He'd always been afraid that Charlie's stories for the paper would eventually put him in danger. 'Reckless' is how Hayward described his son. I knew just what he meant. I'd read some of those stories, too. Charlie Hayward never pulled any punches. Only this time he'd gravely underestimated his quarry. Hayward went on to say that if Charlie had been killed, he wouldn't rest until whoever was responsible got what was coming to them. I told him I'd keep digging, starting immediately with another look at Charlie's apartment. I wanted to make sure whoever was listening in knew where I was headed next. Then back out on the front porch, just before leaving, I suggested he might want to stay close to home until we knew more fully what we were up against."

The circumstances surrounding Matt Doyle's death came next:

"Despite what the coroner concluded, Matt's death can undoubtedly be attributed to the two Germans he photographed. Later that afternoon, I phoned Alie in Atlanta about my concern that her brother had been murdered. Though she and her father hadn't been close for many years, she insisted on flying out to LA to offer him her moral support. In the meantime, I called Northrop under the pretext of being Hoffmann's stock broker. My gut said he was long gone, and his secretary confirmed it. I was told he'd been on extended vacation since around the first of the month. This would've been at the same time that Charlie Hayward went missing. Coincidence? Not on your life."

61

Murphy went on to explain about the key his secretary had discovered and the lock that it fit.

He extracted the manila envelope from the briefcase at his feet and emptied the contents onto the table.

"This is what they were after all along. It's my sense that once the newspaper's lawyers would've found out about what Charlie planned to expose, they'd have forced him to turn over his documentation to the FBI. I think he realized that, as well, and for that eventuality, he compiled everything and sent it to his post office box as a security precaution.

"When the Germans, posing as police officers, searched Charlie's office at the *Times*, his copy girl may've told them that he used a tape recorder for story interviews, because she informed me of that when I went there. So they had to figure that their secret wasn't safe until they found those tapes. And they struck out with Marjorie Kane. Hence, their intent was to keep close tabs on me, in case I turned them up. Which I did, after I gave them the slip. He gestured to the items in front of him. "What are here are Charlie Hayward's own notes, the materials he received from Gordon Kane, and recordings of his interviews. The allegation is that Klaus Hoffmann is a

Communist spy, an imposter, the real man having been killed during the last months of the war. And six people have been killed to keep that fact from coming to light."

Special Agent Simpson fingered one of the tapes and said to Murphy, "My office will get the ball rolling on this stuff, ASAP. But I'm curious. Once you knew what you had, why didn't you come to us directly?"

Murphy thought a moment. "Yes, well, first of all, with Hoffmann already gone, I reasoned another day wouldn't make any difference. Also, by involving the feds, there would be delays in moving forward while they evaluated the situation. I felt personally responsible for the deaths of Marjorie Kane and Matt Doyle, and any delays would likely mean their killers would simply crawl back into their holes. So I devised a plan to hopefully flush them into the open for the police to nab. Sort of a 'Hail Mary' pass.

"Knowing that Hayward's phones were tapped, I called him yesterday morning from the motel. His spirits seemed buoyed up by the news that I'd contacted Alie, and that she was in town. I explained how we'd hit gold dust when we found Charlie's cache of backup documentation for a story he'd been writing for the newspaper. And that it involved Northrop. I indicated that Alie would be taking that material to the FBI after a few more inquiries. And as part of that, we needed to get his impressions of a man who he would've known while he worked there. However, I still made it a point not to identify Hoffmann, though Hayward asked.

"He suggested that we meet right away; that he was anxious to see his daughter. I told him there were other considerations to take into account, but to not ask what they were. I said I'd call again with the location of where we'd meet—somewhere safe and out of the way. Hayward said he understood my concerns completely, considering what had transpired thus far, and would wait for my call. At that moment, I was certain he knew that I was trying to draw out whoever was listening in.

"Afterward, Alie took Tara under her wing while I scouted a suitable location to accommodate my plan in the event that things panned out the way I hoped. I settled on the north end of the Hollywood Reservoir. And the rain worked to my advantage. The place was deserted. After the gates to the reservoir were locked at about nine-thirty last night, I phoned Hayward. It rang six or seven times before he picked up. That's when I realized something was wrong. His words were halting, as if he were being told what to say. I asked him if he was all right. 'Just a little tired,' he said. I gave him my location. He said to give him and Alberto—that was his houseboy—an hour because of the storm. When he started to say something else, the line went dead. That's when I suspected the worse. Then I called here. Lieutenant Snyder can recount the subsequent events."

Which Snyder did in "Cinemascope and Technicolor," as they said in Hollywood.

When he'd concluded, Murphy said, "It seems obvious to me that Hayward was killed simply because he knew as much as he did. There may've been some thought that they could bring Hoffmann back, as if nothing had happened, once all ties to him had been eliminated. In any event, Hayward and his houseboy were last night's most recent victims."

Simpson skidded his chair back across the linoleum and slowly got to his feet. He rolled his neck and stretched. All eyes were on him.

He then said to Murphy, "From what I'd been told before coming here this morning, I had you and Agent Hayward checked out. You both had stellar Army careers. First-rate investigators by all accounts, though I believe allowing females into the FBI will prove to be folly. But that aside, Murphy, the fact that it only took a week to wrap up this case speaks to your skills. I doubt the Bureau, with all its resources, could've done better. Rather, I know it couldn't have. You're right; we approach our investigations cautiously. We don't like going through the motions, only to lose a case in court. Again, congratulations."

Murphy wondered where this was headed and started looking for a monkey wrench in Simpson's back pocket. He didn't have long to wait before Simpson threw it.

"But as I listened to your account, I couldn't help but wonder if it represented 'the whole truth and nothing but the truth,' or if some of the details might be part of an elaborate campfire story."

Murphy was about to respond, but Chief Parker beat him to the punch.

"What's that supposed to mean?"

"From what's been explained, I believe Klaus Hoffmann is, undoubtedly, a spy. Someone way back when dropped the ball on that one, all right. But experience tells me that foreign agents seldom act alone. Now, as I said, Murphy's no amateur. I think he also uncovered Hoffmann's accomplice but has chosen to conceal that identity for what I believe to be obvious reasons." Simpson glared at Alie. "Rearrange Murphy's story a little, maybe add a few things he left out, and this collaborator emerges as none other than Clayton Hayward."

"*What?*" Parker roared. He looked over at Alie, then said, "Miss Hayward may feel she can't challenge a superior, but I'm under no such constraint. How *dare* you! How dare you sully the name of a man revered in this city, as was his father before him. Clayton Hayward generously supported every worthy cause that was brought to him. He was a pillar of the community. A saint. And now you stand there and accuse him of being a spy who had his own son killed? *My God!* Did you find a decoder ring in that box of Cracker Jack where you also got your badge? You owe Miss Hayward an apology, and this meeting isn't going forward until she gets one."

The room fell silent.

Simpson then said, "I suspect Benedict Arnold was well-respected, too. No doubt his treachery came as a surprise to those who admired him."

"I'll take that as a refusal," Parker said evenly. He then turned to Captain Morse. "Ask your secretary to get hold of the Justice Department, and have the call transferred in here."

Morse left the room.

Simpson took his seat again and asked Parker, "What are

you doing?"

"I'm going to speak to John about you."

"John *who?*"

"*John* Edgar Hoover. We've been friends for many years. He stayed at my home when he came out here in April on a matter of international importance. And I'll bet he didn't even inform *you* that he was in town."

Simpson remained stoic.

Parker continued. "I'm going to ask him just how shallow the candidate pool was that you could've been chosen to head the LA Field Office. And when I'm done, you'll be packing your bags for Bumfuck, Alaska." He turned to Alie. "Please pardon my language."

Captain Morse returned, took the phone from the adjacent credenza, and placed it in front of Parker.

"Justice is holding on line two."

Parker picked up the receiver and stabbed the flashing red Hold button.

"Justice Department? Put me through to the FBI." A pause, then, "Yes, would you please connect me with the Director's Office?" Another pause. "Wait one." He placed his hand over the mouthpiece and looked at Simpson. "She wants to know who's calling." Parker was apparently giving him one more opportunity to relent.

Simpson scowled at him—a staring contest of sorts.

Parker shrugged. "Okay, it's your funeral. Make sure you dress warm for those dog sled rides."

Simpson said nothing.

Agent Stoddard suddenly reached across the table and disconnected the call.

When he sat back, he said to Parker, "No need for brinkmanship." Then to Alie, "What was said about your late father was insensitive and untimely. Please accept our sincere apologies." He looked over at Simpson. "Russ?"

Simpson acknowledged his assistant with a grunt.

62

The next days and weeks were hectic. Alie took extended leave from the Bureau to settle her father's affairs, beginning with a memorial service for him and her brother at St. Brendan Catholic Church, where the family had once regularly attended. Attendance swelled to standing room only. Every civic group and charitable organization in the county was represented. Alie was taken aback by the lives her father had touched in a good way through his philanthropy. Ironic, she thought: how even despicable people could rise above their own sorry lives to ease the suffering of others. Charlie had left his mark, as well, as friends and co-workers—Shannon Rigby among then—stood and remembered him as a champion of the underdog and a fierce combatant in the war against social injustice.

Clayton Hayward's will had equally divided his estate between his son and daughter. Officially, Charlie was only missing; thus, his share would be held in trust until such time as he could be declared legally dead. Alie's portion ran into eight figures and would've made her the richest agent in the Bureau's history, but she had no interest in her father's money. At least not for herself; rather, she would establish a foundation to support the kind of causes embraced by him and her brother.

***

Matthew Doyle's ex-wife, Rachel, had been notified by Miami police the Monday morning following his death. It wasn't until Friday, however, that she showed up in LA, accompanied by her boyfriend, a handsomely swarthy kid half her age.

During the interim, the FBI had put a hold on Doyle's body and instructed the coroner to take another look. A more rigorous toxicology screen turned up trace amounts of a tranquilizer used to dart wild animals, sometimes with fatal consequences if the dosage was incorrect. Thomas Noguchi amended the initial report to indicate that Doyle's coronary thrombosis was likely triggered by that tranquilizing agent.

While with the LAPD, Doyle had procured a private life insurance policy beyond what the city had provided, listing his wife as sole beneficiary. Death by natural causes was worth $25,000 to her. The double indemnity clause bumped that amount to $50,000 if foul play was involved. Rachel and Enrique were ecstatic when they found out; because the possibility of collecting on her husband's insurance was the only reason they'd made the trip. She even refused to claim his body, leaving Murphy to arrange a burial.

As he and Tara stood at the graveside, Murphy thought it ironic that even after their divorce, Matt never stopped loving Rachel. She, on the other hand, apparently couldn't have cared less about him—in life *or* death.

The FBI had plenty on its plate and moved immediately to establish the identities of four people. Through channels, the U.S. Embassy in Czechoslovakia found a student photograph of Klaus Hoffmann taken at Prague's Technical University before the war. Granted, he'd been younger and in good health then, but there was no doubt it was the same man as in the picture provided to Gordon Kane by Hoffmann's supposed lover.

Of the two sets of fingerprints lifted from the dead Germans, only those belonging to one Gretta Rosenberg were identified. Her Interpol file was sketchy at best: a Nazi concentration camp survivor, recruited by the KGB in the mid-

1950s, and trained to protect the interests of Mother Russia. Her code name was "Edelweiss," after the delicate alpine wildflower. Ironic, considering she'd been a cold-blooded assassin with a slew of kills to her credit.

As for the imposter's true identity and current whereabouts, the FBI drew a blank. It was confirmed that initially he had, indeed, flown to Mexico—Mexico City, to be precise—but afterward the trail had gone cold.

Half a dozen agents subsequently descended on Northrop Aircraft to interview administrators and co-workers. In one way or another, all were incredulous: *Klaus Hoffmann, a Soviet agent? There has to be some mistake.* In his defense, they pointed out that he'd done more to advance American aviation than anyone since the Wright Brothers.

Which had made him a unique asset to the Soviets, the FBI countered. Whatever technology he'd developed for Uncle Sam, he'd also passed along to his buddies behind the Iron Curtain. The list of projects he'd been part of over twenty years was sobering: from elite fighter aircraft to surface-to-air missile systems. No machine of war was invincible. Each had an "Achilles' heel" that, if known, could be exploited by the enemy. With the conflict in Vietnam heating up, the potential damage to the United States and its allies was incalculable at the moment.

As the investigation proceeded at Northrop, other agents searched Hoffmann's beachside home in Redondo but found not a shred of evidence linking him to clandestine activities. By virtue of the dirty dishes in the sink, it was concluded that he'd left in a hurry. And finding his Mercedes-Benz sports car in the garage indicated he'd had help.

Special Agent Simpson then turned his attention to Clayton Hayward. Since meeting with Chief Parker, where he'd suffered a defeat of sorts, his mind was still made up about Hayward and Hoffmann having worked as a team. Armed with a broadly-based search warrant, issued by a federal judge with whom he played golf twice a month, Simpson obtained Hayward's phone records, going back years, comparing them to

Hoffmann's. The only number in common belonged to Northrop. However, this came as no surprise to Simpson. Tradecraft would've dictated that any contact between them would've been in person or through an intermediary.

Hayward's bank and investment records were reviewed. Whatever motivation Hayward had had to betray his country, it wasn't money. And all of it seemingly from investing in American companies. No infusion of funds from foreign sources. Simpson pushed back against the doubt that began to creep into his brain. Hayward had to be guilty. It was the only scenario that made sense.

Alie was still in residence when Simpson and his men stormed the house in Bel Air like an enemy beachhead. One agent was detailed to take her outside by the pool while the others turned every room upside down. Alie held her breath the entire time—or so it seemed to her. She'd already been through the house from top to bottom for anything that incriminated her father and had found absolutely nothing. He'd apparently been very good at concealing his nefarious activities. But perhaps she had overlooked something.

Simpson had taken malicious pleasure in leaving the place in shambles, but all had been for naught. He lingered on the porch while his minions returned to their waiting vehicles. Alie stood by his side, trying not to betray the butterflies in her stomach.

"You think you're pretty slick, don't you?" he hissed. "But you and Murphy haven't pulled the wool over *my* eyes. Sure, maybe I'll never be able to prove it, but your father was dirty, and you know it. And as for the Cuban houseboy, we've checked, and he doesn't seem to have had a past. That tells me he was in on it, too."

Alie knew Simpson was only doing his job, even felt guilty for covering up her father's crimes, but his demeaning behavior toward her boiled her blood. She thought twice about even responding to him but couldn't hold back.

"You know, there's a psychological term for perceiving everyone as an enemy: 'paranoid delusion.' Maybe you ought to see a shrink." She then turned, walked back into the house, and slammed the door.

The Johnson Administration had been quick to voice its outrage with Soviet Premier Alexei Kosygin that American citizens had been murdered by Red agents to keep a clandestine operation from coming to light. As expected, the finger-pointing was met with flat denials of complicity. Nevertheless, shortly after the allegations had been lodged, the Kremlin recalled its longstanding ambassador, citing ill health. Washington's rumor mill held that the action was a direct result of the embassy having botched the cover-up following Hoffmann's detection and subjecting the Soviet Union to embarrassment in the world press.

In two weeks' time from the meeting on the Hoffmann affair, Chief William Parker would find himself embroiled in an incident that garnered the headlines of every major newspaper in America, eclipsing any revelation of local espionage.

The "Watts Rebellion," as it would eventually be called, began innocuously enough when a young black man was pulled over by a white Highway Patrol officer on suspicion of driving while intoxicated. What exactly happened next is subject to speculation. Officers called for backup reported it one way; the crowd that had gathered saw it another. The truth lay somewhere in between; nevertheless, during the next six days, forty some square miles of South Central Los Angeles were turned into a war zone, necessitating the National Guard being activated by the governor to assist police efforts in quelling the violence.

In the end—no thanks to Parker's public remarks, referring to black residents as "monkeys"—religious and community leaders negotiated a cease fire, exacting from public officials promises of meaningful dialog to address the powder keg that had set off the incident: a hundred years of discriminating practices in the city.

For Parker's part, it could be said that he never recovered

professionally. Demands for his resignation became louder, and though the mayor of Los Angeles refused to give in to political pressure and replace him, Parker's days of running roughshod were through. Stress from feeling that he was being undermined took its toll, and less than a year later, he died of a heart attack at the age of sixty-one.

63

Knowing that Special Agent Simpson hadn't bought his story about the role that Clayton Hayward had played, Murphy expected to be brought in and grilled, with Simpson trying to pick apart the "official" version of events. That never happened. Maybe Simpson concluded that Murphy was unbreakable, and if he was going to show Hayward to be Hoffmann's accomplice, he'd have to find the proof elsewhere. In the end, much to his chagrin, Simpson couldn't come up with it.

Getting back into the swing of things, Murphy had reopened the office and was trying to get on top of what he and Doyle had had in the hopper. To that end, he'd come in a little after six a.m. Tara hadn't stayed over the night before, and he hadn't slept worth a damn—he never did when she wasn't around.

He tinkered with a couple of pending reports, then set them aside and retrieved a file folder from a side drawer in his desk, the same file that Doyle had given him that fateful day at Farmer's Market, the police file on Michael O'Neill's murder. He glanced at his watch just before pulling the phone closer to him. Was the time difference between California and Paris eight or nine hours?

He consulted the address book he took from the top drawer and dialed the overseas number. It was answered on the first ring.

"Interpol."

Switchboard operators for the International Police Organization were always multi-lingual, owing to the offices of member nations represented there. English, French, and German were predominately spoken, with Italian and Spanish rounding out the list. The operator would wait for the caller to say something, so she'd know what language to use.

"Connect me with the British Office, please."

"Certainly, sir. Whom may I say is calling?" Her accent wasn't quite German and not quite French. Murphy figured the Alsace-Lorraine region on the border between the two countries.

"Jack Murphy," he answered.

A couple of clicks, then, "Jack? Is it really you?"

"Hello, Audrey. It's been a while."

"Are you still on the job? We all heard you'd retired."

"Well, you heard right. I'm a private investigator now—in Los Angeles, of all places. And before you ask, let me tell you it's nothing like the movies."

She laughed. "You always were a card, Jack."

"Listen, is Nigel about? I need to speak with him on a matter that's come up here."

Nigel Cooper was England's resident Interpol investigator. He and Murphy had crossed paths many times in pursuit of their respective police duties in Europe—Murphy for Uncle Sam's Army and Cooper for Queen and Country.

"Living in the Colonies, you wouldn't have heard," she said.

"Heard what?"

"It happened all so suddenly. Nigel's no longer with us."

"*What?* He died?"

Audrey laughed again. "No, you silly man. He was called home to be knighted by Her Majesty. For his role in that little classified affair last year that you and he were part of."

She was referring to *Operation Red Star*, a brilliantly conceived plan by Soviet hardliners to breach the Iron Curtain and roll across Western Europe before NATO forces could react. And it might have worked had it not been for some zero-hour police work, with Murphy in the lead.

"Oh, so that's it, huh? Nigel gets a knighthood from a grateful nation, and what do I get? A bullet in the shoulder, a week in the hospital, and a hand shake from General Lemnitzer. If I'd been French, I'd have at least gotten a kiss on both cheeks. Life's so unfair."

"You can say that again, Jack. I like my job here; I know I'm good at it. But Nigel's replacement wants his own Girl Friday. Thinks it would be better to have a 'clean break' with the past. If I only thought that was true... She arrived last week for me to show the ropes before I shove off for new duties at Scotland Yard. As for *her* duties, I'm not sure. She doesn't take shorthand and only types with two fingers. She is, however, quite beautiful. She'll never have to buy her own lunch or dinner; I'm sure of that. There'll be a line of suitors from the lobby to her desk—that is, if she and the boss don't already have an arrangement. I rather fancy that's the case.

"In any event, David has left for the day. David Langston is his name. MI5. The rumor is that he was passed over for a job back home that he really wanted. This assignment is a consolation prize for him, and his heart isn't in it. Should I leave a message that you'd like to speak with him?"

"No, I specifically need Nigel. Would you happen to have a number where he can be reached? Or would that constitute a breach of the Official Secrets Act?"

"It would be if I gave it to anyone else. I'm sure he'll be pleased to hear from you. He always said you were the best investigator he'd ever known."

She recited the phone number, and after she'd repeated it for good measure, she said, "It was nice to talk to you again, Jack. If you'd called two days from now, I'd have been gone."

"It was serendipitous, all right. I doubt I could've gotten Nigel's number from the new Miss Moneypenny," of James

310

Bond fame.

Audrey laughed. "You know how to flatter a girl, don't you?"

Murphy wasted no time dialing the number he'd obtained.

"Cooper Residence." Very proper.

"I'd like to speak with Nigel, if he's around."

"*Sir* Nigel," a soft rebuke, "is having his afternoon tea and cannot be disturbed."

"He'll *want* to be disturbed. Tell him Jack Murphy is on the line—long distance from Los Angeles. I'll wait."

Murphy heard the phone receiver being put down. In the background he heard voices but couldn't make out what was being said.

A moment later, Cooper picked up the phone.

"Jack, ol' boy. What a surprise."

"The surprise was all mine when Audrey informed me of your good fortune."

"Grand gal, that Audrey. How is she? My replacement taking good care of her, I presume."

"You presume wrong. She's being dumped for a shiny new model, one who can't type or take dictation, but exhibits other qualities. Audrey is being transferred to Scotland Yard."

"Well, we shall all have to get together for dinner sometime. Talk about old times."

"I'd like nothing better, but right now I have a 'rather sticky wicket,' as you'd put it, to deal with, and you're the only person I know who might be able to sort out a matter that has its roots going back to the war.

"Sounds intriguing."

"Do you have pen and paper handy?"

Murphy heard a drawer open and close.

"I do now. Shoot, as you Yanks say."

"The man's name was Michael Maguire. I have reason to believe he was aiding and abetting the Germans. Liquor salesman from Belfast. Travel allowed him to spy on Allied installations. The dust had barely settled after the war, when your guys went after Nazi collaborators. The wife got killed in a police raid, but Maguire and his teenage daughter escaped to the United States, apparently with the help of ex-Nazis who appreciated his loyalty. They settled in Los Angeles and changed their name to O'Neill."

"Sounds about right. There were some in the IRA who hated us enough to climb into bed with Hitler and his bunch. We tracked down as many as we could, but some slipped through the cracks. Sounds like this Maguire was one of them. But so what? Water under the bridge, so to speak. No one would be interested in him now."

"That's where you're wrong. Someone was interested enough to *kill* him. March eighteenth of this year. Police couldn't find a motive. Not burglary, not robbery, no known enemies. But I think he was executed."

"What would make you conclude that?"

"The two bullets dug out of his body were 7.5 millimeter."

Silence for a moment on Cooper's end, then, "Huh, that *is* odd."

"My reaction, too. A couple days ago I went to a gun store and asked if they stocked that caliber. The clerk said no, adding that he doubted any other store would, either. Called it 'exotic' ammunition."

"Off hand, only one weapon that takes a 7.5 millimeter bullet comes to mind: a Schmidt revolver. Swiss military and police use them."

"Could it be fitted with a silencer?"

"Most revolvers can, even if not factory issued. Why?"

"Because no one in the near vicinity of the crime heard any shots. The police were quick to move the case off the front burner when they couldn't immediately find a smoking gun. Unlike Europe, homicides are commonplace here. And a good number go unsolved."

"Okay, so where do you fit in? What is your interest in a dead Nazi collaborator?"

"Simple. Two days ago I became engaged to his daughter."

"Really? I never figured you for the marrying type."

"I know exactly what you mean. I was burned the first time

out. Got the 'Dear John' in North Africa. Vowed not to get sucked in again. But meeting Tara...well...I'd have been a fool to walk away. Anyway, her father would never discuss his wartime activities. She put together what I've told you by researching the era in the library. But just before he was killed, he attempted to contact her at her job. She wasn't there, so he left a message that it was urgent he speak with her."

"Did she tell that to the police?"

"Yes. It's in the case file, but there was really nothing to pursue. Listen, Nigel. Had he lived, he would've been my father-in-law. I need to know who killed him and why."

Nigel cleared his voice. "You realize I no longer have unfettered access to the files where this kind of information might reside."

"What's the sense of being a Knight of the Realm if you can't lean on people who *do* have access?"

"Well spoken, lad. It has been dreadfully dull around here, anyway. Now where can I reach you with what I find—*if* there is anything to be found?"

Murphy gave him his office and home phone numbers.

"It's important for Tara and me to get this behind us. It's been bad enough living with the knowledge that her father was an enemy agent during the war. But his unsolved murder weighs her down even more."

64

Two weeks passed and nothing from Nigel Cooper. When the call finally did come, it came at 2 a.m. on a Friday. Murphy nearly knocked over the lamp as he reached for the bedside phone.

"Hello," he said groggily.

"Jack? Nigel. You sound tired."

"That's because it's the middle of the night."

"Those damn time zones. I can never get them straight. That explains why there was no answer at your office."

"Yes, well, hold on a minute. I don't want to wake Tara."

Murphy carried the phone—tethered to the wall by a long cord—to the hall beyond the bedroom and closed the door behind him. He then sat on the floor in the dark.

"Okay. What's the scoop? Or did you draw a blank?"

"No, we had a file on Maguire, all right. But your fiancée's assessment of her father is only partly correct."

"What do you mean?"

"Michael Maguire was recruited by the Germans, that is true enough, but he had been working for us as an informant inside the IRA since the mid-thirties. On recommendation of the IRA's top dogs, the Germans approached him to do a little intelligence gathering for them. The pitch they used was designed to exploit his supposed political leanings: 'You scratch our backs, and when we are running things, Hitler will grant Northern Ireland its independence.'

"Maguire jumped at the opportunity to do double duty. And by all accounts, he was fearless. If his Nazi handlers had found out, they would have executed him on the spot. And if the IRA caught wind of his collaboration with us, he would have suffered a similar fate. In fact, he narrowly avoided detection on several occasions. But his luck ran out some months after Germany's surrender. A faction of the IRA, headed by a firebrand named Sean Patrick Ryan, put two and two together. Ryan bombed Maguire's house. Maguire and his daughter weren't home, but his wife was. You could have put her charred remains in a cigar box with room to spare.

"The ashes were still smoldering when we spirited father and daughter out of Belfast. They were provided new identities, and eventually relocated to Los Angeles. Then King and Country fronted the money to open a drinking establishment. We maintained regular communication with him at first. Just to insure the transition went smoothly. After a time, the contact ceased. Then out of the blue, on the afternoon of March seventeenth of this year, he walked into the British Consulate in Los Angeles. Said it was an emergency and demanded to speak with a case officer.

"Now, it had been seventeen years since anyone had been in touch with him. No one at the consulate knew anything about him *or* his circumstances. And there certainly were not any case officers, as he had known them, in residence. In time, a junior attaché consented to sit down with him. Maguire—or should I say O'Neill—explained his situation and then said that just that morning, he had seen the man who had killed his wife. He went on to say that he had subsequently followed Ryan to a downtown hotel where he was registered under the false name of Paul Flannery. He then gave a complete description of the man.

"It's obvious from the report that O'Neill was unaware that

315

Ryan, apart from having been a stooge for the Nazis, had now become the principal enforcer for the IRA and an assassin for hire by anyone who could pay his fee. Interpol was convinced that his lair was in Zurich, but no one had ever been successful at locating it."

"Did O'Neill connect the dots; that *he* might be the reason Ryan was in LA?"

"He made it clear that he did not believe in coincidences. He was assured that the proper authorities would be contacted and that, in the meantime, he should consider our offer of protection by staying at the consulate until the threat had been neutralized. He refused, saying that he was more concerned for his daughter's safety and needed to warn her. He also stated he could take care of himself, if it came to that."

"That may explain why the police found a Walther PPK at the crime scene, unfired and with only his fingerprints on it."

"No surprise. Ryan would never have given him any chance to defend himself. In hindsight, O'Neill should have been detained by our people, even forcibly, if necessary."

"How did Ryan find him after all those years?"

"Good question, and one to which there is no definitive answer. There are those in the service of the Queen who are sympathetic to the IRA's cause. Our best guess is that one of them stumbled onto O'Neill's whereabouts and passed the information along. In any event, Ryan made a fatal mistake. He put too much stock in his invisibility. Anyone else would have made the hit and been on the next plane out. But Ryan stayed another day, just long enough for our extraction team to make him disappear for good.

"A conversation then took place between our Foreign Office and your Mr. Hoover. He did not appreciate a British covert operation in America, but applauded the outcome. It was Hoover's idea to leave O'Neill's death on the books as an unsolved crime. His feeling was that word of an IRA-inspired assassination in the United States would only stir up feelings among Irish Americans, whose sympathies were already deeply divided.

"We understand that Hoover traveled to Los Angeles the following month and spoke directly with the local authorities about mothballing the case. It was also decided that O'Neill's daughter should be kept in the dark. I now see the flaw in that rationale. That is why I have told you everything. Nothing is going to bring her father back, but at least she will have the complete story."

After Murphy thanked Cooper and disconnected the call, he was just getting to his feet when the bedroom door opened.

"What are you doing out here, Jack? Is anything wrong?"

"No, I'm fine. I had a phone call from an old friend and didn't want to wake you."

"Who'd call at this time of night?"

"Why don't we make some coffee, and I'll tell you all about him. What he had to say is going to change your life."

When Murphy had completed the story, Tara was in tears.

Between sobs, she managed to say, "If only he'd told me. All those years thinking he was a Nazi spy. I feel so ashamed."

"In his way, he wanted to protect you from the past."

"He was courageous, wasn't he?"

"To the very end. And few people will ever know about it. That's the way it is with silent heroes."

Murphy got up from the kitchen table and put their now empty cups in the sink. When he turned around, Tara moved in close and put her arms around his neck.

"I love you with all my heart. Without you, the truth would've remained hidden. How can I ever thank you enough?"

Murphy patted her bottom with both hands.

"I'm sure I can think of something."